SABERS FROM THE BRAZOS

SECOND OF A TWO- PART SAGA

THE LAST BULLET

BY

ERMAL WALDEN
WILLIAMSON

Giant Shadow Publishing

1

Copyright © 2007 by Ermal Walden Williamson
ISBN-13 978-0-9801270-1-0
ISBN-10 0-9801270-1-7

Printed in the United States of America

The Last Bullet is published by:

Giant Shadow Publishing
www.ermal.com
Branson, MO 65616
An imprint of Seven Locks Press
Santa Ana, CA

Production Credits:

Editors: Jo Mayberry, Paula Cravens, Paul Press, Pat and Cheryl Pruett

Design, Layout and Production by: Seven Locks Press
Front Cover Photo by: Phil
Flag on the Cover: © 2007 Paula Cravens

DEDICATED TO

The officers of Terry's Rangers
Colonel Benjamin Franklin Terry
Colonel Thomas Saltus Lubbock
Albert Sidney Johnston
General John Austin Wharton
General Thomas Harrison

And to

My show partner and friend, Paula Cravens
"America's Yodeling Sweetheart"
whose creative insights made this book possible.

A disclaimer: This is a historical novel based upon facts and is intended for entertainment without any prejudice or bias.

Praises for

THE LAST BULLET

By

Ermal Walden Williamson

"This captivating account comes as close to living history as one is likely to find. Ermal's characters come alive amidst the dramatic backdrop of the Old South during the war. He has woven the lives and events together into a wonderful read."

Jeffrey Dixon Murrah
None but Texians: A History of Terry's Texas Rangers

The Last Bullet. "Ermal Walden Williamson has completed a saga about a segment of the Civil War, which illustrates his artistic ability to write with historic accuracy while keeping the reader interested in what lies around the corner. His dialogue is excellent, making for interesting and exciting reading."

Larry Johns / High Sonoran Style Magazine.

ACKNOWLEDGMENTS

There are perhaps thousands of books and essays written about the American Civil War, or the War Between the States. This is a novel, which is intended to entertain as well as enlighten the reader with a well of knowledge.

Being reared in the South with Negro schoolmates and friends, and having served for a time in the U. S. Marines out of South Carolina, I like to leave the reader with insights that I think about how both sides of the Civil War might have felt towards each side and their separate causes.

I want to specially acknowledge Jeff Murrah for his many suggestions for making my work a truly historical novel.

I want to acknowledge my editors, Jo Mayberry, Conan Tigard, Pat and Cheryl Pruett, and Paul Press.

I want to give great appreciation to Sidney Bennett of Tennessee, and to Rhonda Stearns of Wyoming for their wonderful help in providing me with the much-needed information for these parts of America.

Acknowledgement goes to a friend, Abe Carson,

CHAPTER 1

MARKING TIME ON
THE SHELBYVILLE PIKE

6 February 1862 -16 February 1862

Geneneral Albert Sidney Johnston led his brigade on a miserable winter march from Nashville through Shelbyville on his way to Corinth, and Terry's Texas Rangers brought up the rear. The days never got better. Freezing rain and cold wreaked more havoc upon the brigade. Johnston avoided *Jimmy*, Major Thomas Harrison, as much as possible, for he had heard through the lines about the Rangers' continual resentment towards the Major.

And it was no small reason why Major Harrison grew to hate Matt Jorgensen and Steve Andrews, both under-officers in the Confederacy, all the more because they were still the favorite sons. They had proved time and again that they were more courageous in fighting than he was. After all, he had retreated when the men smelled easy victory, when the Rangers were prepared and anxious to fight.

Harrison was a little over five feet tall with a Napoleonic attitude in leadership. Still feeling the bitterness towards Colonel John Wharton for Colonel John Lubbock passing him up to succeed him in command, Harrison now thought back with regret to when General Patrick Ronayne Cleburne advised him to pass up a skirmish. Because of it, he believed it cost him his chance to lead Terry's Texas Rangers to a victory battle.

Terry's Texas Rangers had earned a grand reputation that sparked up interest and enthusiasm along their march from Nashville, through Shelbyville and Decatur, to Corinth. Their stories of fame spread throughout both the north and the south as the *Devil's Rangers* who could not be stopped by Satan himself. Harrison's name was not mentioned, except in some circles where it was cursed.

At times, even Colonel Wharton had doubts about Harrison's ability to properly lead in battle, but because of Harrison's friendship with Terry and Johnston and his previous service in the Mexican War, Wharton kept him as Field Commander. Major William Mitchell took over as Acting Commander of "A Company", the company Harrison vacated for his present position.

The rains came down fiercely that next winter day in February while the company was bivouacking. Perhaps, because of these unrelenting days, Harrison's attitude grew worse and his temper grew shorter. He was particularly resentful towards Matt and Steve this day when he had little to do but to think.

As Field Commander, he went over Mitchell's head and ordered O'Riley to summon the two Lieutenants to his tent. Sergeant Major John Foster O'Riley sensed his displeasure as he had seen Harrison drinking earlier and saw the effects when he was addressed to get Matt and Steve. True to the Confederacy and its military, O'Riley took the order in proper style, waded out into the watered field and marched to Matt's tent. Matt put on his slicker and followed O'Riley to Steve's tent.

The two men bade O'Riley the balance of the day and walked briskly up the hill to meet with Harrison. The rain came down harder without any letup in sight. No one but O'Riley knew of the meeting.

"You sent for us, Major?" Matt asked, throwing the rain off his slicker before entering the tent. He held the flap up for Steve to slide under.

The two gentlemen saw right away that Harrison was far from being sober. A partially filled, uncorked bottle of whiskey laid on his cot.

Harrison turned around and almost fell, but broke his falling forward by grabbing the tent pole. He straightened up, threw his shoulders back and looked at the two men who stood at attention in his presence. He was in full uniform, all neat and tidy. He knew his principles of being a disciplined officer, even though he grew lax of being self-disciplined because of his drinking.

"You know I hate both of you!" he said belligerently. "You know that?"

"Yes, Major," Matt returned.

"You, too, Lieutenant Andrews?"

"We suspected as much," Steve answered.

"Then why don't you get out of the Rangers?"

"Thought about it some," Matt responded.

"Well?"

"We like the men. Good men. Think they like the way we work them."

Steve agreed. "We work well together."

"Well, it's that or my fury! Which will it be?" Harrison asked, wiping his mouth with his bared hand.

"Well, we're not leaving the Rangers, Major," Matt said straight forward, "so guess we'll have to put up with your fury."

"Yes, Sir," Steve added. "Whatever thet might be."

Harrison rubbed his eyes and said, "I want you to get your company up and drill them," Harrison ordered. "Immediately!"

"What for, Major?" Matt fired back, stepping out of attention.

"Never know when we'll be fighting those sons-of-devils in the rain. Get 'em up and in their saddles. Right now!"

Matt and Steve looked at each, turned and opened the flap of the tent. They looked at the soaked fields and the dark clouds filled with rain.

"It's not goin' to stop rainin' for a few days," Matt said, turning back to Harrison. "If we wait for a break in the weather, we'll show you real drillin'."

"You'll show it to me, now, Lieutenant. Now!"

"Beg your pardon, Major," Steve countered. "We've got sick men down there, some already dead which we've buried. You can't be serious about drilling in this freezin' rain?"

"You're wasting my time, Lieutenant," Harrison snarled back at them.

"Our becoming heroes mean thet much to you? To hate us so much thet we have to kill our men by drilling in this freezin' rain?"

"Your men? Your men? The hell they are. They're my men and they were mine before you came in. You're gawdam puny cowboys and you don't know nothing about being an officer." He bent down and picked up his bottle of whiskey, brought it up to his mouth and swigged the remainder down in a couple of swallows. He wiped his mouth with the hand holding the empty bottle. "I'm a lawyer. What the hell are you? Nothing."

He walked up to Matt and looked at him hard. "I fired shotguns, too. I fought with Davis' Rifles in the Mexican War. I fought as a Captain with Benjamin Franklin Terry when this gawdam war started. I don't have to prove anything to anybody.

As he turned his back to the men, he threw the bottle on the cot. The remainder of the contents drained out of it. "Terry liked you because you could ride a horse pretty good. That's all. Hell, I don't give a damn about horses." He quickly turned back again and pointed his finger at the two Lieutenants. "But I can ride as well or better'n you two."

Matt looked at Harrison and then back at Steve. "Is this why he turned back at Jimtown?" he queried to Steve with his jaw dropped down to his knees.

"I think it sure as hell is, chum," Steve answered, falling out of attention.

"I'll be dipped," Matt added. "He's afraid of horses. Thet's why Terry had us made officers in his company, because he couldn't ride as well as his own men. Because his men would show him up. Remember when they showed off at the Nashville Fair. Where was he all thet time?"

"Back in his gawdam tent. And you call us puny?"

Harrison's hair stood thick on the back of his neck as his blood boiled. "Don't give me that rot. I followed General Cleburne's advice. He said it wasn't a sure victory. And let me tell you something." He walked up to Matt's chest and looked up at him. "I don't go charging into battle just for the hell of it. You got that, mister? I don't risk my neck for the hell of it. Walking away from Matt, he turned on to Steve. "I'll be here when a lot of these officers are gone and buried. I'll be a general because I used my gawdam head, not my spurs."

"You turned and ran because you were afraid of gettin' killed?" Matt asked, slapping his leg with his hat. "And we're supposed to risk our necks fighting under a commander with your kind of fear. Hell, you go drill your own company." He looked at Steve. "I wanna puke. Let's go get some air."

"You're still at attention, Lieutenant," Harrison ordered, rapidly stopping Matt and Steve from going out the tent with his inebriated voice. "You are officers under my command and you will do exactly as I say or I'll see that you're court-martialed. Do you hear me?"

"Yes, Sir," Matt returned and stood at attention facing the Major.

Steve answered with him, "Yes, Sir."

"Don't give me those smirks, you yellow liver bastards," Harrison fired back. "Wipe them off."

Matt and Steve stood erect with somber faces. "What is it you want from us, Sir?" Matt asked.

"I want you to take Company A and drill them. I want you to show me that they can pick up a woman's hankie at a full gallop with their gawdam teeth. I want to see every soldier mount, dismount and mount again at full gallop." He took a cigar from his vest and stuck it between his teeth and bit off the end.

"Is thet all, Sir?" Matt asked without blinking an eye.

"For now, yes.

"Then I respectively answer your stupid request, Sir," Matt barked back. "You can take it and shove it up your military ass."

Steve's jaw dropped a little with a slight grin, but Harrison's jaw dropped down to his knees and his cigar hit the floor.

Harrison could take it no more. He picked up his empty bottle and threw it at Matt, hitting him across the chest but not hard enough to do any harm.

Matt winced but immediately straightened up so as not to please Harrison.

"You, Mister Jorgensen, will do as I ordered."

"No, Sir," Matt said as he stood at attention.

"What?" Harrison yelled. "You will take your men and drill them."

"No, Sir," Steve agreed, coming to attention.

Harrison's face bloated and saliva ran its course down his chin. He unsuccessfully grabbed his slicker, lost it and walked out into the rain without his hat. He stood there sopping wet and summoned the two men to follow him.

Matt and Steve followed him out in their slickers.

"Sergeant O'Riley!" Harrison called out. There was no answer. Again he called out, "Sergeant O'Riley! On the double, man!"

The rain drowned out his voice for any to hear, but O'Riley. He knew it was Harrison's craggy sound and paid no attention to it.

Harrison marched the two men to O'Riley's tent and pulled the flap back. "Outside, Sergeant!" he barked his orders.

O'Riley came out with his slicker on and saluted Harrison. "I was jest gettin' me slicker on, Sir." He looked at Matt and Steve and wondered what was working in Harrison's mind. "Yes, Sir," he reported.

"Put these men under arrest for insubordination."

"Insubordination, Sir?"

"You heard me, Sergeant. I want them in full gear and without their horses to mark time on the Shelbyville Pike. If they refuse, shoot them."

"Shoot 'em, Sir?" O'Riley asked with his eyes wide open enough to see the whole universe and then some. He noticed that Harrison was uncovered and soaken wet from head to toe. He sneezed and O'Riley replied, "God bless you, Sir." Then he asked, "The Shelbyville Pike, Sir?"

Harrison looked at the two men, clasped his hands in back of him and continued, "Unless they agree to obey my commands."

Matt looked at O'Riley, shrugged his shoulders but said nothing.

Steve looked straight away and waited to hear more from Harrison. It never came.

Harrison turned and marched back up the hill to his tent.

"What did you do, lads?" O'Riley asked, wiping his face from the rain with his hand.

"It's not what we did, Sergeant," Matt replied walking up towards the Shelbyville Pike.

"It's what we won't do," Steve added.

"You disobeyed his command, Sir?"

"I don't see them marking time, Sergeant," Harrison yelled from his walk up the hill. "Make them mark time right now or you'll be doing it with them."

"Yes, Sir," O'Riley answered. "Right away, Sir." He yelled out at a Corporal nearby. "Corporal Donaldson!"

"Yes, Sir," Donaldson sounded out and came running to the side of O'Riley.

"Get another one of youse and put these men under arrest."

"Huh?" He stared at O'Riley for a moment, looked at the two gentlemen, wide-eyed.

"Youse heard me, son. Put them under arrest. They're goin' to mark time."

"Yes, Sir," Donaldson obeyed and motioned for another Corporal to assist him. Without having to coerce Matt and Steve, they walked behind the two officers. "Mark time, Sir."

O'Riley looked up the hill at Harrison and then at the two men. "Let's go, gentlemen. I mean, Sirs." When they reached Shelbyville Pike, he stopped them and started marking time with them. "Whatever youse done, I don't want to be markin' time wid yu in this freakin' rain."

Marking time was an order whereby a soldier would keep the time of a marching step by alternately moving his feet without advancing any.

"How long, Sergeant?" Donaldson asked, marking time with the Lieutenants.

"How long, Sir?" O'Riley called up to Harrison as the men began their trek.

The flap of Harrison's tent shut without an answer from the Major.

The men kept marking time through the afternoon, resting in periods of five to ten minutes at a time, up until Company A came out for chow. Two fresh Corporals relieved the two Corporals in shifts. Much of the time, they turned their backs when one of the Lieutenants had to rest and kept him out of Harrison's sight.

O'Riley returned after chow and sat on a post and watched the routine with a wink of approval.

Private McTavvit walked up to the two officers as they marked time, and addressed them, "Lieutenant Andrews, Sir. Lieutenant Jorgensen, Sir."

O'Riley intervened, "Bring 'em some food, Private. On the double."

"Chow down, Private," Matt answered, keeping his eyes straight ahead while marking time.

"Man I'm so starved I'd eat anythin'," Steve remarked out of the side of his mouth. "An' keep it out of the rain," he ordered

Several of the Rangers from Company A walked around the Lieutenants, asking what was going on and received no answers.

"Who the hell knows?" Troy asked, standing and watching. "The mud here is shoe mouth deep. I'm cold as hell. You men must be freezin', Sir."

O'Riley saw Harrison's tent open, got up and ran over to the two men. "All right, you men," he barked to the others, "get to your chow line or you'll not be gettin' any."

The tent flap closed without Harrison coming out, to the relief of O'Riley.

McTavvit returned quickly with food. "Here youse go, Sirs," McTavvit said secretly, slipping each man a piece of pork, which he brought back from the chow line.

They took it gladly and stuffed into their mouths.

O'Riley turned his back and joined the chow line. "Youse keep an eye on them," he ordered McTavvit and Troy.

Before the sun went down, O'Riley returned and released the officers and walked them to Matt's tent. "Harrison. Major Harrison said youse had enough punishment for the day. Here. For youse two." He pulled a full bottle of whiskey out from under his slicker, uncorked it and gave it to Matt. "And this be a-comin' from me, Sirs."

"What about mornin'?" Matt asked, slugging down a drink from the bottle.

"He says, says he, thet if the men are in their saddles fust thing, you don't have to mark time no more." He continued, walking Steve to his tent.

Sleep came fast and easy for the two men now dried off and under blankets. The whiskey helped warm their insides. Steve suffered more from the cold than Matt perhaps because Matt had experienced worse winters in Montana, but the cold bit into him, too like the fangs of a snake into soft butter. They shivered through the night in their separate tents. Matt's mind stayed on Ginny.

The morning came early as usual in winter as her sun kept behind the blankets of the season. Strong and determined, the two Lietenants were up and had chowed down before any sign of life showed at Harrison's tent. They wore an extra pair of long johns and pants along with two shirts and their jackets to keep them warm that day. They had the forthrightness to think ahead and wore two pairs of woolen socks, and they applied extra rope to keep their slickers down and the rain out.

Heavy sleet fell that day and the temperature caused the deep mud to freeze. Matt and Steve were happy to be back on the Shelbyville Pike away from the fields of mud. When Harrison threw open the flap of his tent, he looked down and saw them marking time. He grunted and belched, threw the flap down and went back inside his tent.

The men of Company A stood around and watched. The Lieutenants made no mention of the conditions of their detention.

The disciplinary routine hit Steve hard before noon and he fell. Matt picked him up and the two kept marking time.

Colonel Wharton was cognizant of what was happening and asked officers of the other companies to keep him informed of the progress. He wished to stay away from getting involved.

A group of Rangers from Company A huddled together and began to talk among themselves. When they saw Matt also fall, they ran as a well-trained unit and rescued both worn men from marking time.

"It's not me doin's," O'Riley countered when confronted by the Rangers from Company A. "Help me pick 'em up, lads."

Wharton watched from outside his tent. *Harrison has been asking for it for some time and I'm afraid this might be the time*, Wharton said aloud to himself, rubbing his hands together outside his tent and bringing his cape up around the back of his neck.

"What the hell's goin' on?" Troy yelled out. "Tell me, Sarge."

"All right, but youse didn't hear it from me," O'Riley answered, helping McTavvit hold up Steve. "But, the Major said thet they refused an order to make youse men to drill in this freezin' rain. They said it was a stupid command, and I agree. But who am I?"

"They what?" another Ranger asked, drying Matt's hands and face with a rag. "This ain't fit weather for no drillin'."

"Many of our men are in bed with camp fever," another disgruntled Ranger added, helping Troy keep Matt on his feet.

The men were assisting the Lieutenants back to their tents when Troy caught sight of Harrison marching down the Pike towards them. "Here comes the bastard, now." He turned Matt over to one of the other Rangers and rolled up his sleeves. "If it's a fight he's a wantin', he's come to the right place."

O'Riley grabbed a hold of his arm and stopped him. "You'll not be fightin' an officer, and him bein' your Commandin' Officer, too." he barked.

"Who'll be stoppin' me?" Troy growled back. "You?"

"It's me duty."

Two of the Rangers caught O'Riley by his arms and pinned him back from stopping Troy. A dozen other Rangers came up the Pike and sided in with Troy.

McTavvit and three others continued carrying Matt and Steve back to their tents.

"Those men are under arrest!" barked Harrison in his high tenor voice. "Put them down, now!"

The Rangers continued carrying the Lieutenants without stopping. "You'll have to shoot us, Sir," a Ranger yelled out. He was small, the same height as Harrison, a little thinner and sported dark red hair.

"And I'll do just that if you don't put them down." He brought out his pearl-handled Navy, cocked it and aimed it in their directions.

"Shoot me first, Sir," McTavvit answered, steadying his hold on Steve.

"And me," the red-headed Ranger added.

Troy and the other Rangers ran to Harrison in double time, some with their pistols out of their holsters.

Wharton witnessed the mutiny that was taking place and quickly summoned Captain "Pat" Christian of Company K, the officer closest to his tent at the time.

"Take some of your men and stop whatever is going on there, Lieutenant," Wharton commanded. "Get Harrison out of there and have him report to me."

Christian commanded some of his men nearby to ride with him. They mounted as a unit and rode hard and fast towards Harrison who stood still, watching the fracas.

"Hold on there, Rangers," Christian ordered with his Colt 51 aimed directly at Troy.

"This bastard was . . ." Troy lit into them but was stopped by O'Riley.

"What he's tryin' to say, Sir," O'Riley said at attention, saluting his commanding officer, "is thet our good officer, Major Harrison was presuming to treat these two fine officers so inconsiderately."

"From where I sit, Sergeant," Christian said, staying his pistol on Troy, "you men are committing mutiny. Are you not?"

Christian and the men behind him held their weapons ready. They were prepared to fire at Troy and the others if they saw any overt action on their part.

McTavvit and his men kept walking to the tents, carrying Matt and Steve.

"Are you not?" Christian reiterated loudly above the rain.

"No Sir, they're not," O'Riley answered. "They're jest seein' thet these two men get medical attention. Thet's all, Sir."

Troy and the Company A Rangers stood their ground ready to do bout with Harrison still knowing that any move could be disastrous at the moment and not at all in their favor.

"Major," Christian addressed Harrison without relinquishing his control for the moment, "you're in command. What do you want us to do?"

Harrison looked steely-eyed at Troy and the others and kept his Navy pointed at them. "You men realize that mutiny is punishable by death? Do you not?"

"Yes Sir, we does," O'Riley said.

"You're not in this, Sarge," Troy said, grabbing his saluting arm and bringing it down. "It's our fight."

"And am I not part of your company, now I be a askin' ye? And me your Sergeant." His arm went back into a salute and he kept it there.

"You best be listening to your Sergeant, Private," Harrison said sharply and to the point. "In a moment you're going to be dead if you so much as twitch an eyebrow."

"Oh, no, Sir," O'Riley interrupted. "They won't fight ye. Me word on it." He kneed Troy hard in the groin, causing him to react in pain. "Oh, my, did you hurt yourself, now?" He took his saluting hand, strong and beefy as it was, and brought it hard across Troy's face. "And what would ye be fallin' down in the road for, Private?" He excused himself to the officers in front of him and bent down as if to help Troy up, grabbed a good hold on his throat and then whispered in his ear, "You keep your gawdam mouth shut, Private, or we'll all be killed. And you'll be the furst cause I'll do the honors me self."

He released his strong hold on Troy and let Troy come up by himself. "He's sayin' all's forgiven, Sir."

"Is that right, Private?" Harrison asked, uncocking his pistol.

"Yes, Sir," Troy answered and painfully stood at attention. The Rangers behind him followed suit.

"Then I suggest you get back to your tents," Harrison growled. He looked angrily at the men and holstered his Navy. "See to it that the Lieutenants are cared for. I want them to report back to me when they're up and on their feet again."

Troy gritted his teeth and let the blood from the Sarge's hard fist flow down his chin while he still remained at attention.

"Thank you, Captain Christian," Harrison said. "Carry on."

"Yes, Sir," Christian answered. "By your leave, Sir, I'd like to check in on the Lieutenants myself."

"Do that, Christian," Harrison answered. He turned and walked back up the hill towards his tent when he caught the stern look from Wharton standing outside his headquarters, motioning for him to come to his tent. When he reached Wharton's tent, he followed him and ducked inside.

Matt never found out what if any discipline was given Harrison for his act unbecoming an officer, but he and Steve were not bothered by his commands for several days. And from that day forward, Harrison was no longer called Jimmy for he had earned a new name, "the Mark Time Major". The fact of the matter was, Wharton never took a liking to him, either.

The two lieutenants were back on their feet the next day and the sun shone for the first time in many days. The company moved out towards Georgia.

"What kept you goin', chum?" Steve asked as they rode the high ground that was still filled with gaping holes of mud. Their animals shook the cold as they pushed on.

"Ginny," Matt answered.

"Ginny?"

"All the time we marked time, I saw her lovely face and beautiful smile, Steve. Jest like it was when we first sat down by the river together. I never told you this, but she gave me a good whoppin'."

"Ginny did? Now you've got my interest."

"Wull, it's like this. Remember when I told you about ridin' for the first time into Tennessee and caught sight of a slaver usin' a whip on this Negro?"

"Yeah," Steve answered. "Ginny whupped ya."

"Now, me not knowin' about slaves and such, I figured the black man was bein' beat up for no account. I rode up and told the man, his name was Al, and we became friends later. I told him to stop whoppin' him. He didn't listen to me so I plumb shot the whip right out of his hand."

"And then what?"

"Rode off. Thought I was far enough away, I sat myself down for a spell under an apple tree, grabbed one to eat, and almost went to sleep. Along came Ginny with this here Al and another man, real mean cuss. The man we killed back in Nacogdoches. He took my gun away."

"Well, what d'ya do?"

"I looked at her all duded up in dark clothes with a whip in her hand. I didn't 'spect she would lay into me with the whip. I kinda thought we'd hit it off so to speak. But she did. Whopped me right across my chest."

"She whopped you with her whip? Wow!"

"Yep. And I took it. And then she saw I wasn't cryin' or nothin', told the other men to git, and she took me down by the river."

"Interestin'."

20

"It was. She cleaned me all up see, and I put some tree moss on the cuts and the next thing I knew, I was in love. I s'pose I fell head over heels in love with her the moment I saw her."

"Did cha kiss her, or anythin'?"

"Won't say." Matt smiled and blushed a little for telling as much as he had. "We spent most a year together. I beat up thet one Sin fella who was the boss of her plantation and took over his job. Ginny's dad taught me about cotton and all. We had one hell of a time together. Thought I'd marry her and settle down."

"Why didn't cha?"

"Almost did. Christmas time, we had a big party, dance and all. Her dad and I got stone drunk so his date drove us home. Thet's when this bastard showed up with a coupla goonies and caught Jim and me. Thet's her dad, Jim. They caught us drunk and beat the holy crap out of us.

"This Sin fella, the guy whose job I took away, he tried to rape Ginny right then and there. Almost killed me for takin' her away from him."

"Was she all right? I mean, did anythin' happen?"

"Nope, thanks to the black folk who were my friends and all. The slaves who worked on the plantation. Ya see, I treated them like we're all alike. Could never see any difference. Hell, not any of our fault we're different color from one another. So we all learned to work together, and I got rid of the whips."

Steve smiled. "You were sayin' about Ginny. Was she all right?"

"The black folk came to our rescue. I had a big knot on my head and Jim was out for the count. The slaves got after Sin and his two cronies and beat 'em up." Matt sat back in his saddle and laughed. "You should 'av seen 'em, Steve. They lit into 'em. One got killed and the other, they tied up and put him in a pigsty until the sheriff came by the next day."

"And Sin got away?" Steve took his wad of tobacco from his shirt pocket, sliced it and then offered the wad to Matt.

Matt took the wad and continued. "He made a mistake. He fired a shot into the crowd. That's what got them all stirred up. Then he rode out like his tail was on fire. Only thing was . . ." He sliced off a piece of tobacco and placed it between his teeth, then he gave the wad back to Steve.

"What's thet?"

"The shot had hit and killed Bertha, our house Negro."

"Oh, hell."

"No one was so well-liked than her. We didn't know she'd been shot 'til later after she tended to Ginny and Sylvia, Jim's girl. She patched me and Jim up, and jest walked outside and died."

"Blast! And thet's the man we shot and killed?"

"Yep."

"And now I know where Ginny comes in," Steve said, trying to outdistance Matt in spitting. "And here I've been tryin' to saddle you with my sister. Sorry about thet, chum."

"No need for apologies. Hell, your sister's one fine lookin' filly. I'd be a fool not to want her for a wife, had I not got Ginny."

Steve spat and stared at Matt. "In your mind, Matt."

"No, Steve. I've still got her. I know they said she was dead, but she's out there somewhere. I can feel her presence every day. It's something I can't rightly explain. Jest know it."

Matt spit out his wad to the wind, nudged Skeeter and rode away to join his company of Rangers. "See you at chow," he yelled back at Steve.

CHAPTER 2

HOW DRY THE WIND

It was late March in Tennessee. Lieutenant Matthew Jorgensen kept his eyes glued for any signs of the Federals as he stood beside an old picket fence that lined the roadway for seemingly hundreds of miles. Rain trickled down the overhead branches and limbs of the trees that sheltered the countryside. Skeeter stood ground-reined at Matt's side. Matt kept the brass hardware polished and the leather on his saddle clean. He watched as the rain bubbled on them and grit his teeth. His sharp mind and keen eyes traced the countryside for the enemy, but his heart was still searching for Ginny.

Steve sauntered up to Matt and offered him a tin of coffee. "Sign of any activity?"

"Nah. Just a dirty, muddy road leading to nowhere," Matt returned. "Just thinkin'."

"'Bout?"

"Thet tree on thet hillside over yonder reminds me of where I first met Ginny. Jest thinkin' about her."

"Good way to get your head blown off."

"Yeah. I've had my eyes and ears tuned. No sight or sound of any Blue Belly. I could smell 'em."

"Coffee's not all thet hot. Better drink it."

Matt gulped a few swigs and threw the rest away. "Time to ride."

They turned and walked back to camp where O'Riley had two squads of men rallied for a march. Mounting their steeds at the post, they rode over to Harrison, who was standing in front of his tent.

Reining up in front of him, Matt informed him. "We're taking advantage of the weather to weed out some Feds."

"Two squads? Both of you?" Harrison asked. "What if we're attacked?"

"Pray thet we're not, Sir," Matt returned and saluted.

"Be back by noon." Harrison returned the salute to both gentlemen and went back inside his tent.

The hatred of "Company A" for Harrison hadn't diminished their spirit any. Matt and Steve saw to that. With layovers, the Rangers found no such thing as idle time, not with these two young and brash lieutenants. One thing for sure was, the men knew Matt and Steve were the best officers, and they intended to keep it that way, even through tough training and discipline.

The weather was still cold and drizzling intermittently for the next few weeks. Young recruits came on board as well as did more of the healed and treated veterans who returned to the field of battle. The Lieutenants' task at training increased. At times, the Rangers didn't know who they despised most, the Lieutenants, O'Riley . . . or Harrison.

Matt mounted and rode over to a squad of men who had returned from the hospital where Steve had been addressing them. He reined up and listened to Steve.

Matt crossed his leg over his saddle and rolled his makings as he listened and looked proudly at Steve.

"You've all got shotguns. We've got enough shells to win this war. Use them. If you get shot again, I don't want it to be because you ran out of shells. Sarge will make sure you get what you need.

"We'll come in from behind our men, ride fast and low. Use your Navys first. Most of you have at least two pistols, if not three or more. I would advise you who do not have an extra pistol of any kind that you get another one, or at least carry an extra cylinder. Some of you already have. Agin', I don't want you to run out of shot.

"When you get within fifteen yards, use your shotguns. Not before and not until! Do you hear me? Not before and not until!"

"Yes, Sir!" came the unison response from the Rangers.

"He doesn't have a heart," a Ranger voiced out loud enough for even Matt to hear.

"I'll vouch for thet," Matt answered. His voice lightened things up a little.

"Of course," Steve continued, "we wait until we're right in the blue boys' faces before we shoot 'em."

The Rangers' laughter died down some for they knew he was serious.

"Lieutenant Jorgensen," Steve called out. "You want to add anything to what I jest said?"

Matt rode out into the arena in a slow walk and eyed the returnees. "How'd you get it?" he asked the first man he came across, referring to his bandaged shoulder.

"They stuck my horse with a bayonet, much like they did to Colonel Terry's horse, Sir," the Ranger reported. "We fell and I rolled. Thet's when the blue belly got me in the shoulder. I turned and shot him full blast with my shotgun."

"You okay?"

"Hurts a little, but I'll be okay, Sir."

Matt rode a little further and stopped at a man kneeling in the grass. "How about you, Ranger? Where'd they get you?"

"In me arse," came the reply to the resounding echo of laughter.

"Seems thet both men had their backs to the Federals. What's the answer?"

"Don't fall off your horse?" one Ranger answered.

"No, you'll fall off your horse alright," Matt continued, "but when you do, roll away from it like this Ranger did, but come up quick with your pistol or shotgun cocked. And don't stick your arse up in the air."

Matt rode Skeeter out away, turned and galloped back towards the men. He reined up and laid Skeeter down, rolled out of the saddle and came up with a pistol cocked. "And this thing had better be cocked and ready to fire." He fired two rounds for effect.

The Rangers were impressed.

"Lieutenant Jorgensen isn't trying to show off just to be heard," Steve shouted to the Rangers. "We learned the importance of this maneuver from our first day out. We weren't impressed with a lot of the men at thet time. Clumsiness can get cha killed."

"You men are the leaders in this heah War," Matt said, dusting the dirt from his clothes. "And I might add, you're only as good as your horse. So treat him kindly."

"Mount up!" Steve ordered and rode to the center of the arena.

Matt mounted up on Skeeter and joined him.

"We're gonna do a few dry runs. So line up jest like you would in a real battle."

The two Lieutenants watched as the men formed a line of some twenty seasoned Rangers still suffering the pangs of war.

"And we pitied ourselves for having to mark time in the rain," Matt remarked.

"Cold, freezin' rain," Steve added. He looked at the men ready to charge and said, "One thing to remember, Rangers. You're the best. Now show me! Listen to my commands and ride to the end of this clearing and stop. Turn and come back without waiting for any order from me, jest as fast as you can. The last one back gets latrine duty."

The men were ready.

"All right men," Steve yelled out, "trot!"

The men followed the command carefully and rode the fairway as a tight and disciplined unit.

"Canter!" Steve yelled. He watched the men spur their horses lightly. Then he gave the signal and let out his loudest command, "Charge!"

The Rangers rode to the end of the clearing with their pistols in hand. Approaching the end of the field, they bent low so as not to be seen by the pretended enemy. They rose up and fired their pistols. Then replacing their weapons with their shotguns, they aimed them as if they were shooting, stopped, turned and galloped back fast to their original positions.

When they finished, Steve turned to Matt and asked, "Who was last?"

"Damned if I know. They all came in together."

"Dismount!" Steve ordered. "Take over, Sergeant!"

O'Riley yelled out, "Tighten your girth!" When he saw they had done as he said, he continued, "Mount up!"

This went on again and again for many days. The men hated it, but their leaders knew the importance of it. They knew they had to be the best. They also thought they'd get rest when it rained, and it did rain. But they saw no rest.

The Texians picketed Johnston's left front and flank in a heavy rain. They prepared themselves for a surprise attack against the Federals. It never came that night.

4 April 1862

The rain stopped the next day and the sun showed her face. The dry spell didn't last long, but the Rangers thought it would be a good time to test their weapons.

Several of the Rangers approached Wharton as he walked by them one day. "Colonel Wharton," one of the Rangers asked, "the sun's out. We'd like your permission to fire our weapons to check them out, Sir. It'd make us feel easier to reload them with fresh charges."

Wharton looked around and up at the sun. Forgetting for the moment about his preparedness for any surprise attack upon the Federals, looked straight away where he saw the field was empty.

"Hell. Don't see why not," he replied. "Go ahead, Rangers." He walked back to his tent and slipped inside.

The Rangers were one happy bunch, firing off their weapons and checking to make sure they were operating correctly and the powder was dry. However, Wharton nearly lost the element of surprise.

Lieutenant General Leonidas Polk, thinking that the battle had commenced, quickly brought up a brigade of infantry.

"What in the hell?" he yelled out from a distance.

A West Pointer and former room partner to Jefferson Davis, Leonidus Polk had resigned his commission in his senior year and became a bishop. At the advent of the Civil War, President Davis persuaded Polk to accept a commission in the Confederate Army, in which, after Shiloh, he joined up with the Army of the Tennessee.

Needless to say, Polk carried some weight, but he was impatient with men training all the time. He didn't feel the need for it, and being a nervous individual, complained constantly about it.

"It's coming from the Rangers' camp, Sir," a sergeant reported to him.

"Those infernal Yankee skirmishes. Take some men and find out. If you need more, send for help."

"Yes, Sir," the Sergeant replied and quickly rounded up some of his men. "Let's get the lead out."

When the Sergeant discovered that the men who were shooting were just checking their rifles, he reported it back to Polk.

Polk then reported the incident to General Bragg. "Braxton, I think Wharton has gone too far."

"How's that, Leon?"

"We're within shouting distance of the enemy, and he's having his men shooting their weapons."

"And?"

"Well, hell, they're giving our position away."

"And you think they don't already know where we are?" Bragg asked, lighting a cigar.

"Yes, but to confirm it with our shooting guns needlessly only makes matters worse. I'm asking you to discipline him."

"What for, man? Shooting guns is part of this man's army. We do shoot guns, now don't we?"

"Sir, I respectfully request that you discipline him. Arrest him and the entire regiment. If we encounter a needless battle because of his carelessness, I will personally write that in my journal that you, Sir, allowed it."

"And you would be right," Bragg answered, exhaling his cigar smoke towards Polk. "All right, I'll talk to him." He called out, "Sergeant!"

"Don't just talk to him, Braxton. Arrest the son-of-a-bitch."

"O'Riley was within sound of Bragg's voice and immediately entered the tent with a proper salute. "Yes, Sir."

"Tell Colonel Wharton, I'd like to see him. And tell him to stop the shooting. Unless of course it's at the enemy."

O'Riley saluted and left to summon Wharton who caught sight of Polk leaving Bragg's headquarters.

Wharton entered the tent, removed his hat, and addressed Bragg. "Yes, Sir. You wanted to see me."

"Yes, John. I just received word that you're having your men fire their weapons when we're close the enemy lines."

"Yes, Sir. Since the rain let up, our men wanted to test their weapons. I saw nothing wrong with it since we can see the enemy's camp and they can see us. Thought it'd throw a little scare into them."

"Well, we now know that the Federals know about us for sure," Bragg returned. "Let's not give our Federal soldiers any reason to get up and start attacking us."

"Yes, Sir," Wharton agreed. "Polk complaining again?"

Bragg nodded and took another puff on the cigar. Other officers have voiced it, too.

"Hell, General," Wharton said as he removed his gloves, "who would have thought otherwise? Our first clear day and . . ."

"I know, John, "Bragg interrupted. "The timing was off."

"We're all a little jittery. I hate to say this, but I have to put you under arrest."

"What?"

"Just for the next battle. You and your men will have to sit out this one."

"Polk! He got to you."

"Some do. Comes with the territory."

Wharton stood for a moment, straightened up, saluted Bragg and received his salute. He started to leave, stopped at the entrance and said, "We've already checked out our weapons and the men are cleaning them, now, Braxton."

"Sorry, John."

Wharton turned again and left.

"John." Bragg called him back.

"Yes, Sir?"

"Oh, nothing. Except, you know of course, I was charged by one of your peers to so arrest you. I would have overlooked the arrest. You know that. Don't you?"

Wharton stopped, thought for a moment, and then nodded in agreement.

Watching Wharton walk away in anger, he murmured to himself under his breath, You're *the best man I've got, dammit. You just thought about the safety of your men at a wrong time.*

Wharton rejoined his men. His address to them was simple. "Sometimes I suppose I don't use good judgment. There's no room in our outfit for bad judgment. I shouldn't have let you fire your weapons, knowing damn well that we were within close parameters of our enemy. I acted unwisely. Because of this, we will sit this next battle out."

An air of anxiety swept over the men as they began to talk among themselves.

"Hold up!" Wharton yelled out. "Sure. We'll sit it out, but know this, men. We will erase this wrong in the next battle. Trust me."

It was the same General Polk who, when he was later ordered to attack Chickamauga, failed to comply with the order. As a consequence, Bragg ordered him at that time to face a court-martial. *"I'll be a son-of-a- . . . ",* Bragg said to himself.

"Commanding a brigade can be quite tedious at times." He lit his cigar and sat down. *"Quite tedious."*

The roads always seemed to stay muddy, an advantage for good stout steeds such as the Kentucky stock the Rangers had over both the Federal cavalry and foot soldiers. This was particularly the case when the Rangers rode through the woods over leaves that camouflaged the mud beneath them. The horses proved their worth and hardly ever faltered.

Usually a patrol or a squad rode out through the woods at the first sign of smoke in the air and ferreted some Federal soldiers out of their nests where they were setting up offensive positions.

It made no difference whether the company of Yankees was small or large, the Rangers swept down upon them with their shotguns at close range. They were proud of their reputation as fast and furious devils and wanted to keep it that way. The two lieutenants not only encouraged it, they demanded it.

When the Rangers weren't chasing the Federals, the Federals were chasing the Rangers through the woods. Had it not been for the dead and wounded, the cat and mouse chase would have been rather fun for many. However, as it was, many a mother on both sides would never see her son again.

Skirmishes were on the increase by the Rangers as they traveled to Georgia as their objective. General Albert Sidney Johnston vowed to not only protect Georgia with his brigade but to route out the Federals and chase them north.

CHAPTER 3

THE THIRD BRAZORIAN SABER

Matt and Steve found their place by a cottonwood and adjusted their eyes to the scene around them. The sight of a church, a small, unpretentious edifice of hewn logs that occupied the brow of a hill with a commanding prospect made the setting seem a little holier than it was.

"I don't figure it cost much to make," Steve whispered. "There's no stained window or carvings or anythin' fancy like. Hell, the people around here are few and far between. They'd have to come for miles to attend services. Can't seat mor'n fifty, I'd say."

"Why?" Matt whispered.

"Yeah. Like I said, who'd a thought?"

"I don't mean the General," Matt corrected him. "I mean this bloody gawd awful, boot kickin', ever lovin' war. A while ago I was in the arms of my girl in another cotton field. Then I went chasin' a killer. And now, I'm here by an abandoned church in a cotton field a hunert miles from nowhere. Don't figure. No cotton growing either" Then he looked out and smiled. "They grow corn and beans. Of course, the peach blossoms make the field real pretty like."

Steve hooched himself up against a cottonwood and took out his makings. "Want some?"

Matt eyed Steve taking his tobacco out of his pocket. "It's the peach blossoms that make this place beautiful. Real pretty like in full daylight. But the moon makes them pretty, too."

Steve offered a slice of chaw to Matt. "Can't sleep." He looked out into the field where the moon seemed to play tricks with the shadows on the ground. "Wonder how many are out there?"

"Too damn many." Matt bit into his tobacco and relaxed for the moment.

But the next few days were not for his relaxation. He waited and watched for something to happen.

As he stood beside the church early Sunday morning, he saw the silhouette of a tall man walk inside. He trekked over to where the man entered and quietly followed him. Once inside, he saw him kneel down to pray. The man was Confederate General Albert Sidney Johnston. Matt joined him respectfully by bowing his head. He listened but heard nothing audible.

The man rose and, seeing Matt, ordered him, "Prepare for battle, Lieutenant." General Johnston then turned and walked out of the church. "Thanks for joining me."

Matt stayed for a moment, looked at the church's plain-glass window to the early light of dawn outside and said to himself, *A man as great as this comes in and prays. Why? What good does it do? Pa always taught me that prayer is in the power of man, and that Whoever or Whatever is over this cockeyed world of ours simply ignores us anyway. He does what He wants to do, when and where.* He found his eyes slightly closed as his hand gripped the back of a pew. Before he realizeed it, he whispered a prayer. *I'm only a man, Lord, who doesn't know nothin' about You or anythin' but . . .* He opened his eyes and gripped the Navy Colt at his side.

The shadow of another man draped Matt's body and made him aware of his presence. It was that of Chaplain Robert F. Bunting. "Want me to put an *amen* to it, Matt?"

"What?" Matt turned towards the chaplain and removed his hand from the handle of his colt. "Oh, Chaplain. I was jest sayin' a word." He fidgeted a little. "General Johnston was jest here."

"Need me to help you?"

"No. No, Chaplain. I'll be all right. Thanks. Gotta get back to my men."

"It's almost time for my services. I'd like for you to stay."

Matt excused himself and left the tent. Bunting bowed his head, prayed for a moment, and ended it with, *Amen.*

General Johnston had not taken into account for the severity of the weather. The rains came down heavy that night and muddied up the roads and fields as well as his plans to attack. His army sluggishly moved towards Pittsburg Landing. His and General Beauregard's fear was that they would lose the element of surprise and Major General Don Carlos Buell would group up with General Grant at the Tennessee with a more powerful force. Yet it did not phase Johnston's determination to plan strategically for a victorious battle, knowing that the enemy was still pretty much spread out and disorganized.

Wharton was convinced that the Rangers could ride to hell and back in the rain and mud with their thoroughbreds.

Late that afternoon, Johnston's Brigade smelled the smoke of Federal campfires. Terry's Rangers camped in the woods immediately across an old cotton field just short of where they spotted a Federals' camp. They kept out of sight and quieted their horses and other noises from the troops. The air fell dismally and deathly quiet.

The brigade threw out a heavy picket in the direction of the enemy and lay upon their arms during the night, prepared for action at the call of the bugle. The night passed slowly with the echo of the insects resounding throughout the fields.

6 April 1862

General Johnston ordered his troops into offensive position against the Union Army of Tennessee under General Grant along the Tennessee River. He realized he had lost valuable time in getting the formation of troops and artillery into place without the Federals knowing it. Because of this, Johnston had lost some of the element of surprise on his side.

"Bring 'em up! Bring 'em up!" a lieutenant barked at the artillery soldiers as they moved the canons into position.

Johnston had chosen the hillside for a barrage of attacks carefully, but the men, for some reason or another, had difficulty with positioning their canons.

"Get the damn canon loaded," a canon commander ordered his men, realizing he was slipping behind the others as they prepared their canon for the onslaught.

Once in place, the barrage from his artillery filled the afternoon air with a sense of urgency as the ground shook from the thunderous noise of the canons. Astride his great white stallion, Johnston waved his saber and yelled out, "I will lead these Kentuckians and Tennesseans into the fight." He looked over at Wharton standing ready with his men. "Well, Wharton," he said, slipping on his gauntlets, "what are you waiting for? I'm releasing you, so get in there with Walker and let's get this war over with."

Colonel Wharton, now released from his arrest, led the cavalry charge against the Federal left. Colonel Harvey Walker attacked against the right.

Colonel Calvin Walker led the infantry offensive down the middle while Johnston's guns loped their barrage overhead. When they saw the full force of the Federals, their eyes opened wide for they had not anticipated a force many times their own size, although they were the charging army. Walker's infantry met the Federals in hand-to-hand combat, and at the sound of the horses' hooves, they got under cover to let the cavalry ride through.

When Matt and Steve followed with their cavalry units down the middle of the arena and got ahead of the infantry. They fell upon the Federals like a colossal herd of buffalo. They gave out the fiercest yell that cut through the smoke-filled air. The rest of Terry's Rangers quickly spurred their steeds and rode up from every ravine and from behind tents and forage fast and furious. The Federals showed great fear, and when the hoof beats pounded louder and louder, they fired their volleys at the ensuing cavalry. Once they fired, they retreated.

Matt and Steve plunged their steeds through the lines with A Company and fragmented their defense with hard and quick shotgun blasts. They found the Federals slow to reload and fire again once they wasted their first shots at a distance. The rest of the Rangers followed and opened the gorge wider with their shotguns for Johnston's infantry to follow. The Rangers continued charging and scattered the Union soldiers out of hiding and into the open fields.

Walker's infantry rose and fired at Grant's army. Minni balls flew like swarms of hornets through the air, hitting everything in sight, peeling bark off the trees, kicking up dirt and breaking up bodies.

General Johnston's ride with his brigade impressed the Rangers, for he appeared to be everywhere. Storming forward, the Confederates found the Federal position not as fortified as they had expected. Johnston had achieved almost total surprise on his part against the Federals. By mid-morning, the Confederates seemed within easy reach of victory, overrunning one frontline Federal division and capturing its camp.

Shiloh Church seemed to be a pivotal point for both sides and the Federals were not willing to give up ground even though Johnston's brigade pummeled their right. They seemed weakened at times to almost breaking, but by some strange miracle it seemed the Federals fought harder.

Tremendous casualties piled up for both sides.

Johnston's brigade came to a momentary halt at a place his men called the "hornet's nest" in front of Sarah Bell's peach orchard. Nothing spectacular about this landmark, but both sides were unwilling to give it away. Johnston's right flank eventually caused Grant to give ground, but instead of driving them away from the river as Johnston had planned, the Confederates drove them to the river. As brilliant a military tactician Johnston appeared to be, he could not fathom how his charge drove the Federals to the river. It was a move he had not anticipated. He looked to capture them running the perimeter instead.

"Damnation!" he yelled out. "There's no way we're going to get in there to beat them."

The ground was a boggy ravine where Grant's troops found good coverage behind trees. Neither man nor beast could march to meet them except in single file, which meant sure death. The rains made it impractical, if almost impossible, to amass an attack, for the troops would be picked off one by one.

Johnston signaled for Wharton.

"Yes, Sir," Wharton answered.

"What I'm looking at, John is something you're going to have to do to save this messed-up attack. As I see it, if they suspect an attempt by us to route them out of there, they're going to have to build a solid front, repulse our army from every rock and tree they can find like guerillas and fight with the last breath in them which could be crucial to my brigade."

"Am I still under arrest?" Wharton asked.

"What'd you think? Get in there and fight."

"Yes, Sir!"

Wharton turned his steed and rode fast and hard towards Matt.

"Take them through, Matt," Wharton yelled out.

A minni ball struck and killed a Ranger who was riding beside Wharton. Another minni ball caught Wharton in the right leg, knocking him out of the saddle.

"Matt," Wharton cried out as he rose and leaned against his horse. "Lead the offensive for us."

"You're hit, Sir," Matt noted, riding up to Wharton.

"You've got to get our Rangers in there and out, alive."

"Yes Sir," Matt replied. "We'll do 'er." Matt spurred Skeeter forward, commanding the Rangers to ride through the Federals. He realized the risk and pushed his men fast and furiously into the ravine, firing off their weapons and disorganizing the hidden troops. Once in, the Rangers turned, reloaded and fired again as they returned to their safety. Some died, but the Federals felt their anger.

When they returned to camp, Wharton was sitting in a straight back, waiting for their report.

"Colonel Wharton, Sir," Matt addressed him as he reined up at the post. "How's your leg?"

"Good clean wound, Matt," Wharton answered, offering him and Steve each a cigar. "Not as bad as it appeared to be." He smiled, and then asked, "How was it?"

"Like you said, Sir," Matt returned. "We scattered them and caused them to run. We lost a few. They lost more."

The night rested but Wharton's Rangers didn't. Though wounded, Wharton commanded a heavy picket to be set up. The men stayed alert.

General Johnston caught sight of General Beauregard who still looked pale and sickly, wiping saliva from his mouth with his bandana. He rode over and confronted him, angrily. "I told you, G. T.," Johnston shouted to him. "I told you that if they got to the river, this would happen."

"Thanks for your vote of confidence, Albert," Beauregard shouted back. "That's why I had our men fight in three successive parallel lines, to keep them from getting to the river. It would have worked if we were fighting in the open on a clear day. We're not. We're fighting across uneven land, woods and now this gawdam mud."

In the gray light of dawn, a small Federal reconnaissance patrol discovered Johnston's army deployed for battle astride the Corinth road, just a mile beyond the forward Federal camps. Before they could return to camp, Matt's squad of Rangers sent them to their Maker.

Matt returned with the detailed information they obtained from the field back to Johnston.

Pointing to the north side of the Tennessee with his lit cigar, Johnston informed Grant's position to Colonels Wharton and Major Harrison along with Calvin Harvey Walker of the

Third Tennessee Infantry. "Grant is over there, gentlemen. And, with sixty-thousand troops, give or take a hundred, Sherman is to the right of us."

He looked at Wharton and asked, "Your leg alright?"

"Healing up real nice," he answered.

"Are we going to wait for him to attack?" Walker asked about Grant, watching Johnston chew on his cigar. Walker was a determinant six-footer and considered to be one of the best infantry leaders in Johnston's command. His question was rhetorical in that he knew Johnston was not a patient man who would await an attack. He also knew that Generals Grant and Sherman were also impatient leaders and would attack at the drop of a hat. The wait for both sides appeared to soon be over.

General Ulysses S. Grant, and General William Tecumseh Sherman, Commander of the Fifth Division of the Army of the Tennessee were the two great Commanders of the Federal forces that stood between Johnston and victory.

"There's no word from our men about Buell, but I don't intend to underestimate him," Johnston continued. He knew the two Yankee Commanders were not about to sit on their haunches and wait to be attacked. He knew it. He did not fear General Buell any; he just realized that he was the catalyst who kept him from making his next move. He waited, but his waiting moments were near an end.

An Ohio-born, Indiana-raised West Pointer, commanding the Army of the Ohio, Major General Don Carlos Buell had been posted to the infantry. He had prior-battle experience serving in the Seminole and Mexican wars.

"Damnation!" Johnston slammed his fist down on his desk. "I'm not waiting any longer. I aim to take my newly christened Army of the Mississippi and launch an offensive. I'm going to make Grant retreat into the swamps, and then I'll cross over the Tennessee and beat the living hell out of Buell before he can join up with Grant. That the way you see it, gentlemen?"

"We encountered some Feds this morning, General," Wharton reported. He referred to Matt's skirmish. "We took them by surprise. I don't think it's going to be a great battle."

"Colonel Wharton, don't ever underestimate the enemy. Who you encountered was probably an encampment of unsuspecting Union soldiers." He waved his cigar, turned and pointed it at Wharton. "All the same, John. Congratulations. Now, would you like to expound on that?"

"Yes, Sir. The best news is that we defeated them and made them run. As I saw it, the Federals were in position of attack and not concerned about their defense. They were so disoriented, so scattered, that all we had to do was ride right through them.

"The way I figure it, General," Wharton continued with much stamina in his speech, "the field is wide open. We should simply march down the middle with full force."

Johnston clasped his hands behind his back, turned around and, removing his cigar from his lips, said, "That's the expected. We do the unexpected. I'm going to show you some strategies, Colonel. By damnation, you will see the best fighting you've ever witnessed, or my name isn't Sidney Johnston. We're going to scatter them with our artillery and, when they try to regroup, we're going to move the canons up closer and give them another barrage. Then we're going to charge through them with some of your Rangers on both sides," he smiled, "and your best men will follow me down the middle."

"General," Wharton addressed him, "why is this battle so gawdam important?"

"Railroad, Colonel," Johnston answered. "There's a railroad crossing there, the Memphis and Charleston, Wharton that is strategically located. It's the western Confederacy's most important rail junction. Our concern is transportation." He went to the map on his desk and used his cigar to direct the points of his objective.

"About 20 miles distant from the bend of the Tennessee, near Pittsburg Landing, right here. It crosses the Mobile and Ohio at Corinth, in the northeastern corner of Mississippi. Now why do you suspect it's important, John?"

"No need telling you, General," Wharton replied in an easy voice, "Corinth is our mobilization center for our troops through Bowling Green."

"And Mobile, Pensacola, and Virginia," Johnston continued. "One of our jobs is to fortify the eastern and northern approaches to the city. Make it impossible for Grant to get in. That's the easy part. What he wants to do is come right up the rails and destroy us. We're not going to let that happen.

"Gentlemen. If Grant gets through," Johnston warned, "it'll push the South's victory further back and prolong the war indefinitely."

"How is General Beauregard, Sir?" Wharton asked. "He's not in this meeting. Am I to presume he's not feeling well?"

"G. T. is under the weather, else he'd be here with us. However, even with his absence, we agree that this is going to be our victory."

"G. T." was the abbreviated name General Beauregard preferred to be called by his officers. General Pierre Gustave Toutant Beauregard, Johnston's second in command, stood barely 5 foot 7 inches tall, weighed 150 pounds, and sported a full beard and moustache. He was also the fourth officer in command of the Confederate Army. He had seen battle in the Mexican War, was present at Fort Sumter as well as the first at Manassas with Terry and Lubbock. On this day, he laid sick in his tent, too weak to attend the all-important meeting. However, he was briefed on it and discussed it with General Johnston ahead of the meeting.

"Yes, Sir," Wharton agreed. "Where do you have the Rangers in your plan, General?" Wharton asked, stroking his beard with his left hand and holding tight to the handle of his saber with his right.

Johnston stood up and straightened his back as if in pain. He was not a young man and the strain of bending over the map plans pained him greatly.

"Colonel Walker here will brief you on that.

Walker stepped in and eyed Wharton and Harrison carefully.

"Before the smoke clears and after my men have gone in."

He then looked at Wharton sternly and, at the same time, watched the concern of Major Harrison in the background. He walked over to Harrison and placed his hand on his shoulder.

"I hear you're a hard-nosed bastard, Harrison," Walker said with tight lips. "I want you to take your Rangers and ride through my infantry."

"Through your infantry, Harvey?" Harrison resounded. "That's certain suicide for your men. Not to mention dangerous for mine."

"Aren't you listening, Major? Grant will not be prepared for a cavalry assault while fighting hand-to-hand, I assure you. Not with cannons volleying overhead." He turned and walked back to the center of the men and directed his attention to all the officers. "My infantry will do their job way ahead of your horse soldiers. But, I don't want my infantry chewed up. I want you to ride your men hot and heavy. Put on a show that you've been bragging about all this time.

"I understand you consider your men the best in this outfit, and I know I have the best damned infantry."

Johnston interrupted. "Terry was my closest friend. I bragged to high heaven about his Rangers."

"You tell me what you want, Colonel," Harrison answered, chomping down on a cigar.

"Good. When you see my infantry marching through the smoke that will mean they've encountered hand-to-hand combat. I want your men to ride like they've never ridden before. Ride through our infantry and plow the field."

"Through your infantry, General?" Harrison re-iterated.

"They will be expecing your men charging through. They'll pull to the side and fall down. Don't worry about them. I want you to smack the hell out of those sons-of-Yankees. You got that, Major?"

Harrison eyed Walker with dead seriousness. Walker gave it right back.

"I know you can get the job done, Harrison," Johnston stepped in. "This is what you've been training the Rangers to do. Being an attorney just gave you some insight. You're more of a soldier, now."

"I thank you for your confidence in me, General," Harrison replied.

"The rest of our men, General?" Wharton asked.

"Take the rest of your regiment and ride the perimeter around my troops. You know how to do your job better than me."

"Yes, General," Wharton answered, looking at Harrison, "We know our jobs."

"My concern is to win this battle," Johnston said, taking a cigar out of his vest pocket. "And I don't want to lose any more men than I have to. My brigade is the best in this war. With you two out there, let's just watch what the hell happens."

Wharton whipped out a match, struck it and lit the General's cigar. "Yes, General."

"Tom," Johnston addressed Harrison, "if you come out of this alive, you'll probably wind up the Governor of Texas." He laughed. "I hear that's your ambition."

"Sir?" Harrison came back with a slight grin. He took the pipe from his mouth, packed fresh tobacco into the bowl and lit it. Johnston watched him as he gave him a moment of egotistical pride.

"Who the hell told you, if I may ask?" Harrison countered.

"Colonel Terry never kept secrets from me," Johnston answered as he dragged on his cigar. Addressing the other officers, he said, "Now, I know you two Colonels can learn a little from Harrison. Don't pamper your men. I also heard about them calling Harrison here some gawd-awful name. What is it?"

"'Mark time', General," Wharton answered.

"Hell of a name. You made two officers mark time in the freezing rain. Why?"

"Discipline, General," Harrison answered. "They were insubordinate as a couple of shave-tail louies and tried to make me look bad in front of my men."

"Did it work?"

"The Rangers hate me more than ever."

"Will the officers follow you?"

"Yes, General,' Harrison answered, "they'll certainly follow me . . . without question."

"And the men?"

"They'll ride to hell and back with those officers to show how much they hate me."

"See what I mean, Walker? Wharton?" Johnston paced the floor, bracing his back with his hands to straighten his spine. "And that's why they're going to ride with my troops. Full charge when the time comes, by gawd. And you'll see that my infantry gets the support from the sides, Colonels!"

General Johnston was the second officer in the Confederate Army and was complimented by many officers as being one of the most brilliant strategists of the war. His charge was to lead the campaign at Pittsburg Landing near Shiloh Church, Tennessee.

"First light, be ready, gentlemen!"

The officers watched Johnston return their salutes and all, except Harrison, left the tent.

"I'll be a son of a leaping frog," Walker whispered over to Wharton. "He says little to us and gives praise to Harrison." The men turned their eyes back to the tent.

Harrison saluted Johnston, pivoted on his heels, and with a smirk on his face, followed the rest of the officers, keeping far enough behind them so as not to be included in their conversation.

Wharton commented, "The hell he did. The old man knows about Harrison. That you can bet on. Why else would he be sending out a lawyer to do a soldier's job?"

"I just hope he does what I told him to do," Walker added. "Else, my men are going to get chewed up lying there in the dirt."

"Ride through your infantry? With Jorgensen and Andrews," Wharton returned, "you can bet on it. And you can rest assured, Harrison will simply hide behind their shotguns."

"Sergeant!" Harrison yelled out.

O'Riley, who was stationed outside the tent in his usual place, turned up immediately and responded. "Yes, Sir!"

"Find Lieutenants Jorgensen and Andrews and get them over to my tent on the double."

Once inside Harrison's tent, Matt stood anxiously waiting for Harrison to ask about the ensuing battle with the Federals. The Major did not disappoint him.

"The infantry's going in solid?" Matt asked. "When do we charge?"

"Whenever Johnston damn well feels we can without endangering his men," Harrison replied. "Captains Walker and Mitchell will ride the parameter, so you better do your best."

"Where're we goin' to be?" Steve asked.

"We're going to pave the road right down the middle of Grant's ass," Harrison answered. "Johnston's infantry will be prepared for us to come through. They'll either pull to the side or lie down. We'll ride through them with canon balls loping overhead."

Matt showed much concern in the furrows of his brow as he listened closely and began to put the pieces together. He sensed that Harrison got the message from the colonels that they were setting him up for what he had done to them on Shelbyville Pike. He and Steve believed that, without officially disciplining Harrison, they were letting him lead the charge. Now it was time to see if this mighty Major was up to his stature, a man fit to lead the finest company of horse soldiers in the Confederacy. Their concern however was also for their safety as the Rangers were under his command.

"Down the middle?" Matt asked, taking cigar from his shirt pocket. He watched Harrison's hands move nervously about and his lips quiver.

"Your company will follow my ass, Mister Jorgensen," Harrison answered with a smirk. "And you're going to be right beside him, Mister Andrews. I don't want you in front of me, or beside me. If I fart, I want you to hear it. Do I make myself clear?"

"Yes, Major," Matt answered, lighting his cigar.

Matt and Steve were dismissed and each returned to their companies. Steve caught up with the humor and the seriousness of the meeting as they walked. "*If I fart, I want you to hear it.* Hell, he could fart and the whole damn county would hear it."

Before they reached their company, O'Riley rode down upon them. "Sirs," he said as he reined up, "the General wants you at his tent."

"Gentlemen," Johnston addressed his officers, smacking the palm of his left hand with his fist. "I've just learned that Buell has not united his Army of the Ohio."

Union Federalist General Buell was under Sherman's command and was to have met up with General Ulysses S. Grant for a full-blown attack.

"In fact," Johnston continued, courting a slight grin, "the whole Union army under Grant is spread out and it appears that he is unprepared to meet our onslaught. How the hell they plan on taking the Memphis and Charleston Railroad with such an army is beyond my apprehension. But I'm not one to look a gift horse in the mouth."

He turned and took a drag on his cigar, and with a slight lilt in his voice, he continued. "We have a great edge on the enemy. This report," he gloated as he showed it to the men from a distance, "shows that they have no idea of the imminent danger they're in. Well, gentlemen, we strike at first light.

"We will advance upon Pittsburg Landing with our 44,000 or so men and surprise the hell out of Grant, cut his army off from retreat to the Tennessee River and drive the Federals west into the swamps of Owl Creek. I know I don't have to explain the urgency of the situation, gentlemen. We have to accomplish this before Buell comes in or anyone else with reserves.

"Gentlemen," he said with his cigar held tight between his teeth and his arms behind his back, "victory is close. We've finally got the son-of-a-bitch where we want him." He watched the men pondering on what he had said, and then added, "Well, gentlemen. What are we waiting for?"

Harrison smiled and moved out with the rest.

They rolled out the artillery that evening and prepared for the brigade to go forward. They had word that both Sherman and Grant were at the Tennessee River.

Johnston's intent was to have his men go in first with the smoothers for long range and the Howitzers line up in front for shorter but deadlier force.

"What your Howitzers can't do, we'll damn sure make certain the Napoleons do. When the Feds advance, use them at two-thousand yards."

Johnston considered the Napoleon, a kind of hybrid of the two canons that could fire shot or shell, the best artillery piece in the army.

"Beg your pardon, Sir, but it won't go thet far, General." Captain John Walker stood erect in his leather shirt and big sombrero, looked towards the enemy line and squinted.

"Fire a few solids for effect," Johnston instructed. "It'll bust up the sod and know we're within range. It'll do."

"Just be sure to keep the Howitzers up front," Johnston commanded his artillery commanders. "Don't want them behind us like our guns."

"Hell," one of the artillery soldiers said lowly as he rolled the Howitzer in place, "we knowed thet. They're not like our guns."

"No they're not, Sergeant," Johnston came back. "Remember that and we'll keep from shooting up our own men. Those are explosive shells you're using, not solid shot. They're canisters filled with several hundred musket balls in each one."

"Yes, Sir," the soldier returned. "Sorry for my remark."

"They'll blast the hell out of 'em," one infantryman who stood aside remarked. "Make our job a little easier."

Laughter rolled through the ranks. Canons played a big part in the campaign, but not enough. They knew it would be a war of canons from both sides. Then it was up to the infantry.

"Come to," Captain Walker shouted. The Captain then addressed Johnston, "I'm sorry, General. I'll see that he's disciplined."

"No need, Captain. Just aim that gun raised high, Sergeant and we'll do all right.

General Johnston had the infantry stand ready behind his big guns, while Wharton had the Rangers in columns and in line formations following the infantry.

Matt rode in front and within earshot of Wharton where he heard Wharton discuss the situation further with Harrison.

Still commanding his troops to fiercely override Grant's army with his right flank, Johnston was knocked out of the saddle by an infantryman's bullet.

"Our General's been hit!" a medic yelled out as he stopped to help the General. Seeing blood filling up Johnston's boots, he quickly tore the trousers and saw the blood gushing from a severed artery behind his right knee. He unsuccessfully tried to apply a simple tourniquet, as Johnston was still giving orders and interfered with his attempt.

"Get on with it, Private," Johnston ordered the medic. "I'll get the bleeding stopped. Attend to the others."

Steve quickly turned his steed towards the Union soldier who fired the shot. As the soldier tried to reload, Steve rode down on him. Realizing he too hadn't reloaded his shotgun, Steve unsheathed his Bowie and threw it with lightning accuracy. It caught the man's jugular and killed him instantly.

Reluctantly, the medic left his Commander and, obeying his command, ran back to the spot in the unit and continued his fight. A minni ball quickly felled him before he could explain to others about Johnston's condition.

Johnston tied his neckerchief around his thigh, and, writhing in pain, thinking he had stopped the bleeding, remounted his steed. He looked at his brigade with pride as it moved against Grant's army.

"We're going to stop you, Grant," he yelled. "This is my day of victory."

Seeing Johnston was back in the saddle, Steve innocently believed the wound must have been superficial and, without further delay, dismounted and retrieved his Bowie. After remounting, he continued riding through the Federal forces.

The neckerchief around Johnston's leg fell to the ground. The bleeding hadn't stopped. Johnston continued leading his frontal charge, not realizing his energy was being sapped from him with every drop of blood that spilled on the ground from his wound.

Matt noticed Johnston's unsteadiness in the saddle, turned Skeeter and rode him to the weakened General's side. He leaped from his fast-gaited horse and rushed to aid the General, catching him just as he fell from his horse.

Cradling the General's head with his hands, he looked into his eyes.

"Quick, man," Johnston barely ordered with his eyes half closed, "get me back on my horse."

Matt tried in vain to stop the bleeding with a tourniquet on his thigh, using his Bowie to tighten it.

Steve reined up, dismounted quickly and knelt at the General's side.

"It didn't look that serious," Steve said. "Seeing the boy leave, I figured he was alright."

"Yes, I believe it's quite serious," Johnston said, softly and painfully.

Upon seeing the two Lieutenants off their mounts, Harrison rode over to them. Breaking his ride at the General's side, he looked down at Johnston's body.

"No use, Captain," Johnston said to Matt in a weak and craggy voice as he looked up into Matt's eyes   "Tell Colonel Wharton to regroup and charge again."   He coughed out his last words slowly. "Get those . . . sons-of-bitches."

Harrison watched as the General's eyes rolled back into his head. His body went limp.

"Is he dead?" Harrison asked.

"Yes, Sir," Matt replied, removing his hat.

Steve and Harrison also removed their hats out of respect.

"He said to regroup and charge those sons-of-bitches again," Matt said, looking into Harrison's hard, cold eyes.

"I heard," Harrison said, gritting his teeth.

"He addressed Matt as 'Captain', Sir", Steve said, reseating his hat on his head.

"Harrison gave a look of consternation and then barked at Steve. "Mount up and get back in the battle, mister." Seeing a slight hesitancy on the part of the two officers, he barked louder, "Now, dammit!" He looked towards the enemy. "I'll inform Colonel Wharton of the General's death. Like the General said, we're going to kill every last one of those sons-of-bitches.

Matt laid the General's head back down and picked up his reins. He and Steve looked with astonishment at an iron man who seemed to have no pity for the enemy, and showed little remorse for the dead.

"Privates," Matt commanded two Rangers close by, "stay with the General and await a detail."

"We're going right back through the middle, gentlemen," Harrison ordered. He looked strongly into Matt's eyes. Nothing else had to be said.

Quickly, the two lieutenants joined their company in front once again. The rebel yell of A Company was stronger than ever for they had a hard cause once again which reminded them of Terry's death earlier, except, this time it was a general of a brigade and the close friend of Colonel Benjamin Terry.

Colonel Wharton awaited Harrison's report. When he received it, he bent his head and solemnly said, "Too bad." He swallowed hard. "Damn good man. The best."

The death of General Albert Sidney Johnston, perhaps the best military mind in the Confederacy, changed the course of history. For without his military ingenuity, the tide was turned with the victory going to Grant.

Wharton looked around as if into space. "Well, G. T.'s in command now," he said, sitting astride his horse and holding the reins loose in his hand while blood trickled down his leg. "I'll inform him about the General. Tom, have a detail pick up the General's body."

"Yes, Sir," Harrison replied, and sent a note with his courier. "Take him to the hospital."

"Is he the same Beauregard that fought at Sumter's Fort?" Steve whispered at Matt as they rode near.

"From what I hear,' Matt answered, shrugging his shoulders.

"He a Frenchman?" Steve asked.

"He's a West Pointer," Wharton explained, as he rode past Steve.

Because of his size, short in stature, G. T. was called 'Little Napoleon'. It seemed that he and Harrison had something in common.

"Hope he's a good leader," Steve returned.

Chaplain Robert F. Bunting stood at the head of General Johnston's flag-draped coffin with his saber laid across it. "General Albert Sidney Johnston is now laid to rest," he said, closing the Bible. He continued. "To say that he is now with the Lord is to be almost blasphemous."

Matt's bowed head rose up and his eyes opened and looked towards the chaplain as he listened intently to every word.

The chaplain continued. "With that I mean, General Johnston led a religious life and his exemplary style of command is definite proof that he has always been with the Lord. How else could he have commanded such a brilliant brigade as he had and not been a man of God. As with David of old, Gideon and the rest of the heroes of the Bible, so it is with General Albert Sidney Johnston."

Matt hung onto every word and placed them into his subconscious as he continued to stare at the coffin.

After the services, he watched Chaplain Bunting take the folded Bonnie Blue along with the General's saber and walk towards his tent. Stepping up in his gait, Matt sided the chaplain. "Mind if I walk with you, Chaplain?"

"Oh, Matt. Not at all. Not at all. In fact, I was hoping I'd have a chance to talk with you."

"Anything special?" Matt asked.

"Come on in and let's talk, Matt."

The two gentlemen entered the tent where Bunting placed the flag on the cot. Matt watched him as he took the General's saber, and opened a locker box to place it inside. Matt caught the glimpse of the handles of two other sabers sticking with the blades neatly wrapped in cloth.

"You're the first, Matt."

"What do you mean?" Matt asked, staring at the sabers.

Bunting leaned the lid of the box back as he took some linen cloth and wrapped the General's saber with it. He laid it down beside the box, and then removed one of the sabers. "This one belonged to Colonel Benjamin Franklin Terry." He handed it respectfully to Matt.

Matt took it, sat down on the cot next to the flag, looked at the flag for a moment and then gently rubbed the handle of the saber. "Terry's saber?"

"Yes." Bunting then took the next saber out and showed it to Matt. "And this one was Colonel John Lubbock's."

"You mean, you've been keeping these?" Matt asked, handing the saber back to Bunting.

"We're writing history, Matt," Bunting answered, returning the saber to the box along with Johnston's. "Each saber represents a great man. I call them *the Brazorian Sabers* namely because they represent the men from Brazoria County. Terry, Lubbock and now, General Johnston."

Matt leaned into Bunting and watched him close the box and sit down in a chair opposite him. "What do you aim to do with them?" Matt asked curiously, taking a well-worn handkerchief from his pocket. Taking advantage of Bunting with his back turned, he quickly wiped a tear from his eye, hoping Bunting would not see it.

"If I'm still alive after this War is over, and I hope it's soon, I plan on making a memorial of them so that the South will remember them."

"All three great men," Matt continued. "I mean, not jest great, but the best."

"Yes, Matt. The best. And I don't want their memories to die here on the battlefield."

"Then may I ask you a question. One thet's been on my mind for a long time?"

"About?"

"Why? If there's a God in Heaven, why did He let these men get killed, and let me live?" Matt stood up, crumpled his handkerchief and stuffed it back into his pocket. "I mean, I'm nothing. Nobody. I don't even belong here."

Bunting sat quiet, staring at Matt's back. "Where do you belong, Matt?"

Matt turned around. "In a grave somewhere, out there. Terry." Matt pointed hard to the men around him. "He belongs here. Lubbock, and now Johnston. Chaplain, I watched Johnston kneel and pray just before the battle."

"I know. I was there, remember?"

"Then why did God let him die?"

"Why did God let you live, Matt? Think about it." Bunting stood up, walked over to Matt and placed his hand on his shoulder. Looking out at the camp with Matt, Bunting continued. "You said, 'if there's a God'. Don't you believe in God?"

Matt remained silent for a moment. Then he answered him, "But I didn't pray."

"In your own amicable way, you did, Matt. And I know you believe in God, Matt. Oh, you might not call him God, or Lord, but I know you believe in Him. If you believe, then you must realize that He can do whatever He chooses to do. We can't question His reasoning."

Matt turned and looked into Bunting's gentle eyes. "Thet's jest it. We can't do anything, but He can do everything. Then what's the sense of prayer? General Johnston was a God-fearing man. He prayed to God for victory. I heard him."

"And he was victorious, Matt. Time and time again, he was victorious."

"But this time, he died. He died!" Matt showed his side of empathy for a great man as he cried.

"Let it out, Matt. Once in a while, we need to cry. All of us."

Matt turned swiftly as if to hide his tears, smacked his hand with his fist, and walked out of the tent.

Bunting followed him and walked down the hillside with him. The two of them came to rest at the river's bank. Bunting watched Matt take out a cigar and light it. Bunting looked over at

Johnston's coffin still lying in the back of a wagon. He watched as two soldiers climbed aboard and drove off with it.

"If that's all there is to life, Matt, then we are most to be pitied. There goes one of the greatest generals of all time." He removed his hat in respect. Matt kept his hat on until he turned and saw Bunting standing there with his hat in his hand. He turned, faced the wagon with the coffin, and removed his hat.

"You see, Matt. God does not intervene for us every time we call upon Him."

"Thet's what my pa always taught me," Matt responded, still watching the wagon roll down the road.

"That's what we want to think, Matt. This is God's world. He has a plan and purpose for each and everything. We might not understand everything about what He does or does not do." As the wagon disappeared around the bend, he placed his hat back on his head. "Just like Terry's brother, Frank. He died the same day. Remember the saying, *God rains on the just and the unjust.* Oh, we can certainly question God, but the answer has to come from within us."

Matt replaced his hat and threw away his cigar. "Then what's the sense of praying?" He walked off.

April 6, 1862

Wharton met with Beauregard and then had Harrison called to his side.

"G. T. wants us to protect the left flank of the army to the bridge across Owl Creek," Wharton continued.

. Wharton knew the terrain and figured he could have his men move behind the enemy line to a field where he intended to form the charge.

"A charge?" Harrison countered. "Doesn't G. T. know there are trees and creeks on these grounds. He has eyes, doesn't he?"

"He's using good tactics, Major. You and he should see eye to eye about things." He looked at Harrison and eyed his stature.

"What d'ya mean?" Harrison asked, watching Wharton's eyes scale his body.

"Napoleon tactics, Major. Napoleon tactics."

Harrison grumped.

"He's good at planning, Major. I respect him." Then he smiled and looked Harrison in his eyes. "Ever go pheasant hunting?"

"Often." Harrison answered. He sat tall and straight which gave him the appearance of a tall leader and matched Wharton's stance..

"This is something like that. I know there are some squads of Federals out there. I want you and your men to ride over near Hurly's on the Purdy and Pittsburg road, get behind enemy lines and flush out whoever's there."

The wound gave Whareton pain and he grunted the rest of his words. "Let's ride, Rangers!."

"All right, Rangers," Harrison ordered those around him. "Have the companies ready to move out!"

"Yes, Sir," Matt replied and mounted Skeeter. He and Steve followed Harrison back to the rest of the Rangers and led their men back into battle.

The soldiers rode single file down a ravine, and when they reached their destination they found it occupied by the enemy reserve, supposedly two infantry regiments. Union soldiers came at them like bees from a disturbed hive. Matt turned in his saddle and fired his shotgun in their direction, hoping to stay off any soldier his eyes couldn't see. He saw several bodies fall as the shot tore into their flesh. His company engaged more Federals than they had anticipated who had hid behind every tree and forage.

"Where the hell did these bastards come from?" Steve yelled out, firing his Navy.

A minni ball whizzed past Matt's face as he saw the scared eyes of the soldier who fired it. He whipped out his .36 and shot the soldier.

Harrison fired at Federals as they tried to bring him down from his horse. Killing had become second nature for him as he saw the men fall in front of him. He thrust forward for the thrill of victory as he felt strength in the company of warring Rangers. At times he was caught up in the rebel yell and felt the excitement of a good fight.

Steve fired and killed one infantryman who jumped on the back of Matt's horse. Matt recognized the deed and gave a nod of thanks back at Steve.

Clinton Terry, Colonel Terrys' brother and a volunteer aide for Wharton, rode towards Shiloh church away from the battle. He was taught that his position was to stay alive wherever possible to keep the commanders informed. He would have made it had it not been for an expert marksman. A minnie ball caught him in his back. He fell from his horse and before he could stand up again, a Federal infantryman ran and plunged his bayonet into his midsection.

Matt stopped reloading, took his Bowie and threw it at the infantryman. The Bowie swiftly found its target in the infantryman's back. It was not in time to save Clinton. Matt dismounted, and upon seeing that Clinton was dead, walked over to the dead Union infantryman and removed his Bowie.

The rain poured down harder as if to cleanse the battlefield of its blood.

When Matt saw two soldiers attacking his Commander, Colonel Wharton, he grabbed his reins, mounted and spurred Skeeter towards Wharton. A bayonet thrust in his direction barely missed Matt as he dove and knocked two bayonet-wielding soldiers down with his body.

Steve came to his rescue and used the butt of his shotgun to knock the one soldier on the head who had tried his bayonet on Matt. He turned his shotgun and fired at the other man, killing him instantly.

Wharton's horse was hit with a bayonet and fell. Wharton rolled away from the horse and scampered to the safety of a tree in the slush and mud.

Matt remounted Skeeter and rode to his rescue with the reins in his mouth, firing his shotgun and his Navy at the soldiers running towards Wharton. One of the Federals' shot blast hit Wharton's right leg.

Seeing Matt's heroic ride, Harrison rode his horse into the side of Matt's steed, shoving him out of the way. He quickly dismounted and went to Wharton's aid. Reaching for his neckerchief from around his neck, he discovered he had tied it around his head.

Matt reached for his but remembered he had left it with Johnston.

Harrison removed his from his head, and quickly applied it tight with his Bowie to Wharton's wound, stopping the bleeding.

"Wish I had been in time to have stopped the General's bleeding," he said as he tied a knot. "He simply bled to death."

"Thanks, Tom." Wharton politely said.

"Get the Colonel a horse!" Harrison ordered Matt.

Matt gritted his teeth in anger, and then quickly complied. He turned Skeeter around and, finding an empty horse, brought it to Wharton. Wharton mounted his new steed, thanked Harrison for staying by his side and rode to the rear of the line to analyze the situation.

Matt and Steve continued in combat as Captain Mitchell and Company K rode in and joined the fight.

They rode over and greeted him while the Federal forces were still clashing with him. Steve grabbed a hold of the head of a Federal soldier and held on to it while the man's eyes bulged.

"Glad to see you, Mitch." Steve greeted him with grit teeth as he held onto his prisoner. He removed the infantryman's hat and banged him with the butt of his Navy. "He weighed too much."

"Thought you men were in danger when I saw heads pop up all over the field," Mitchell said with a smile. "Then when they rose up like Phoenixes everywhere, we thought you'd need some help. Where's your leader?"

"Ridin' this way," Steve said, watching Harrison lope towards them.

"Mitch," Harrison yelled out. "Good that you came. Colonel Wharton's at the rear, injured. Not sure how bad. I have to ride back to him."

"My men will help out here until the others join us," Mitch replied firmly.

"Glad to have you." Harrison turned his steed and spurred him towards the rear where Wharton was waiting.

Wharton sat his horse, favoring his right leg. He removed his hand from it when Harrison approached him.

"I'll be all right, Major," Wharton advised him. "Get to your men."

"Sorry to disobey you, John," Harrison said as he dismounted. "But we don't want two killed, and so close together."

Harrison commanded a couple of the Rangers to ride with the injured Major Wharton back to Shiloh church for treatment. He examined Wharton's leg, took his bandana off and cleaned the blood away. "It's still bleeding a little. Hold it tight, and I'll have some men get you back to the hospital."

Harrison watched as Wharton agreed and the men hauled him off towards the church. "Make sure someone takes care of him," Harrison commanded, then turned his steed and joined the rest of the Rangers.

An infantryman lunged at Mitchell and brought him down to the ground where he used his rifle as a club, breaking his right arm.

Matt was fast with his Navy and fired at the infantryman wounding him. He dismounted and, seeing the infantryman rising, kicked him in the face. He picked him up again and plowed his fist squarely into his face. The man went down and out.

Steve dismounted and helped Mitchell back up on his horse. Once he saw the Captain was secured in his saddle, he smacked the rump of the horse with his rifle and sent him galloping towards the rear.

"His arm's busted!" Steve cried out.

Harrison saw waves of fresh Federal troops sweeping towards them, firing at them in every direction. The Rangers could do nothing but dismount and fight on foot.

Finally, a wearied and fatigued Beauregard gave the call; a call the Rangers hated. "Retreat!"

The Rangers stayed behind as ordered and spent the rest of the day covering the Confederate retreat.

In the evening, the Rangers regrouped. The cavalry came walking on foot with their horses in tow. It had been a fierce day of guerilla warfare, digging out every Federal soldier hidden throughout the fields. Many were killed or wounded. Many fled to fight another day.

Harrison had proven himself a hero in the eyes of his men that day. Again, the men picketed during the night.

Matt and Steve found temporary solace as they hid in the church's shadows from the moonlight where they watched their men bring the wounded in one door and the dead out the other. The wounded were brought and laid on the bare wooden floor where once pews were. The pews had been removed to make tables and for other camp use by their soldiers.

A few of the makeshift tables accompanied the bodies of soldiers the doctors worked on to repair their wounds. Blood spilled down between the cracks. Stench was everywhere; even the outside air was filled with it, although the church smelled worse.

Matt's view through the church's opened door saw the moon's light filtered through the church's one glass window. It seeped through the slits at the bottom of one of its closed doors.

Monday 7 April 1862

The sun shining in his eyes and the fact that his stomach was empty kept Matt from sleeping in the next morning. He rose and walked around the camp to find food. He came upon Wharton sitting outside the church, still favoring his leg. Harrison was by his side.

"Your wound any better?" Matt asked. He could see that the bleeding had stopped as the blood was dried on his trousers and there was no flesh blood.

Steve stumbled in to where the men were and joined some other officers who had gathered around Wharton.

Disillusioned that the battle was over, Wharton called his subordinates to a meeting. He was still suffering from his painful wound.

"Gentlemen," he addressed the officers, "as you can see, I'm a little out of commission." The men grinned; some laughed. "I'm not in position to ride. So, I've turned the command temporarily over to Harrison." Wharton held tight to his bandaged leg. "He'll do right by you. Follow him."

Matt looked at Wharton whom he had come to admire for his intelligence and courage on the battlefield. But he remembered when Harrison took away his glory of saving Wharton's life when he shoved his horse out of the way.

"Yes," Matt said with tight lips, "we will."

"I know of your dislike for each other, Matt," Wharton said. "Here. Read my report. It might make a difference."

Matt took the papers from Wharton and read them. The orders were addressed to the Texas Rangers.

I respectfully refer you to Major Harrison's report of a brilliant charge, gallantly led by himself, upon the enemy's cavalry and infantry on Tuesday evening. The nature of the ground rendered a charge practicable, and the men and officers behaved with great courage.
John A. WHARTON,
Colonel, Commanding Texas Rangers

Nothing was mentioned about Matt and Steve leading the charge with Harrison. Matt folded the papers and handed them back to Wharton.

"With your permission, Colonel," Harrison addressed him, "I'll meet with my officers now."

"Might be the right time," Wharton said, dismissing him.

"We'll see you when we return, Sir," Harrison replied.

Immediately, Major Harrison called the officers to a meeting in his tent. "Gentlemen," he addressed the standing officers, "G. T. is now in command of this brigade. Colonel Wharton's on his way to the hospital in Corinth."

"Thet makes you a Colonel?" Matt asked, taking his makings out of his pocket.

"Not yet, Captain Jorgensen." He took a cigar from his pocket, bit the end off and lit it.

"Gentlemen. I was with General Johnston when he died. His last words were to promote Lieutenant Jorgensen here to captain. I saw the courage and bravery demonstrated by this man. It gives me great honor to carry out General Johnston's last order."

"The hell . . ." Steve's jaw dropped.

Matt butted up against Steve and kept him quiet.

"He displayed a great amount of courage when I attempted to save the General. In fact, Jorgensen sort of helped me by keeping the enemy from getting to me when I rushed to aid the Colonel."

Steve turned and motioned towards the battle arena and said, "I told you back there . . ."

Matt interrupted Steve again with a kick in his shins. "Thank you, Major. It's a pleasure serving under you."

Matt looked at Harrison like a dog gritting his teeth for a fight with a cat. He waited for him to make his move.

Instead, Harrison smiled, took another drag from his cigar and said, "I thought you'd like your promotion." He turned and walked away, arrogantly.

Harrison quickly gave orders for the men to mount and form an offensive. Matt's feelings were still in a bad way for Harrison taking the glory for rushing to Wharton's aid when he shoved his horse out of the way. However, he put it behind him and commanded his troops.

The fight began and continued throughout the day. The Rangers gave they rebel yell, and charged into the Federals again and again. Harrison was one proud officer, for the Rangers gave one of their best performances of the campaign. Matt and Steve reminded them of General Johnston, and now Colonel Wharton.

They were also helped by one Colonel Nathaniel Bedford Forrest who led his two-hundred or so horsemen into the battle against General William Tecumseh Sherman's two regiments of Infantry and one cavalry. All in all, that afternoon saw only two Rangers killed. A proud Forrest turned in his saddle only to feel the pain of a bullet as it creased his arm. But he stopped Sherman's troops with the Rangers' shotgun tactics.

Grant's tactics began with Buell that day, having him lead four divisions to repair the line along the Memphis and Charleston Railroad towards Chattanooga.

What Buell didn't expect was Matt and Steve waiting for him. Terry's Rangers swept down upon his supply line with lightning speed that completely caught them by surprise.

"Who the hell are these devils?" Buell shouted as he called his army to retreat.

The swift skirmish over, Buell retreated and Matt and Steve commanded their Rangers back to Shiloh.

With Grant's beefed up brigade, the day started to look bleak for Terry's Rangers, and for that matter, for Beauregard's Brigade.

"Wonder what our new Commander's plans are now?" Matt asked Harrison as he and Steve caught up to him leaving his tent.

"He's sitting with his head between his knees, as I see it," Steve noted, looking across the field into Beauregard's tent where one of the flaps was wide open.

Harrison didn't reply but Matt and Steve watched him quickstep over to Beauregard's tent. General Braxton Bragg met with him and the two went in together.

"Bring the troops in," Beauregard commanded his Council of War.

The meeting proved futile, for Beauregard was too sick to do the officers any good. The sweat on his brow and the trembling of his body were evidence to the officers that their near victory that day was about to be given away the next.

"Sir," Harrison addressed Beauregard, "we met General Buell's army, demolished their supply train and caused them to retreat. My men walloped the hell out of them."

"Buell?" Beauregard asked haltingly. "I'm not too concerned about him. We fought Grant and licked him yesterday. Now, from what I've been told by my couriers, he has fresh troops in from Crump's Landing and they're combined with Buell's. I don't know how many, but you can rest assured, they're too many for us."

"Dammit, G.T.," Bragg interrupted, standing. "We had Grant right where Johnston wanted him. We could have won the finest victory thus far, had he lived.

"I won't argue that. With General Johnston's Brigade, that bloody day has got to be one of the Ranger's most glorious moments," Bragg agreed. "The Federals knew they were in imminent danger that Saturday, let me tell you." He looked at Beauregard and the others around him and continued, "But, damn! When Buell showed up, Grant turned the tide on us."

Beauregard came back. "And as you know, that's war. Now they'll come at us like fire lapping up the side of a wooden wall. Braxton, I want you to take our men right a way and establish a defense."

"Yes, Sir!"

Braxton knew the command before it was given, but to manage to rally 30,000 of Beauregard's badly disorganized Confederates and mount a surprisingly destructive defense against the Federals was a lot to hope for. He thought to himself, *Hell! Johnston's gone. G. T. sicker than hell. And I'm to hold this thing together. Damn!* He straightened up, called his subordinates in and got the ball rolling.

Grant had been heavily reinforced during the night by the arrival of General Don Carlos Buell's Army of the Ohio. Buell, being not too brave a man, reached Pittsburgh Landing and crossed the river to file into line on the Union left. Witnessing the fugitives from Grant's army cowering behind trees and brush around the river bank, he had the vanity to believe that it was his army alone that saved Grant from defeat. However, it was also coupled with the timely appearance of a reserve division from Grant's army, led by Major General Lewis Wallace. Grant's army was now reinforced and ready for battle.

With all of that, he renewed the fighting with an aggressive counterattack and overpowered Beauregard's Brigade, forcing it to retreat to Corinth, Mississippi.

At the same time, it was to Matt's chagrin because a wounded Wharton only saw Harrison as the man who saved his butt and therefore became the hero.

"How's our friend, Nathan?" Steve asked, lighting up his makings as he and Matt rode toward Corinth with their beaten command.

"Oh, he's healed up. Can't keep him down, I recken." Then he looked back at the church. "It's Wharton who's taking time to heal."

"And Mitch?"

"Don't know about him, yet. He's lying on a cot, resting, I suppose."

Matt looked back down the road they were riding and thought about Harrison. *He even got a letter of commendation from Wharton,* he thought to himself. He joined Steve and rolled his makings. Turning to the wind they rode on. "Hell. That's war."

CHAPTER 4

G. T. BOWS OUT

Captain Wood from K Company caught up with Harrison and asked, "What are your orders, Sir?"

"We're moving out to Corinth. That's all. Get back to your men."

Wood turned and was instantly hit by a miniball. He fell dead. Another flew by and hit the side of the tree, just missing Harrison.

Harrison quickly yelled out, "Mount up! Mount up, dammit!" and ran like a bat out of hell for his horse.

More volleys hit the woods.

With lightning speed, the Rangers hit their saddles and rode.

"You don't have to tell me twice," Steve said, galloping through the thickets towards his company.

Beauregard was alerted, and with help from two of his fellow officers, mounted up and rode with the Rangers. He faltered in the saddle but stayed on. His infantrymen returned fire, making good his escape.

The Rangers rolled like thunder through the woods as more shots whizzed past them. They out rode the bullets and into safety. The infantrymen made sure of their safety by staying behind and firing volleys at the Federals.

Beauregard was so sick that he felt like he was ready to die. That night proved to be a bad night for him as he had already given everything he tried to eat back to its origination, and now weak and without Johnston, he felt the fear of defeat. The expected came early and swift before the sun had a chance to rise.

Harrison rode up to his tent and dismounted. He was met by two of Beauregard's staff.

"He's not fit to fight," one of them said, stopping Harrison. "He's called for a retreat."

"Can he ride?" Harrison asked, trying to see inside the tent.

"I'll ride," Beauregard said in a weakened voice from inside. "Someone get me my horse."

However, unbeknownst to Beauregard, he was out of danger of being pursued by the Federals any further, for fate was smiling upon them. Union Officer General Buell cowardly failed to follow up the retreating brigade, and for this he was later relieved of his command by General Grant.

Because Beauregard withdrew his now disorganized brigade to their fortified stronghold at Corinth, it allowed Grant's army to move in and take possession of the grisly battlefield of the dead and dying. Grant was simply satisfied with claiming victory over the Confederates for the moment.

Monday, 29 May 1862

Corinth had been a haven for quite some time, but now Beauregard, because of his illness and feeling unfit to properly command, thought that he could see its end. When he got wind that the Union Army's General Halleck was moving into Corinth, he called General Bragg to conference.

"I have no intention of fighting Halleck," Beauregard told Bragg, as Bragg sat down inside his headquarters. "We've had Corinth for as long as I can remember. It's time we left."

Taking a cigar out of his pocket and lighting it, Bragg answered him. "We're without water. Our rations are low. That would be my order."

"Then see to it, Braxton. I'm not in any condition to order our men."

In a brief meeting with the officers, Bragg advised them about the imminent attack they were expecting from General Halleck. "I know we could beat the hell out of them, but under these conditions, no water and our rations are dwindling, G. T. has ordered us to evacuate. I've concurred. We'll head for Tupelo."

Th brigade fel back towards the Mobile and Ohio Railroad to Tupelo, Mississippi. They swiftly left the town. When the Federals moved in the next day expecting a full-blown battle, they found themselves in a deserted town.

Weakened by continual illness, Beauregard, feeling that he would recover quickly, temporarily turned over his command to General Bragg. Beauregard's condition worsened, and the take-over command soon became permanent for Bragg.

CHAPTER 5

A GENERAL NAMED
NATHAN BEDFORD FORREST

10 June 1862

While Union Brigadier General James Negley advanced toward Chattanooga, threatening the Confederate government, Confederate Brigadier General Nathan Bedford Forrest was commissioned to organize a cavalry brigade to raid middle Tennessee and Kentucky. Being one of the best horsemen himself, his first thought was Terry's Texas Rangers because he wanted only the elite to ride with him. He had heard about Matt and Steve and called upon their expertise.

Fortuitously, Matt and Steve had heard about the General for a long time, and knew about his reputation as a horseman and a fighter. Matt even thought of Forrest as a legend through the ranks. When he finally got his first glimpse of the General, he was not disappointed.

It took a month for the two young officers to rendezvous with General Forrest, but when they rode into camp at Chatanooga, the first thing out of Matt's mouth when he saw him, was "Now there is a general,"

Steve ordered his company to halt. "Yo!" He looked around at his men and announced to them, "We're in Chatanooga, men. Look alive. You're going to be inspected by the great General."

Matt reined up, straddled his saddle, took out his chaw and sliced it, giving Steve a piece. "Yes sir, I'd hate to come up against him." He recognized the General mainly from reports he had heard about him and knew this had to be him. Forrest was every bit the striking figure of a heroic general on a horse.

"What makes you think he's better'n us, Matt?" Steve asked, wallowing the chaw inside his cheeks. Then he took off his hat and wiped the hatband with his bandana.

"A good horse soldier can spot a better man than he is instinctively friend, and right now I can see our superior." Then he looked over at Steve and added with a smile, "Or at least our equal."

He spit to the wind and, with Steve, rode over to meet the general.

Forrest was six-foot-two, dark complected and wore a mustache and goatee. His language was rough, being reared through the ranks from a private. When it was discovered that he was a plantation owner and a millionaire, he was immediately elevated in rank.

He watched the two men ride towards him and waited until he saw them rein up and salute him. Returning the salute, he addressed them. "You ride well. I watched you from a distance. Fine animals."

"Thank you, Sir," Matt returned. Captain Matt Jorgensen and Lieutenant Steve Andrews at your disposal.

"Good! Your men, I take it, are the Terry's Texas Rangers."

"Yes, Sir," Matt answered, looking around at the Rangers cutting up around newly acquired friends.

"It is my understanding that you have trained the Rangers well."

The Rangers sat tall in their saddles and gave their officers a show of approval by straightening their backs.

Matt rubbed his nose and answered, "Well, we try, Sir."

"I need you to work your men hard again and again. We've got Buell to deal with."

"Major General Don Carlos Buell?" Steve asked.

"You know him?" Forrest returned.

"Met him," Matt answered. "Not much of a man, but can be dangerous just doing nothing. He cost us a battle just by his being late and careless to boot."

Matt was referring to the time that Buell showed up late for Grant's retreat, but just by sheer numbers, still helped Grant regroup his army and move the Confederates out of the battle zone. Matt and Steve knew now that their archenemy was back in action.

"Well, for your information, his Army of the Ohio is a big threat to Chattanooga."

Later that day, they met another friendly face, Colonel John Wharton leading Colonel James Morrison's First Georgia Rangers.

"Where the hell did you come from?" Forrest asked as Wharton sided him.

"Good to see you, too, Nathan," Wharton greeted him.

"John, it's always good to see your smiling face. Heard you were recuperating in Corinth before Grant took over.

"Yep. As you can see, fit as a fiddle."

"Your orders?"

" Chattanooga," Wharton replied, "same as yours."

"You know the odds are against us?"

""Yeah. Wouldn't have it any other way. But, we're not here to sit out a war, but to make it bad for the enemy." Wharton looked around at Forrest's growing army and said, "I count a thousand at least."

"More or less," Forrest came back with half a grin. "I mustered in the Army of Tennessee under a thousand. With Terry's Texas Rangers, and you now, I'd say roughly thirteen hundred." He motioned with his gloved hand the arrival of Matt and Steve riding up to them. "Speaking of the Rangers, I think you know these two fine gentlemen. Major Jorgensen and Captain Andrews."

"I know them, well, Nathan." Wharton greeted the two men. "Matt. Steve. How are you?"

"Fine," Matt returned, "and raring for more action. Looks like ol' home week to me."

"They've served with me through Shiloh and more," Wharton informed Nathan. "Hell, you were there. You know."

"And now we're together once more, so let's get on with it."

Forrest gave the order to his Sergeant Major to set up a meeting of his corps of officers. Matt, Steve and Wharton joined the rest of Forrest's staff as they planned their maneuvers for the next day, and the next. They quickly found out that Forrest didn't earn his reputation by sitting on his haunches.

At the meeting, Wharton asked, "What's happening in Chattanooga that's got us together like this?"

"As you already know, gentlemen, I'm here to organize a cavalry brigade. Ya'll seem to be included."

"But, what the hell for," Wharton pushed Forrest further. "Sounded real important when I was ordered to join you." He looked over at Matt and Steve. "Didn't' know you two boys would be here, too."

"Same as you, John," Matt answered. "Steve and I were instructed to leave our training units and take out some Rangers to join Nathan."

"Well, gentlemen," Forrest started in, strutting in front of them with a quirt in his hand. "The situation is this. We're headed to Murfreesboro."

"I heard that," Wharton returned. "What are your plans?"

"It's an important Union supply center on the Nashville & Chattanooga Railroad. The Murfreesboro garrison is camped in three locations. As I understand, they're located all around town. It's not going to be an easy job. We're going to have to hit all three locations at the same time, and hit them hard, making sure every inch of the city is covered with our men."

Forrest stopped pacing, turned and looked the officers straight on. "'As you all know, war means killing," he said, " and the way to kill is to get there first with the most men. We're going to get there first and surprise the hell out of our enemy. But, our objective is to take property, not lives. Unfortunately, lives will be lost." He looked down and then back at the men and added, "on both sides."

"I'm told that General Crittenden will be there to meet us," Wharton informed the officers.

"Yes, that's my information, too. Your units will hit the outlying areas, John," Nathan answered, "while mine will directly confront Crittenden."

Federal officer, Brigadier General Thomas T. Crittenden was the man sent to Chattanooga to insure the success in maintaining the supply center.

"From my reports, he has not arrived, as yet," Forrest suggested, striking his quirt on his leg as he continued to pace in front of the officers. "All I know of this gentleman is that he is not a West Pointer." Then he laughed. "Well, hell, neither am I."

"But you're all soldier, Sir," Matt pointed out, "and that's the difference."

"Don't know about his army intelligence either, Matt, but thanks for your vote of confidence."

"Do we know how fortified they are?" Matt asked, biting off a chaw.

"I'm told that they have four units, comprising of infantry, cavalry, and artillery."

"And we're going in against a fortified army with us on horses?" Steve asked, ."With only fourteen hundred horsemen?"

"Steve," Forrest addressed him curiously, "seems to me that you have a slight problem with numbers."

Steve rose to his feet and looked at Forrest, and then at the rest of the officers, and back at Forrest again. "Yes, Sir," he answered. "Terry's Rangers and Colonel Wharton here, well . . ."

Matt stood up and interrupted Steve. "What I think Steve is trying to say is that we have trained our men in the art of combat. And now you say, you don't want much killing, and yet you want to capture an entire garrison. Respectively, might I ask, with what, Sir?"

Forrest looked at Matt, and the two men locked themselves into eye to eye contact. "Matt, have ou ever played poker? Yes. Yes, of course you have. We all have. What I'm saying is, do you know the power, the power, Matt of a strong *bluff?*"

Matt knew he was looking into the eyes of his alter ego, his idol, his own spirit so to speak, his own soul while he was listening to Forrest. Nathan Bedford Forrest. Cerainly he knew the power of a strong bluff. He had played out many a hand with a bluff. And now he was witnessing how an almighty general was about to reveal a secret to success on the battlefield with a bluff.

"You and I know the insurmountable odds we face. I'm not going to lie to you. We're going in against a stronghold, fortified with canons, infantrymen, and cavalry, and commanded by what we have heard to be one of the Union's finest generals, I suppose. Now that in and of itself would scare the hell out of any offensive army. But," he continued, "we're going in to defeat him by incapacitating his thinking ability, his power to make decisions by our using *scare tactics*. We're going in before he has time to organize his new command, and we're going in fast and hard. We're going to shock the hell out of them, Mister."

He looked at the officers' faces one more time, bent low and added, "Got a confession to make, gentlemen. This is not a new tactic of mine. Remember Washington on his attack against Cornwallis? He went in on Christmas Eve, across the Delaware when everyone was concentrating on the holiday. He shocked the hell out of them. And gentlemen, I repeat, we are going to shock the hell out of Crittenden's forces, too, just like Washington. We're going to disrupt his ability to think fast and catch him with his pants down."

"We've done the same with Terry," Wharton added. "It cost him his life."

"Don't think I've forgotten. And Johnston's. But, gentlemen, that's why I've called you to my aid. I need you to help me win this battle. It calls for our collective strength. But more important, I'm counting on your fighting expertise. Hell, I could have gotten any number of officers to help me win this battle. I wanted the best. I never thought for a moment that I could pull this off alone." Then he looked into the faces of each of the officers who were entranced at the words coming from the mouth of a fantastic general. "I don't intend on becoming a statistic, or a martyr."

"Now, here's my strategy. We'll hit the saddles at two in the morning. That'll get us at our objective before dawn. Crittenden should be there and just snoring away. If he's not there, all the better. By four-thirty, I want to be lighting my cigar. Understood?"

Heads nodded as Forrest continued his tirade. "The territory is filled with farmers who are not in this war. I want of you to take some men and ride ahead of us, route them out and arm them. Make them ride with us, if they have horses. If not, make them walk, but get them to the court house."

Steve took in every word the General was saying. He was a good learner, and realizing he was sitting at the feet of General Nathan Bedord Forrest, he locked every word in his mind. "My company can handle that, Sir."

"Good, Steve." Nathan placed his hand on his shoulder. ""The jail has to be full. I need it broken down and I want the prisoners armed. March them out to join us. Who'll it be?"

"I'll do thet, General," Matt called out.

"I don't have to tell you, it has to be fast. Remember, Matt, I don't want them to have time to think about what side they're fighting on. They'll be asleep and you'll scare the hell out of them. Just get them out and arm them."

He did an about face, and walked menacingly towards the opening in the tent, turned and stood strong and straight, looking back at the officers. "Niggers. God there must be hundreds of them."

"I'm following you, Nathan," Wharton spoke up. "My men would love the chance.

"Ride out at the same time as Steve. I'll have cannons firing over the court house by the time you get there. And I'll use every available firepower at my disposal to disrupt the enemy while each of you do your task." Forrest moved back into the tent. "You'll have your job cut out for you, each and every one of you."

Then he asked, "The main goal is what, gentlemen?"

"To take the supply center away from the Federals," Matt answered.

"How?"

"With their pants down," Steve chimed in.

"And gentlemen," Forrest smiled at the officers, "you have one day to whip your men into shape so they'll know what to do. Matt and Steve, I want you to go in with shotguns blazing and your pistols too hot to handle. I want so much confusion that they'll think Lee's entire Army hit them. Keep their blue-capped heads down so they don't see what's going on. So explain that to your men, and we should win this battle in short order. Understood?"

Matt understood all too well, for he was excited about fighting under Forrest's leadership. This was a great opportunity for him, and he did not want to disappoint him. He was excited about witnessing a battlefield strategy unlike his own, with a bluff. He knew he was watching history in the making. But, he had thoughts that it could fail, which he quickly pushed out of his mind. His thoughts strayed to remembering how Terry and Johnston, two great leaders, also, were killed. He prayed that it would not happen to Forrest.

At that moment, in his heart, he said a silent prayer. *Lord. I know I'm not a man of prayer. Though my mother taught me to do so. My father believed more in the work of his hands and to let You bring in the harvest. But, like this man jest said, you intervene when we call upon you. Trouble is, I don't really know how to call upon you. Just hear my heart when I say, I would lay down my life for this man's safety. Hope I won't have to, but I want you to know, it means a lot to me to keep this man alive.* He continued listening as Forrest talked, understanding what he was saying so it didn't interfere with his own personal thoughts. *I pray for this our victory, not because we're any better than the other man, but because we have to move on. And I believe that if we win this battle without much killing, it will be a lesson for me to remember for the rest of my life. For I don't get any pleasure out of taking another man's life.* He reflected the day he took Sin's life in a gun fight. And the first time he brought down a man in battle too late to prevent Terry's death. *But I swear here and now to protect this man's life with mine, if it comes to thet.*

"Any doubts?" Forrest asked the officers.

"No, Sir," Matt returned. "By God, it will be a successful battle."

"By General Nathan Bedford Forrest and Terry's Texas Rangers, Matt."

"And the first Georgia Rangers," Wharton added.

"And the First Georgia Rangers," Forrest agreed with a smile. "God only watches us. He never intervenes unless we absolutely ask Him to."

Matt's thoughts left him and went into the ethereal, the unknown, as he asked himself, *whose side is God on?* And he realized that all along he had been depending on his own strength led by his love for Ginny, and not for his country or for God. He vowed to himself to stay alive to see her once more. He prayed to the wind often, seeking guidance in finding his true love. He also often thought about the futility of war, the stupidity of it all, and the false sense of security he had for fighting a face-less enemy disguised as Federal soldiers.

Forrest looked sternly into the officers' faces. "Gentlemen," he started, "I only have two codes on the battlefield. Firstly, everyone, and I do mean everyone, obeys my commands. Secondly, no one, and I mean no one, leaves the field of battle in the presence of the enemy. Am I understood?"

The officers stood at attention and confirmed their agreement aloud with the General.

"Lastly, gentlemen," Forrest said with a half-grin, "the day we go into Murfreesboro will be my forth-first birthday. I want this victory for my birthday." He continued to look towards the officers with his grin. "Understood?"

"Yes, Sir," the officers shouted in one accord, each feeling victory around the corner.

"I'll be dipped," Matt said, turned and rolled his makings.

With this, the the officers took their orders and delivered them to their men, repeating Forrest's code for battle for all to hear and understand. And understand they did.

Forrest's Raiders with Terry's Rangers and the Georgia First Rangers rehearsed their strategy all the next day, and the next, hitting the sack early on the second day for a pre-dawn battle.

Forrest marched out early that morning towards Murfreesboro, three cavalry units strong. Other horse soldiers joined them along the way, bringing the total number to fourteen hundred men.

13 July 1862

Brigadier General Thomas T. Crittenden took command of the Murfreesboro garrison on the twelth. It was as Forrest had described, camped in three locations around town.

Forrest knew it would be no easy task taking the supply center away from Crittenden's massive army. He was going against unestimadible odds. The enemy was dug in and well fortified. His tactic was to take it by surprise before Crittenden had time to organize his new post.

In the darkness of the morning hour, Forrest's artillary fired off its first volley of cannons over the court house while he, his raiders and Terry's Rangers, under Matt's command, rode into Murfreesboro.

Forrest surmised that the only way he would have a chance, was to use rapid movement to keep the enemy off balance and hope it would do the trick. He wanted Crittenden to believe that there were more than just the fourteen hundred men, and that he would immediately be wiped out if he did not immediately surrender.

General Forrest's attack at Murfreesboro left the Federals the experience of being hit by three well-experienced cavalry units.

Forrest rode in front of his cavalry and reined up at the court house. He turned in his saddle and eyed Matt and Steve near him. "Matt. Free those prisoners."

Matt turned Skeeter around and Steve followed him, riding up the steps of the courthouse. Matt quickly commanded his Rangers to follow him to the doors of the jailhouse. "Break it down!" he commanded them.

With the aid of some foot soldiers, they stormed the jailhouse and broke the bars. When they did, the men poured out into the streets with shouts of victory.

"Give them rifles!" Forrest commanded, ever waving his saber.

Once the door was opened, the Rangers ran in and freed the prisoners, giving each man a weapon. "Get those rifles up here, men! Now! Move it!"

Matt felt Forrest's eyes on him for doing his job well. Forrest knew that he had picked the best men to follow him, and that they would make him look good. Matt was honoring his tactics.

"Fire them in that direction, Mister," Matt ordered as the men filed out of the jail. "And don't aim at those men on horses, dammit. They're on our side. Shoot in that direction." Matt pointed towards the camp of Union soldiers.

Forrest was so confident that his strategy would work, that he rode up the courthouse stairs where Matt had already made his stand. He sat his brilliantly decorated stallion and flared his shining saber for all to see. Matt sided him.

Wharton rode to the General's side. "Nathan, we got the niggers to help us, but to arm them would be asking for trouble. We don't know which side they'll fight on."

"They're citizens of this county, are they not, John?" Forrest fired back at Wharton. "I know sure as hell that the North uses them, and without question. They will fight with us as long as they know we are their masters. Trust me. I know niggers. Now, get them some guns!"

"Yes, Sir." Wharton replied, and, being the professional officer that he was, he rode back to his regiment. "Get the lead out, men." He was quick to answer with action and not with mixed words. "Get those niggers armed!" Wharton waved his Navy Colt in the air and pointed it at the black people. "You people!" he yelled out. "Get a rifle, a pistol, a club and follow us." He watched as black men marched with his Georgia First Rangers, as others climbed back fences to get the chance to hold a rifle.

"What the hell is the Colonel thinkin'?" Steve asked Matt, siding him.

Remembering his experiences on the McBride Plantation, Matt quickly answered, "Well, they can fight, too. And if you ask me, they're not afraid like most of you are," and he quickly added, "some of the time."

They black men were well armed and equipped, and took no little part in the several skirmishes that ensued.

"Listen, blunthead," Matt smarted off to Steve as they rode through the city streets, "good, bad, white or black, he wants them to fight along side of us."

"I guess," Steve replied, shifting in his saddle. "Better'n fightin' agin' us."

By this time, Matt had a Sergeant Major lead some men with a wagon filled with arms to the black men. "You better damn well know how to use these," he said to those who climbed aboard the wagon as his men distributed the arms to the Negroes.

One man well-built and in his twenties was the first on the wagon. "Most us knows how, mastah soldier", he answered with a broad grin. "Youse jest turns us in the right direction."

Matt laughed and then spurred Skeeter back towards Forrest. Steve rejoined him and both men brought their horses to a halt in front of the man himself.

Within minutes, the courthouse was filled with horsemen, farmers, prisoners and black people, and the noise they were making was deafening.

In short order, Forrest took center stage, as he rode into the middle of the courtyard. "General Crittenden. You in the trenches. And you up there on the roof tops. I want you to surrender to me right now. Not five minutes from now. Or I'll be forced to kill every mother-loving one of you."

Matt looked around at the regiment behind him, and the enemy in front of him and sweated as if great drops of fear. He thought to himself. *What the living hell is he talking about? They've got more men than us and, hell, many more I can't see.*

"I did not come all this way to talk," Forrest continued in a strong, determined and yet low voice. "And I sure as hell did not come here to make half a job. I want every one of you, man and boy, to come out of your hiding and surrender your weapons. Now, dammit!" His eyes burned into the elements around him as he watched a few come out of hiding and give up their arms. More began to walk feebly out of their nests, but a few remained hidden.

Steve rode over to where the prisoners were out in the street. He then ordered his men, "Disarm the enemy. Get their arms over to these prisoners." He looked at the prisoners still pouring from their cells and still wondered, *Sure hope the General knows what he's doing.* He turned in his saddle and looked around him, waiting for someone to take him down and break this beautiful setting before him of the enemy throwing down their arms. But the more he looked around, the more he saw victory on their side.

Forrest shouted, "I did not come here to make half a job of it. I want them all!"

His eye went to Wharton and the black people. "Arm those niggers right now!"

Immediately, the Texas' Eighth with Georgia's First joined in with the other horse-soldiers, disarmed Crittenden's army as they surrendered, and equipped the farmers, the black people, and all the citizens in and around Murfreesboro.

It gave further credence that the black men were good with firing rifles, and with accuracy. The black people simply followed orders, not having time to think about whart side they were fighting. They were simply enjoying the fun of soldering.

Matt and Steve watched the farmers and other citizens, too, enjoy the thrill of taking up arms, no matter the age, as Matt eyed an elderly man, humped over, carry a rifle loosely in his right hand as if he were marching to a drummer's beat.

Forrest brought Wharton, Matt and Steve to meet with them. "Advise these poor devils that they are to return home with arms and ammunition to fight against patrols surrounding their farms."

"I want your immediate surrender, General Critenden. Now! Or else I will be forced to kill you."

To the astonishment of Matt and Steve, they witnessed something they had never dreamed possible. General Crittenden came out with some of his men in full surrender for fear of being shot.

"Sir," Matt motioned to Forrest. "Ain't that the General walking towards us?"

"I see him, Matt. Bring him here."

With his arms in the air, General Crittenden surrendered his army to General Forrest.

"Is this your main force?" Crittenden asked.

"Dissapointed, General?" Forrest replied.

"Am I to believe that I was taken in by a group of, of what, cavalry men? Is that all?"

Matt smiled.

Watching Crittenden being taken prisoner, Forrest returned, "Yep!"

"And to whom do I give the credit with this brilliant tactic?", Crittenden asked, surrendering his saber to Forrest.

"My name is General Nathan Bedford Forrest. These are my Rangers."

Wharton leaned into his saddle, sat straight and said, "I am Colonel John Austin Wharton, and these are Georgia's First Rangers."

Crittenden wiped his forehead with his bandana and looked directly at Matt. "And you, Sir. You are one hell of a soldier. My eyes were on you."

Steve sided Matt and the two gentlemen smiled. Matt answered, "Terry's Texas Rangers, General. Terry's Texas Rangers. And, Colonel John Wharton."

Wharton sat tall and rode to Forrest's side and greeted Crittenden with a salute. "General Crittenden."

Forrest looked down at Crittenden and said, "And, now, General Crittenden, move out. You've done lost the battle."

Before the Federals had time to realize that they were the ones who had the largest army an hour ago, more guns, and an entrenched position, now they were made to believe that they numbered the least. But it was too late. The battle had only lasted fifteen minutes, and they had already surrendered to the bluff of one great general, General Nathan Edwards Forrest.

Other Confederate troops continued the attack on the camps of the Union commands, and by late that day, all of the Federal units had given up the battle to General Forrest.

CHAPTER 6

R & R AND A CASE OF KENTUCKY RYE

In the fall of that year, Wharton returned to the brigade where he was promoted to Brigadier General. Harrison became the Regimental Commander of Terry's Texas Rangers. Captain Mitchell of K Company, who had returned from medical treatment for his busted arm, was elevated to the rank of Colonel and succeeded Harrison.

But soon Mitchell's physical condition worsened as gangrene set in and cost him his right arm.

Harrison's hate for Matt and Steve grew more intense for they epitomized greater horsemanship and marksmanship that was close to being equal to that of General Forrest. Harrison never forgot that they were Terry's handpicked cavalry officers and that he had never gained Terry's confidence as an officer like they had. He felt that Terry had only kept him because he was a man of influence and power.

With several weeks of no battles, Matt and Steve had Terry's Rangers working up sweat with constant training.

"Don't they ever give up?" a young Ranger asked, holding onto his saddle.

"You've got new skivvies, Private?" Doc asked. "When they wear through and stick to your skin, then maybe, jest maybe, he'll let up on you." Doc was a man in his thirties but could hold his own among the youngest of them. Being with Terry's Rangers longer than most of the other horsemen, he had the benefit of having hard muscles and tough buttocks. He added, "But don't count on it."

"Reason we're the best," a Private commented. "There isn't a day that goes by that we don't train. Get used to it." He rubbed his buttocks.

December 1, 1862

After having lost a battle to the Federals in Kentucky, General Braxton Bragg marched his troops to Nashville, Tennessee and left for Chickamauga, near Murfreesboro. It was here, at Stone River, where he deployed his troops, now redesignated as the Army of Tennessee, to attack Major General William S. Rosecrans's Union Army of the Cumberland. Rosecrans was General Bragg's main concern for the moment.

General William S. Rosecrans was an 1842 graduate of West Point, being fifth in a class of 56. He stood six feet tall and was immensely popular with his troops who nick-named him "Old Rosy", because, as a devout converted Catholic, he carried a rosary with him and made it a point to hear Mass each morning when possible. And like Bragg, he was a passive general.

The wind was dry and still as Bragg nervously looked over the rise, down the road and waited for his scouts to return. It seemed to him to be too long a wait and he was becoming quite impatient. He was not a man to be kept waiting, but in the meantime didn't use his freed time to his best advantage against the enemy.

He was concerned that somehow the Union army that had followed them out of Kentucky, and who he was waiting to cut apart, might have taken a different route than the one he suspected. He also didn't know the surrounding terrain that well, and relied heavily on his officers' intelligence. He was not interested in attacking Rosecrans. His plan was to take the defensive, and yet the terrain was not suitable for a defense. The ground was open with little coverage from trees.

He was a quiet man who appeared to his officers to be very reserved and mysterious. He had grown to be quite despondent. In the months that Matt knew him, he remembered him as a much younger man, who now appeared to have prematurely aged. He was a very nervous man. Not many officers could reach him in conversation and they feared him rather than respected him. His record for retreats also alienated him from the rank and file under him to where he did not have their respect as a leader to whom they could rely upon. He was distant in his relations with his next in command, General Leonidas Polk, which was not the best position for a man of his power to be in.

Because of his uncertainty about the exact position of his enemy, and because of his lack of confidence, some of his subordinates had about him, he was an intensely frustrated and disturbed man. He watched and waited for a scout to return. For weeks, no one appeared on the horizon. He grew more aggravated and distressed, frustrated with time standing still while not knowing if the enemy was slipping up behind him.

With each impossible order he gave his subordinates only frustrated him more because they somehow saw that the order would never be carried out. They were not happy about taking the defense in unprotected territory. He waited.

Days turned into weeks.

21 December 1862

Christmas approached General Wharton's camp in the Tennessee hills. His command now consisted of seven regiments and a detachment of an eighth, two battalions, two escort companies, and a battery.

Colonel Tom Harrison commanded Terry's Rangers while Wharton withheld a small portion of his brigade as a reserve.

Light snow fell and melted as it hit the ground, and Steve had received his promotion to Captain, matching Matt's rank.

The Rangers were in high spirits as many of their wounded had healed and returned to fight again, showing their loyalty to their regiment and to the South. New recruits joined them but only of the highest caliber as Wharton insisted on having nothing less, and having a good horse would help them muster in to becoming a Ranger. It made O'Riley's job of training them of greater importance, as they came to join, not just any cavalry, but Terry's Texas Rangers. The word had spread from Virginia to Georgia, from Georgia to Kentucky, Kentucky to New Orleans, and from New Orleans to Texas that they were the finest cavalry unit of both sides, *the fierce devils.*

O'Riley packed his pipe and lit it while watching his new men line up for inspection. He had his aides run them through the basics.

In the distance he saw Matt and Steve ride hard and fast towards Wharton's tent. He saw the other officers already there with Wharton, among whom was Harrison.

Wharton greeted them outside as they reined up.

"Yes, Sir!" Matt addressed him.

Wharton's eyes combed the hills. "It's Christmas. Some of the locals have dropped by and said they want to give us a Christmas dinner. One that we'll not forget for a long time. I want you to give your men some R and R. Break out the Kentucky Rye. But, don't let your men get too drunk. I'm depending on you."

"Hell, thet's like sending a rooster in the hen house after it's been castrated," one of the officers piped up.

Steve looked over at Matt and jestered, "How does one castrate a rooster?"

"Beats the hell out of me, Steve," Matt answered with a hearty laugh.

"Thet's it?" Harrison asked.

"No. They'd like to give some of our men a warm night's sleep in their homes, too. Some of them are prepared to take some of our Rangers home for Christmas."

"You're not telling us everything, John," Harrison said, watching Wharton's eyes.

"Tom. I'll tell it to you straight. Gentlemen. General Bragg is not in agreement with me in giving you men some rest, but I talked him into it. We've got word form our scouts. Well, let me put it this way. In a few days, there's going to be hell to pay. They've informed us that the Federals are in those hills around Nashville. I have a feeling in my bones it's Colonel Willich."

"Why do you think thet?" Harrison asked.

"It's been rumored he's been made Brigade Commander, same as me. He's the only one, outside of me, who knows the Tennessee River and these surrounding hills. No, it's him all right.

"He knows exactly where we are. They've camped and they're celebrating. If they move an inch, I'll know it."

"And tomorrow, Sir?" Matt asked.

"I've been told not to expect their move from Nashville for several days. But, you've got a bigger task than ever, Matt. Their cavalry is made up of good thoroughbreds. Tough horses. They've been training, using the same maneuvers that your men are using."

"They've caught on as to how to ride," Harrison said in disgust. "But they know nothing about how we fight."

"Don't bet on it." Wharton lit his cigar and watched his exhaled smoke waft into the air. "They're practicing with shotguns."

"Holy hell!" Steve shouted. "Then we don't have time to go and celebrate with the locals."

"I thought about that, Steve. What's your thinking, Matt?"

"We've been training every day, jest about, for the past four weeks. You know we're ready. Let Steve and me work with some of our men the rest of the day. They deserve the day off. Then, after Christmas, we'll put them into battle readiness."

"Good. Today and tonight and tomorrow, let the Rangers howl at the moon. Come the next day, there will be no let up. You'll be out doing some skirmishes with them, and you'll get a taste of what we've learned."

"Our artillery is clean and covered, Sir," an artillery major informed the General.

"Fine. I'll let General Bragg know that. Well, gentlemen. You know what to do. Merry Christmas."

CHAPTER 7

A SUIT OF ARMOR

Later that day, O'Riley walked surreptitiously up to Harrison's tent, carrying what appeared to be flat iron sheathes.

Within moments O'Riley came out of the tent and ran down to the grounds looking for Matt and Steve.

"Youse seen Captains Jorgensen and Andrews?" he asked flippantly as he passed several of the Rangers.

"Not again," a Ranger said in disgust, watching O'Riley bounce down the meadow.

O'Riley found them running some of their men through the paces. As he passed by a couple of the horse soldiers, he said, "Tighten your girth, girlies. Tighten your girth."

He stood and watched for a while as the men went through their maneuvers. When he heard the command, "Charge!" he recognized Matt's voice. He looked out and witnessed horsemen ride in motion like geese in the sky.

He hit the shoulder of a nearby Private and said, "Thet's me lad. Greater man never lived." He had become a loyal fan of Matt and his talent to work with the men. He often caught himself watching the splendor of the two greatest horsemen he had ever laid eyes upon, Matt of course, being his idol.

"I've seen three horses shot out from under thet man," he said to the Private. "The big one there, Captain Jorgensen. The other man, Captain Andrews, he had a couple, but he could lay a horse down and shoot over the saddle like you never saw before. Yeah."

When the charge was finished, Steve saw O'Riley looking his way, sensing that something was up. He rode over to Matt and the two cantered to the edge of the field and met O'Riley.

"The Colonel want us agin?" Matt asked, reining up.

"Yes, Sir."

"Drinkin'?" Steve asked.

"Never stopped. But, he's sober. Don't be askin' me how he can put it away and stay sober. Him bein' a short fella."

"Take over, O'Riley," Matt said as he and Steve rode up to Harrison's tent.

Once at the tent, they dismounted and went inside.

"You want to see us, Colonel?" Matt asked.

"Yes. Sit down, the two of you. Sit down."

He showed an empty flask in his hand. "O'Riley thinks I've been drinking. I haven't had a drop since Shiloh. So help me."

Matt looked at Steve and shrugged his shoulders. "Never crossed our mind."

"I know. I know how he thinks. And how you two think. Take a couple guys like me and G. T. On the ground, big guys like you swallow us up. But in the saddle . . . in the saddle, we're taller."

"Yes, Sir," Matt answered. "Now, is thet why you called us up? To justify your height?"

"No. No it isn't, smart ass." He squared off with Steve almost eye to eye, and then continued. "Matt and I have an agreement."

"To keep you alive? I know all about it," Steve interrupted.

Well. Whatever he's told you is true" He paced the floor of the tent and tried to choose the right words to say. He appeared quite nervous. "I have to lead our regiment. We have over six hundred good men left and they are looking to me as their *Colonel Terry*. I need help from the two of you."

"We'll side you," Matt said, drawing out his makings.

"I've another idea."

"What's thet?" Matt asked.

Harrison picked up the metal sheathes lying on his cot. "I've had these special made for my legs. They run up to my waist."

Matt and Steve looked at Harrison almost in disbelief. "You're goin' to ride out there like some sort of knight?" Steve asked.

"Wait a minute, Steve," Matt interrupted. "I'm gettin' his drift. Go on, Tom."

"Johnston got it in the leg and bled to death. Wharton got hit in the arm. I'm pretty much protected in those areas."

"What about Colonel Terry?" Matt asked. He got it in the chest."

"As I don't have light enough material that could protect me there, I have to rely on my arms to protect me. Else I would. Figured I'd be stiff and couldn't fight, and I've got to be flexible."

"And so, with us protectin' your ass, and metal sheathes protectin' your legs, you figure you'll come out of this alive?" Matt surmised.

"Don't laugh," Harrison said, wrapping the sheathes around his legs for size. "It'll work." He strapped them around his legs and waist. "See." He proceeded to walk about the tent.

"I'll say one thing about you," Steve said. "You've got guts."

"Well?" Harrison asked, standing fully dressed in his iron pants.

"How do you expect to get up on a horse?" Matt asked.

"You can help me. Let's go out and try them on for size. Just side me and make damn sure I don't fall off.

That was Harrison's Christmas present to himself. Matt and Steve took him out to the back hills away from the view of

94

the Rangers, and with O'Riley's help, got him on his mount. He rode clumsily at first, and his steed felt the extra and unexpected weight on its back. But after awhile, he got adjusted to his new outfit and sat up straight in his saddle.

Matt and Steve stole away for a few hours from training their men to work with him, teaching him how to best handle his weapons while riding heavy on his horse.

When they returned to camp, they found the area filled with local Tennesseans walking, riding in on buckboards, mules and horses. The training ground was made into a dining area. Tables were set with food of all sorts and a variety of all kinds, chicken fried or broiled, biscuits and corn bread, fried potatoes, potato salad, baked potatoes, and pastries of any man's imaginations.

The sound of music filled the air with fiddlers and banjo pickers tuning up their instruments on the other end of the field. Soldiers laid down planks to form a dance floor and children began their playing with one another.

"What in thunder?" Harrison asked as he stood beside his tent, holding on to his new suit of armor.

"Looks to me like a hoedown is about to take place, Colonel," Matt said, laughing aloud at what he was seeing.

"Where's half our men?" Harrison asked.

It seemed obvious to the men that a third of the brigade was nowhere to be found.

"I'll go found out, Sir," O'Riley said and trotted himself down to the area. When he got to the ladies, he was so totally consumed with their hospitality and their offer of food that he never returned to the Colonel.

"Best we go down," Matt said running down the slope to the grounds below.

Harrison stood there with a strange look on his face, then turned and disappeared into his tent.

No one returned to tell him that the local people had permission to put on the feed and the hoedown for the brigade, and that some were even taken to their homes for warm fires and hot meals.

The jug was passed around and the merriment of the men and ladies increased well into the evening. One soldier commented, "This has got to be the Garden of Eden."

Harrison laid in his tent, having finally passed out from celebrating alone with his Irish drink.

Steve enjoyed the festivities by dancing with a bright-eyed girl his age that seemed to enjoy his company as much as he did hers.

A buckboard came around and when Steve looked up, Matt was driving it with a good-looking lady at his side.

"Step up, Captain," Matt said. "We're invited home to a hot meal."

"Now, thet's what I call hospitable," Steve answered. "Do you two know each other?" he asked, hoisting his female companion up into the buckboard.

"Ought ta," she answered. "She's my sister. Ma has vittles ready and pa's got some good liquor and tobaccy for ya."

"Sounds like a right nice invitation, Captain," Steve said, climbing on board. "Man am I gonna enjoy this night."

"Let's go, Dancer." Matt snapped the lines and drove the buckboard away from the party.

The day of awakening came when Harrison rode his mount into the training area in front of his men and the entire brigade the day after Christmas.

O'Riley wiped his mouth with his gloved hand and took his neckerchief and dotted his eyes. "If any of youse laughs, you'll get the back of me hand," he told his men.

It was of no use because everyone laughed, including the General.

That evening, General Wharton toasted with his officers before evening chow. "To Old Iron Sides."

Harrison raised his glass and smirked. *I'm nobody's fool,* he told himself. *It worked in the days of the roundtable. It'll work tomorrow in battle.*

Rosecrans, a highly respected General who had earned the right to be feared by the South, left Nashville on December 26. Bragg was about to learn just how much respect he carried. By the time Rosecrans arrived in Murfreesboro on the evening of 29 December, his army numbered roughly about 45,000 to Bragg's estimated 38,000.

Establishing his defense position, Bragg chose the relatively flat area northwest of the politically influential city, straddling the Stones River. Portions of the terrain were characterized by small but dense cedar forests, making it difficult for infantrymen to fight. Wagons and artillery were handicapped by the short limestone outcroppings, separated by narrow cracks appearing like rows of teeth. Stones River itself meandered northward toward a junction with the Cumberland near Nashville, and divided Bragg's troops. Bragg expected Rosecrans to attack early the next day.

Bragg called in his corp of officers, Lieutenant Generals E. Kirby Smith, Leonidas Polk and William. Joseph Hardee, for a conference.

He quickly realized that to bring Rosecrans out into the opening, he would have to drive Hardee's Corps along with Terry's Texas Rangers deep into the Union's rear.

"Hardee, take your corps and move to the east side of the river."

A West Pointer and one of the first lieutenant generals in the Civil War, Hardee's tactics were by the book; he wrote it. He was about to prove the worth of that book. His men nicknamed him, *Old Reliable*.

Bragg continued, "Leon, situate your corps on the west side".

Matt sauntered close to the tent, picked up a ladle in a bucket of water and began drinking. Putting the ladle back, he moved close to Bragg's tent to listen in on the conference, watching carefully that no one saw him. He gathered bits and pieces but couldn't make out all that was being said.

What he did hear in part was Bragg saying, "A mountain is like the wall of a house full of rat-holes. The rat lies hidden at his hole, ready to pop out when no one is watching. Who can tell what lies hidden behind that wall?" His fear was that of a minnie ball bearing his name on it.

"You know something?" Matt asked Steve after leaving the door of the tent, "I think we've got another Harrison on our hands."

"Yeah?" Steve replied. "What makes you think thet?"

"He sounds scared. He's worrying that Yankees are lurking around trees waiting to get a clean shot at him. Maybe thet's why we're out here in the open. Thet's the way I'm seein' it. He's not a Terry, let me tell ya."

Rosecrans' attack did not come.

CHAPTER 8

THE UNCANNY CAPTURE
OF A GENERAL

31 December 1882

For the next few days, the Rangers met Federal troops with skirmishes, driving them back. Then, on the last day of the year, Wharton had the brigade in defensive position prepared to meet the awaiting Federals.

Rain was the order for the day as if God had sent earth an omen to cleanse the blood that would be spilt. It was cold and wet along the raging rapids of Stones River. Then the Rangers pushed out at dawn in full regalia and marched with the fife and drum to Murfreesboro Pike. They numbered six hundred and ninety men, making it one of the larger regiments of the Confederate army. Harrison rode in front of his men dressed in his new suit of iron.

General Bragg led his brigade out and stopped just west of Stones River outside of Murfreesboro where he caught site of Willich's Brigade across the uneven field of deep crevices, boulders and limestone ledges. Bragg knew that the stream was shallow and his men could ford it at any point. His eyes scoured far out the densely populated woods to search out the positions of soldiers who might be hiding behind the red cedars and oaks, looking for that lone sniper with his name on a bullet. He set up his men and artillery. Bragg's main line of battle was in the edge of the woods, with open ground to the front. He had his troops formed in two lines; the first line protected by entrenchments, and his second line formed some six hundred yards to the rear. With the element of surprise in his corner, he knew victory was his.

"Courier!" General Wharton called out to his dispatcher. "Get Colonel Harrison here on the double."

Harrison was close by, and when summoned, rode without delay to Wharton's side.

It was a sight for Wharton to behold as Harrison rode in, bouncing in his suit of iron.

"Now's your chance to really prove Terry's tactics in using shotguns, Colonel," the General addressed him, holding back any laugh that might be hidden inside him. "We've divided our brigade. General Bragg is going to fire artillery into their lines and do some dispersing of flanks. General Polk will be on the left flank. You're going to take the Rangers to the right where the Union cavalry is mounted. Watch for my saber. As I raise it, Bragg's guns will be waiting for your advance. When I bring my saber down, ride like the devils you are and use your shotguns at close range. This time, the infantry will follow behind."

"Yes, Sir!" Harrison saluted his Commander and rode back to his Rangers.

Reining up in front of Matt and Steve, he said, "Well, Gentlemen. The day has come. Their cavalry is to our right and they look well fortified." He referred to the Federals.

"They've got shotguns," Steve added.

"We've been watching them, Colonel," Matt said. "We've also noticed that they're carrying sabers." He looked down at Harrison's side where he had his hand gripped firm around his saber. "May I suggest you keep yours sheathed, Sir?"

"Let's dispense with our indifferences, Matt," Harrison ordered.

"Beggin' your pardon, Colonel, but it seems it's kinda late for thet."

"What do you want from me?" Harrison asked with his eyes stayed on the Federals.

"You know what I want," Matt answered with his jaw tightened. "Those damn Federals are going to rely on their gawdam sabers. They'll shoot off their shotguns to no effect and turn to their sabers. We don't use sabers. Only Bowies when we have to. You know our strategy only too well. We're gonna ride in and use our shotguns at fifteen yards."

"You want us to ride in and use our shotguns at fifteen yards?" Harrison asked, nervously. "Those men are on thoroughbreds and armed to the teeth. You're mad."

"For a man in a suit of armor, you'll make out all right."

"It won't stop a saber." Harrison put his hand to his throat as if contemplating the feel of the steel blade.

"You want something around your neck?" Matt jested.

"And if we fail?" Harrison asked with his jaw still quivering.

"Damn it, Colonel. This is one hell of a time to be thinkin' about failin'. You're actin' jest like Bragg. Let our men ride in there and chew 'em up. Thet's what we've trained them to do."

Harrison took out a cigar and chomped down hard on it. Cutting it with his teeth, he chewed the end of it. "Take them."

"Yes, Sir!" Matt answered smartly.

"Just remember to watch my ass."

"Haven't I always?"

"Okay. Watch for my saber. When Bragg gives me the signal, give 'em hell!"

"Thet you can be sure of, Sir." Matt and Steve saluted Harrison, turned their mounts and rode through the ranks.

"Close range, men. Fifteen yards." They yelled it to the Company Commanders. When they reached Company K, Matt looked at Captain Mitchell who had only one arm, and said, "You're the bravest Captain I've ever met, Mitchell."

"I'll tie the reins down on my saddle horn, Matt. I've still got one good arm."

Matt and Steve spurred on, waving their hats as they rode back to the front of the lines.

The word from each of the Commanders was, "Follow Matt, gentlemen, and send 'em to hell."

Harrison sat tall in his saddle as his captains rode back and greeted them with an encouraging smile. He leaned in his saddle, creaked in his suit of armor and looked back at his regiment.

"Now boys," he said loudly for even General Wharton to hear, "we'll have some fun. There is a regiment out there preparing to charge us armed with sabers. Let them come close enough to strike and then fill them with buckshot. Watch me!"

1 January 1883

On New Year's Eve, the moment of courage was in Bragg's hands as he sat his mount and yelled out, "Fire!"

The big guns, the Howitzers and the Napoleons, rained heavy metal down the middle upon General A. Willich's Brigade, causing them to draw back and reconnoiter. His cavalry hid in the woods and readied itself

After a season of firing, Matt watched Wharton's saber come down. Harrison, in like manner, brought his arm down as a signal for his men and spurred his mount forward with Matt close to him.

"Trot!" Harrison commanded. With Matt and Steve leading Terry's Texas Rangers, and Harrison sandwiched inside, they trotted out. He yelled out in succession his familiar commands.

"Canter!"

"Charge!"

"Ride you sons-of-the devil! Ride!" Matt yelled. And they did, with a blood-curling rebel yell that shook the earth and toppled the trees.

The rain turned into sleet and the hoofs of the horses churned up the muddy field proving that the Kentucky thoroughbreds were the finest in battle for hardly any of them faltered in the gallant charge.

Willich's officers sent their cavalry to meet the Rangers head on while the infantry lined their weapons and bayonets up at an angle to spear into the horses' flesh of those who got through.

Harrison rode out in front in his suit of armor leading six-hundred and ninety Rangers with Matt and Steve and Company A immediately behind him, armed with shotguns set into their sides and an extra one wrapped around their saddle horns. The other companies spread out across the open field. The Rangers bent low to confuse the Yankee cavalry into thinking the men were either sloppy in their riding, or simply not in their saddles.

When they felt the time had come, the Rangers rose up in their saddles and raised their Navy's into firing positions.

Captain Mitchell rode hard and fast with his reins wrapped around his saddle horn and his shotgun raised high in the air. This was a moment of courage for him and he met the challenge with strength and determination to ride for glory.

The Federal Cavalry was not as prepared, as they thought they were, for the onslaught that was to follow led them to feel the full thrust of Terry's Rangers as they rode like a cyclone into their ranks.

The cavalry units met each other and rode at midfield amidst the smoke from the cannons from both sides and over killed and maimed bodies. The Rangers fired their Navy's and their rifles, but held back on their shotguns.

The Federals discharged their shotguns early with little effect. They waited with sabers drawn to carve up their enemy, but soon found out, and quickly, how the Rangers earned their nickname as *devils*.

The Rangers fired their shotguns and fragmented the Federals' cavalry regiment.

After clearing the enemy's line, the Rangers halted and reloaded their shotguns. Without waiting for orders from Matt, they uniformly rode fast and furiously again towards the Federal infantry line. Again, they caught the Federals with their pants down because the Federals had thought the Rangers would have already been defeated, and that their bayonets would finish off any of those who got through.

The Rangers knew instinctively how to maneuver into battle.   They had all been well trained by two of the finest officers of the Confederate Army and showed it in the line of fire. They were met by two lines of savage bayonets. The front line consisted of Yankees in kneeling positions ready to carve into the horses and hopefully lift the Rangers out of their saddles.

The infantry looked on as the Rangers continued riding like a herd of long horns about to pounce upon them. The men, standing with their bayonets extended between their fellow soldiers' heads, waited with a firm grip on their rifles and a determined stance.

The Rangers rode to within twenty steps of the line and unloaded their twin barrels of twenty buckshot into the thick blue line. Destruction and confusion reined as the Yankees fell upon the ground like a convey of quail flopping all around while others ran for safety, leaving their weapons behind

The Rangers continued pursuing them, slinging their shotguns on their saddle horns and firing their Navy Sixes and other weaponry from their belts and scabbards until they reached the Yankee's reserved force.

"Sound 'recall'," Harrison ordered, reining up.

Steve noticed that Harrison was holding his arm. "Did ya get hit, Sir?"

"Flesh wound," Harrison answered.

"Only place you didn't have protection," Steve replied, laughingly.

"Let's get the hell out of here before their reserved force attacks," Harrison ordered.

The scattered and tired Rangers reloaded and spurred their mounts and raced back to their line together through Willich's disoriented cavalry, echoing the rebel yell they had so proudly yelled during their attack.

In the meantime, Matt had infiltrated the main site where General Willich was headquartered and found the General with three other officers and a courier all looking away from his direction. Assessing the situation, he thought to himself that if he retreated, it could mean certain death as the Yankees could out chase him. On the other hand, he thought, if he went forward, he and any other Ranger near him could also get killed. He chose to play out his hand as it seemingly was dealt him and went forward, and maybe, just maybe, he thought, he could capture himself a famous General. He aimed his shotgun in Willich's direction and clicked the hammers.

"General Willich!" Matt addressed him with tight lips from his mount. "Order your men to lay down their weapons or I'll be forced to blow your head off."

"I'll be damned," Willich said, turning around and facing his enemy. Matt sat his horse directly behind him. "Didn't hear you ride up," Willich confessed, looking around and behind Matt.

"Drop 'em!" Matt said, staring down Willich.

"I'm not a fool." Willich complied and threw up his arms in surrender. "Drop your weapons men." Unbuckling his saber and gun belt, Willich kept looking around in the woods for other troops. Finding none, he asked, "Where are the rest?"

"Mount up, General." Matt quickly realized that he was alone. In his enthusiasm for battle and to capture the Yankee Commander, he forged ahead, thinking other Rangers were following him. Then he remembered that he had given them the liberty of charging at their will back through the lines without his command.

His brow furrowed and perspiration beaded up on his forehead when the stark realization hit him that he was directly in harm's way with only one escape, straight back the way he came with his prisoners in front of him. "The rest of you, move out in my direction!

"Quickly, General," Matt said, moving his steed to their backsides. "My thumb's gettin' a little tired."

Willich mounted up and rode in front of Matt's shotgun. His men mounted and rode beside him.

"I know how good you are with that," Willich said. "Don't let it go off accidentally."

Marching back through the thickets towards the Rangers, Willich again observed that Matt was playing out a solo hand. "I recognize you, Captain. A year ago. Watsonville."

"Slow and easy, General. I don't wanna lose you."

"Your Colonel Terry was killed by one of my men. You asked my permission to bury him."

"You've got a good memory, General."

"I gave you my permission."

"Yes, Sir, you did. And I'm grateful to you for it."

"Enough to let me and my men go?"

"General. You do have a sense of humor. Keep movin'."

"You'll wind up with a medal for this. Perhaps even a promotion," Willich said, looking ahead at what appeared to be some Union soldiers nearby.

"Your head is gonna be my trophy if we don't make it back, General." He sensed one of the officers getting a little antsy towards making a break and said sharply, "Keep him in line, General. He don't seem to care about you."

"He's got us, Colonel. Might just as well go the rest of the way with our heads up."

From a distance, Steve caught site of Matt and realized that he needed help. He gathered some nearby Rangers and rode to his aid firing their weapons at some Federals who were coming to Willich's rescue. The Rangers turned them around and pursued them, chasing them back into the woods..

"I'll be a suck-eyed mule," Steve said as he sided Matt. "I wondered what happened to you."

"I'm like the wind, ol' buddy," Matt said. "Here, there and everywhere. Recognize our friend here?"

"General Willich," Steve yelled out. "You've got the ol' man himself."

"Well, yell out so thet the rest of the Federals know about it and we'll likely lose him."

The Rangers helped Matt get his prize catch of the day back to camp.

In the meantime, Generals Bragg and Wharton looked at their achievement in battle and watched with their officers at the battlefield of dead and wounded. Suddenly, they caught sight of Matt and Steve bringing in General Willich along with other prisoners.

"Sir!" Matt said as he stopped in front of the two Generals. "May I introduce you gentlemen? General Bragg. General Wharton. This here is my good friend, General Willich."

"Thank you, Captain," Bragg returned.

Bragg watched as Willich tried to hide pain as he saluted. "You've been wounded, General."

"Slightly," Willich said, looking at Matt. "Not by this gentleman. Some buckshot in my leg."

"You're to be commended it wasn't in your back," Wharton said as he returned Willich's salute.

"Not likely. I am no coward."

"No, General. I never read that in you," Wharton said.

"Dismount and come on into our tent, General." Bragg motioned for him to enter. "We'll get that leg tended to."

Matt saluted both Generals and then dismounted.

"May I say something, General Bragg?" Matt asked.

"Captain."

"General Willich's army, as you well know, defeated us last year at Watsonville where Colonel Terry was killed."

"Yes, Captain. I'm aware of that."

"What you may not know, Sir, is thet General Willich halted the fighting between us and allowed us to retrieve Colonel Terry's body. He gave Colonel Terry the proper respect and salute afforded an officer."

"Thank you, Captain." Bragg reached out and shook hands with Willich. Wharton did the same.

"It was a good fight, General," Bragg said.

"For us, General Bragg, it was a good fight," Willich returned. "For you and General Wharton, it was a glorious battle. Had it not been for your Rangers, Terry's Texas Rangers, we would not have been defeated."

"You have a point, General Wharton. But I think we still would have won."

The officers smiled and Bragg offered Willich and Wharton each a cigar, taking one himself. He gave three more for Harrison and his two friends.

Matt courteously provided a light for their cigars.

Willich eyed Colonel Harrison. "I see you're out of uniform, Colonel Harrison."

The men smiled, as they knew he was referring to Willich's armor sheaths.

"General." Willich addressed Bragg as he inhaled his cigar in the cool air. He looked at the soldiers on both sides and the effects of the battle. "May I offer? If I had a choice whether to fight with the Union Forces or with Terry's Rangers, do you know what my answer would have been?"

"I'm not sure, General." Bragg walked to his tent where his aide opened the door for the two Generals to enter and waited for Willich to answer.

Pausing outside the tent, Willich turned and looked around at Bragg's regiment. "I am a Federal officer of German descent. I know victory. And now I know defeat." He took a long drag on his cigar to show that he enjoyed it, and then let the smoke drift into the cold air.

"Mein Gott," he said with enthusiasm, looking at Matt and then at the Rangers sitting their mounts around him "I would rather be a Private in that regiment than be a Brigadier General in the Federal army. That's how good they are. No, General. You would not have won without them."

Bragg smiled and Matt laughed. His laugh was echoed by the other officers and men around them.

Bragg entered the headquarters first and then Wharton allowed Willich to enter as was protocol, and then the other Confederate officers followed.

"Would you like some Kentucky bourbon whiskey, General Willich?" Bragg offered as they sat down. "Compliments of the South, Sir."

Matt and Steve waited outside and adjusted their saddles. They could hear the conversation, as they stood silently outside.

"Thank you, General Bragg. I love the fine taste of Kentucky bourbon."

He looked at Harrison, wrinkled up his face and said, "You know, Colonel Harrison. Your armor scared the hell out of my men's horses. Very shrewd tactic."

They toasted their glasses and laughed.

Then Willich looked hard at the Confederate officers.

"What's on your mind?" Bragg asked, finishing his drink. "I'm seeing something I don't like."

"Yes, General Bragg," Willich answered. "I'll tell you. You think by taking me, that you've got Rosecrans, too."

"And . . ."

"Well, let's just say, for the moment, you have me."

Nothing else was said, and eventually General August Willich was led away, a prisoner.

Harrison had no more need for his iron pants. He had gained back a reasonable respect from the Rangers as they quit calling him Mark Time, mainly because he had turned over his command at Murfreesboro to the man who could pull it off, Matt Jorgensen. Although he shared in the victory, he hated it more because Matt was the one who single-handedly brought in the Commanding General.

General Willich was probably right, too in his remark that Terry's Texas Rangers were the key factor in winning the battle. Generals Wharton and Bragg honored Matt in front of the Rangers with a promotion to Major.

Bragg watched as the escorted General was led away. He remarked to himself, *Yes, you son-of-a-bitch, I've got Rosecrans, too. All the way to Nashville.*

CHAPTER 9

ROSEY

That same day, Matt and Steve rallied their company, and with the rest of Bragg's Brigade, pushed the Federals hard down to a river crossing called McFaddens' Ford. The rest of Bragg's troops brought up the rear. Bragg thought he had found the strength in these two men to break Rosecrans for sure.

But Rosecrans did not retreat to Nashville, as Bragg thought. Somehow, the Federals gained strength and rained canon fire down upon Bragg, crushing his brigade. Ostensibly, Bragg's momentary thought of victory distracted his awareness of Rosecrans' renewed strength, and now he was seeing defeat.

"What the hell is happening?" he yelled out, sweating profusely and shivering.

With determination to win, Matt and Steve rode their company through Rosecrans' troops again and again, but, because they only carved a gap into a tired but vengeful army, the opening closed in, and closed in tighter, putting Matt and Steve's company behind them with no possibility of them coming back through their ranks and to the safety of Bragg's army.

The Federals pushed hard towards the main body of Bragg's Brigade. They fired their weapons, and when they ran out of ammunition, they used their bayonets, and then their muskets as clubs.

When the fighting was over, a third of the Rebels bloodied up the river, and within one hour, the battle was over. *A terrible affair, although short*, a member of Bragg's troops described it. The Rangers' hard training paid off only in getting them on the other side of the river and out of harm's way. Matt and Steve witnessed another of Bragg's defeats as they rode the circumference back to camp.

As the smoke cleared away the winter air, the evening went without any further incident. The Tennessee valley, her hills and river, seemed to swallow up the fierceness of the battle with the men from both sides carrying off their dead and wounded.

Although defeated in battle, Bragg's Brigade had captured over two thousand prisoners.

The troops on both sides rested that New Years' Eve. But an angry Matt charged into Harrison's tent, tired and dirty from the fighting, and madder than a wounded bear. "Sir, I respectively ask you, what the hell is Bragg trying to prove?"

Harrison kicked the blankets off his body and sat erect on his cot. "Who the hell are you to come in here and demand anything?" he answered, wiping the sleep from his eyes.

"Bragg called a truce?" Matt asked. "Just because it's New Year's Day?"

"You helped us lick our wounds, and now you ask why we want to rest on New Year's Day." Harrison sat down and looked tiredly up at Matt. "We came to that decision quite amicably."

"Amicably?" Matt retorted. "Amicably?" He opened the flaps of the tent and revealed to Harrison their troops sheltered against the cold the best they could. "These men aren't fighting an *amicable* war, Sir."

113

"Get the hell out of my tent, Major" Harrison threw the covers back over his body and slumped down onto the cot. "Don't say another gawdam word."

Matt brought the flaps down on the tent and stood in front of Bragg. "Terry's Rangers have broken their back, Tom. We could have had them, had Bragg listened to Forrest and not charged in after me."

"You glory hunting son-of-a-bitch."

"I'm not talkin' about glory. I'm talkin' about winning this damn war. We drove through their confusion to defeat them. But, Bragg rode after us, givin' those Yankees no avenue of escape. And thet, Sir, gave them the edge to want to fight harder. And damn if they didn't. Now, if we give them time to rest up, then we've lost our advantage. Right now, they're still fighting in confusion, and thet makes them one weak machine."

"They were cutting up my men with bayonets, mister. And your men were too tired and scared to fight back."

"Not scared, General. Never scared. And only as tired as Rosecrans, General."

Harrison looked with angry eyes at Matt, gritted his teeth and said, "There's a time to fight and a time to rest. I agree with Bragg, and right now, mister, I'm going to sleep."

"All I ask is thet you talk to Bragg, and let us fight on our turf our way. The Terry's Rangers way, Sir."

Harrison watched out of the corner of his eye as Matt's fist grew tighter. He gave one command. "Out!" and went back to sleep.

New Year's Eve found soldiers on both sides of the McFadden Ford lying in the mud and rocks, trying to sleep. Just before *Tattoo*, they stopped and listened to music filtering through the air. The word *Tattoo* came from the closing-time in the inns a hundred years or two before. The cries came, "Doe den tap toe", meaning, "Turn off the taps." It became a time for the men to simply rest and enjoy music.

Matt looked out into the emptiness of the night. "Music. Sounds pretty."

"Our band's playing," Steve replied, stuffing his hands into his pockets to cut the chill of the evening.

"No. More'n thet Steve." Matt pulled his collar up, turned his head to all directions and listened. "It's our band all right, but there's another tune out there. Hear it?"

Both men stopped the noise of the night made by their men and looked around. "There's music coming from the other side of McFadden's Ford, Steve."

"Yeah! I'll be."

As they continued walking, they watched the men, who were all listening to the tunes. One of the soldiers plucked out his cold harmonica and began playing *Dixie* on it. A few of the soldiers around him rose up and started dancing with one another, seemingly having a good time.

"What's your name, soldier?" Matt asked, blowing the cold from his lungs.

The soldier stopped playing for a moment and answered, "Corporal Sam Shea, Sir. First Tennessee Infantry."

"Don't stop. I like your playing."

The young man continued as Matt and Steve walked on.

The armies bivouacked only 700 yards from each other, and their bands started a musical battle that became a non-lethal preview of the next day's events. Northern musicians played *Yankee Doodle* and *Hail, Columbia* and they were answered by *Dixie* and *The Bonnie Blue Flag*.

"It's as if they're all trying to outdo one another, Matt," Steve replied, smiling at the men as they walked by.

"Kinda like a *battle of the bands*," Matt came back. "Thet's it. They're playing hard enough thet they are trying to outdo one another."

Then the soldier who was playing *Dixie* began playing *Home Sweet Home*. Steve joined Matt as he stood next to him, listening to the sweet restrain. Both men realized quickly that he was echoing the bands playing the same turn.

"Well, I'll be," Matt whispered. "Both sides are playing "Home Sweet Home. Shh. Listen."

The night air carried the music throughout the woods, whispering its melodic harmonies on the wings of cheerfulness, dissipating into the chasms of emptiness.

General Wharton summoned Harrison to his tent. "I've been instructed to attack in the morning."

Harrison's eyes opened wide at the news. When he gained his composure, he asked, "Why?" He became lost for words.

"I'm free to pick my targets, and I'm not too sure where I want to be."

"Well, you know if we go back the way we retreated, we're going to run into Rosecran's whole garrison. We'd be demolished."

"I'm thinking about going around them. See what's on the other side. I want to see if we can come in from the rear and stir up some real trouble for them."

"Thinking?"

"I'm thinking we need to take a ride along the Nashville and Murfreesboro Pike, Tom. Rally the Rangers and let's set out at first light."

Bragg slept that night without any changes in his plans for his infantry. Having given Wharton his command for the day, he felt confident victory was on his side. When he woke before dawn the next day, he met with his subordinates.

He was in full regalia as he walked from headquarters towards them. After giving Wharton his leave, he said, "Line 'em up!" he ordered the officers. "We're marching in!"

Matt and Steve had the Rangers in their saddles and ready when the sun beamed through the trees. Matt looked over at Harrison climbing into his saddle. "Changed your mind, did you, Tom?"

Harrison humphed and said, "I thought it over. Wharton and I had a few words and he agreed that it'd be a good time to see what's out there. Probably a waste of time, but like you said, it's better than sitting on our asses."

The *ride* almost proved to no avail, as they rode to keep away from the enemy, as well as to scout out small parties to combat. Then, late afternoon, they came across a rather large wagon train at La Vergne with over a hundred wagons, a cannon, and three hundred mules.

"Alright, Rangers," Wharton commanded Harrison and his officers. "Let's look alive."

The fight was short as the Rangers moved upon the wagon train like angry wasps, taking it without too much of a fight.

"Now what, General?" Harrison asked, sizing up the haul they just took. "How the hell are we going to get these wagons back to our lines?"

Wharton looked over at a puzzled Matt and shrugged his shoulders. He rode around the wagons and received a report back from Harrison. "Ammunition in these," he pointed out to the first few wagons. "Food and clothing in some others. Not much in the rest."

Wharton saw he was wasting time. He quickly commanded them. "Take ten wagons and haul out. Burn the rest. Take them, all the prisoners and animals back to the commissary."

Harrison rode over to his side, took off his hat and wiped the perspiration from his brow. "This is a large haul, John."

"Didn't expect it, did we. I think I must have sent more prisoners to the rear than the total number of my whole Brigade."

The lack of adequate information at General Bragg's headquarters about Rosecrans' forces, however, had left Bragg with a surprise counterattack from men who had their spirit rekindled by a leader who defied defeat, Rosecrans.

Rosecrans' organizational skill and obedience through the ranks made him the great general he was. That night, he consolidated his tired and battered forces, giving his subordinates the assurance of victory.

"The Mother of God is with us," he said, standing with his officers by his side and looking over the Tennessee hills. "I want you to encourage your men in the lines. Make them ready. Make them strong in spirit, for I'm certain Bragg will be thinking the same as me. Heaven help us, and God be with us, I'm fearful that the worst is yet to come." He looked back at his men. "But be assured, God is with us, and victory shall be ours."

One of the officers stood up and toasted to the general with his tin of coffee. "Here's to *Old Rosey.*" The rest of the officers stood up and followed suit.

Rosecrans smiled, accepted the toast, turned and looked out towards Bragg's unit. *Damnnation,* he said to himself, biting his lip, I'll *be glad when it's over*

While his adversary worked through the night, Bragg went to bed without changing troop dispositions at all. He expected to catch Rosecrans in the open on the road back to Nashville on the first day of 1863. He confidently expected to find the Union troops gone from his front on the morning of the 2d. His cavalry had reported the turnpike full of troops and wagons moving toward Nashville. It was not to be.

His surprise came when he found Rosecrans army still in position to give battle on New Year's Day. He was disillusioned that Rosecrans would retreat.

Before Bragg's Brigade got to celebrate, the Union forces were down upon them.

Captain John Walker yelled out, "Where's our army?" He looked around at his men scattering, leaving the wagons behind. Bragg's Brigade rolled through the woods again in defeat, leaving much of his captured artillery and prisoners behind.

The sergeant looked back as Walker looked around at Bragg's scattered soldiers.

"Don't we get to keep any of it?" the Sergeant asked.

"Keep those canons rolling," Walker charged. "Leave the rest."

Captain Walker yelled out. "Where the hell is our army?"

Captain John Walker was no man for retreating. But standing there with his wide sombrero and puffed-out chest, he looked behind at the Union forces and lifted up his heels.

With the Rangers not there to help him, having given Wharton leave earlier to route out Union Forces, Bragg took his remnant and left the battlefield.

Rosecrans claimed his victory proudly. As a tribute to his victory, Rosecrans built the Middle Tennessee Fortress, a station that would serve the Yankees as a supply base for the battles against Chattanooga and later, Atlanta. He stood the victor, a General for all time; a man who became widely respected for his bravery.

It was another victory for Wharton as he routed out the Federals. But for Bragg, he kept some of his over two thousand prisoners, not many, and part of his loot. Not bad for a defeated man.

4 January 1863

Rosecrans watched Bragg's Army of Tennessee move out towards Tullahoma where Bragg established his headquarters. Both sides lost equally as many in the battle, numbering just under twenty thousand soldiers.

CHAPTER 10

A MEXICAN SADDLE FOR WHARTON

The spirit of the Rangers remained high throughout the rest of 1863 under the leadership of General John Austin Wharton. Whatever town they rode through, the women would lean out their windows and cheer them on. "We're proud of Terry's Texas Rangers," one woman shouted. Another ran up to Wharton and begged for her husband to be saved from hanging as a spy. "Please free my little Freddie."

"I'll save him if I'm still alive," Wharton told her.

Mothers provided the Rangers with food, pastry, and glasses of cold buttermilk as they rode by. Older women sat on their porch, some too weak to move, and just cried into their aprons.

"Give 'em you know what," an old man shouted as he leaned against his plow.

Men too old to fight and kids still in school ran along the road and shouted "hoorah's!" until they could run or shout no more.

They all knew Terry's Texas Rangers and they just had to touch them, talk with them, walk with them, or simply smile at them, something to make them feel they, too, were a part of their victories.

A lad rode out on his sorrel with a rifle and a pistol, and to the consternation of his mother, yelled out, "I'm comin' with ya." Oft as not, Wharton would welcome the lad as long as he had a good horse and was a good shot.

"I'll not take him, ma'am," he said to her with hat in hand, "without your permission, and unless he's willing to be the best."

"I'll not stop him, Sir," she said, pushing the hair from her forehead. "And he is the best. His pa taught him."

"Where's your husband?" Wharton asked, looking back towards the house.

"Killed at Shiloh, Sir," she answered. "My son's been waitin' for you to ride by."

Wharton looked into her eye and found no tears. "You're a strong woman."

"I'll cry tonight," she answered. "I have for a long time." She bit her lip and continued, "Bring him back to me."

He nodded his head and said, "I'll do my damndest." He turned away and watched the boy ride his sorrel in line with the rest of the Rangers.

"His name is Robert Allen Colton," the mother added.

Wharton registered the name in his mind, nodded and rode away.

Early February, General Wharton called a special meeting with Colonel Harrison, Matt and Steve in the tent headquarters.

"Gentlemen," Wharton addressed the men as they entered the tent, "please sit down."

"If you don't mind, Sir," Matt replied, "been sittin' all day. Mind if we stand?"

"You may. However, with news like this, you might want to grab hold of something."

"Yes, Sir. We'll still stand."

"Gentlemen," Wharton started in, "when Terry's Rangers connected with Johnston's Brigade, we did so as an independent guerilla regiment, if you please. We had no uniforms. We're still an independent regiment . . . serving with Bragg's brigade now.

"Your skill and expertise with horses and weaponry have helped to mold Terry's Rangers into the finest fighting cavalry the Confederate Army has ever seen."

"Beg your pardon, John," Harrison interrupted. "The finest cavalry regiment in this whole damn war. Both sides will attest to that."

"You gonna promote us, General?" Steve asked, almost expecting a positive reply.

"You'll rate one eventually, Captain. And let me tell you, I would rather do that here and now and keep you in our regiment than anything else."

Matt cleared his throat and looked around at the men in the tent. "Excuse me, General Wharton, Sir. You said, 'keep us' like as if you've got a second choice to get rid of us?"

"Matt," Wharton continued. "I can't keep you. President Davis wants you to start training other companies in our Confederate Army."

"What?" Steve asked, swallowing hard.

"I have to explain, gentlemen. You will be doing the South a bigger favor by taking on this assignment."

"We got rooked into training others, Sir," Matt threw back at Wharton. "We did it to get into Terry's Rangers. We had no choice at thet time. It seems to me, we now have a choice."

"Remember, I was there when Colonel Terry took you under his wing, so to speak," Wharton came back.

Harrison looked at the two men and had ambivalent feelings. First, here was his chance to be rid of them and their glory seeking services. Then, on the other hand, he thought, "Who the hell's gonna buffer me?" He waited with anxiety at what Wharton had to say.

"But, gentlemen, I've been with President Davis in Virginia. We've talked about you before the battle at Murfreesboro. We knew the Federals were copying your strategy and we knew we had to do something about it. Davis instructed me to offer this position to the both of you. No. No, he commanded me to order you to take it."

"Excuse me, General," Steve came back. "Why did you wait until now to tell us? Two months almost?"

"Because I needed your help to clean up what became the finest battle I've ever witnessed. Our Rangers fought better than I've ever seen any cavalry unit fight all because of you two men. Davis gave me this much time. Now he's asking for you."

Matt grit his teeth and looked at Steve.

Steve asked, "Wanna talk about it, Matt?"

"Where do we go next?" Matt asked Wharton.

"Some people are natural born leaders to train as well as soldering," Wharton said. "You're still members of Terry's Texas Rangers, and that you'll wear on your cap. But, you're to work with the First Georgia Cavalry Regiment and get them ready. Sherman and Grant have got to be stopped before they reach Georgia."

"Grant? Again?" Matt asked. "And why Georgia? General, you and I know there are jest as many Federals inside Georgia as there are Southerners. We won't get loyalty there. I'm agin' it."

"We knew you would be, Matt."

"Damn right. We've got thirteen stars on our bars and stripes. One of those ought'n be there. Georgia."

"That's the feelings of most of us Rangers, Matt. You're not alone. This is not my decision. It comes from President Davis."

"Let Sherman and Grant take Georgia for all I care, Sir," Matt came back. "Would serve 'em right. We'll ride right through them anywheres else."

Wharton laughed, took out a handful of cigars, tossed three for the other three men and took one for himself. He knew a cigar would always calm his officers down the best. "Dammit, Matt. We can't afford to lose Georgia. Trust me on this one."

"Have we no other choice?" Matt asked, lighting Wharton's cigar and then his.

"I've got you on a train for Rome, Georgia. You'll leave first thing in the morning." Then he added, "I'll soon see you in Georgia myself, gentlemen."

"You're goin', too?" Matt asked.

"Just as soon as I can."

Matt dragged on his cigar and smiled. "Well, I guess it's all right, then."

Almost immediately, Matt and Steve left for Rome, Georgia which was built on seven hills and situated within a triangle defined by Atlanta, Georgia; Birmingham, Alabama; and Chattanooga, Tennessee. It had several new stores where goods were supplied by steamboats that sailed the Coosa River. Turkeys were the catch of the day, and cotton was the export. They reported to Colonel James J. Morrison. He was a thin man of medium stature with a full head of hair and a rather large bushy beard.

It was not easy for two strangers like Matt and Steve to enter the camp of another cavalry regiment and get full cooperation. Yet, Matt and Steve knew they'd soon be mixing it up with them just like they did with the Rangers when they first joined up. They stepped from the train onto the platform and looked towards the engine as it belched a full gust of steam.

"Gentlemen!" A deep voice filled the air from behind them. It was that of Colonel Morrison of the First Georgia Cavalry Regiment. "Seeing the star on your hats, I'm to presume you are the two men President Davis sent me."

Matt and Steve nodded and saluted the Colonel.

"It's good to see you," Morrison added.

"I'm Major Matt Jorgensen and this is Captain Steve Andrews of Terry's Texas Rangers. Yes, Sir. We're here by President Davis' request."

"Good to have you men with us," Morrison greeted. "I've been expecting your coming earlier. What kept you?"

"Murfreesboro," Matt answered. "And a few others."

"Murfreesboro? I was there."

"Yes, Sir," Matt answered. "I watched your command. You were pretty good."

"Thank you." Morrison smiled and looked Matt over as if in a routine inspection. "I hear that you're the gentleman who captured Willich and his whole damned army?"

"I got General Willich. Yes, Sir. The Rangers helped in getting his whole *damned army*."

"And you're going to help my men learn the same tactics? God is blessing us this day, gentlemen. I welcome your help."

"We're gonna try, Sir" Matt assured him.

"And, please believe me, I do mean I welcome your help. My aid here, Sergeant Major Mallory, will see you to your new quarters. When you're ready, he'll bring you over to my quarters."

"Thank you, Colonel, "Matt replied.

Sergeant Mallory was a bruiser of a man, short and stout in stature who liked to show off his muscles.

"Sirs," he addressed them, "I'll take you to your quarters."

Matt turned and the two of them followed the Sergeant.

After they settled in, they reported back to Colonel Morrison who took them on a tour of the camp.

"This is my cavalry," Morrison said as he showed the periphery of the camp to the two gentlemen. "I call them 'Morrison's Cavalry'. Nothing fancy like Terry's Texas Rangers.

His men were idling their time, sitting around on the grass.

"Sergeant," he yelled out. "Get these men up and in formation. I want them to meet their new trainers."

Sergeant Mallory double stepped to the center of the camp and roused the men into formation. "Dress right!" he yelled out once they lined up. "Attention!"

Colonel Morrison took Matt and Steve and introduced them to his regiment. "At ease, men." Pointing to the duo, he continued. "You'all heard about Murfreesboro. These are two of the men who caused us to win that battle. Major Jorgensen here is the one who single-handedly captured General Willich.

"Now, I don't have any more to say than this. President Jefferson Davis ordered them here to train us how to subdue the enemy, Texas style."

"Sir?" one of the horse soldiers interrupted him with his hand raised. "These men are from Terry's Texas Rangers? The demons?"

"You've got that right, soldier," Morrison answered.

"We've known about their comin', and we're mighty proud to have them with us. Yes, Sir. Mighty proud."

"Well," Morrison said, looking back at the two gentlemen, "looks to me like you've got a captive audience. Gentlemen. They're all yours."

Quickly, Morrison discovered a new way of fighting; the Terry's Texas Rangers' way.

It was at Silver Creek near Rome that they set up training and ran raw recruits as well as seasoned veterans through their paces. Matt and Steve came to be known as the devils that came from hell to separate the men from the boys. Whatever a man could do with a horse, he learned to do more and better. How he used a shotgun, a carbine, or a .36 caliber Navy Colt he learned to do more and better. The impossible became possible.

And not too soon, for three months later, Federal officer Yankee Colonel Abel Straight launched a skirmish against Morrison at Rome.

"If we may be so bold as to make a suggestion, Colonel," Matt said to Morrison as Straight established his position against them, "I'd like to go with an offensive."

"An offensive?" Morrison questioned. "We're here to defend Rome." He thought for a moment and then asked, "What's your plan, Major?"

"I'll take Major Franklin and half the regiment and go around in back of the Federals." Franklin was commander of a regiment that was well-trained by Matt and Steve. "Once in position, you and Steve will take the rest of your regiment. You'll ride like the devils you are through the front lines of the Federals. We'll ride back through them and meet you." Matt drew the plan in the dirt with a twig. "Just one other thing."

"What's that?" Morrison questioned.

"Don't shoot at us as we come through."

And ride they did. The strategy worked. They caught Straight in a pincer with Steve's unit to the front and Matt's unit to the rear.

Straight surmised quickly that he was being attacked by not only Morrison's Cavalry, but reinforcements from another Georgia sector. He turned tail and retreated.

Morrison could only praise Matt and Steve for their ingenuity. "Who would have thought?"

"In battle," Matt interrupted, "we don't have too much time to think. I've found that the quicker we launch our troops against the Federals, the more effective we are. We learned thet from General Sidney Johnston." He looked around and added with a proud grin, "Who in my mind was the greatest general of all time."

The General must have been smiling that day from heaven as he looked down upon two of his best officers borrowing his tactics.

The young officers walked down the road together that evening and talked about old times.

"Still thinkin' about Ginny?" Steve asked.

"As much as ever." Matt answered. "Not when we're trainin' or in battle, though. I learned a long time ago to keep my head clear at those times."

"You won't be mad if I tell you something'?"

"What?"

"Best you read it." Steve handed a post to Matt.

Matt took it out of the envelope and read it. Afterwards, he calmly put it back into the envelope and gave it back to Steve.

"Well?" Steve asked.

"Well, what?"

"Brenda says she's comin' for a visit."

"She's your sister."

"Yeah. But she's kinda fond of you."

"Yep."

"Thet all you got to say?"

"Yep."

"Not mad?"

Matt simply walked away with his hands in his pockets like a school kid. "Brenda," he thought. "Damn."

CHAPTER 11

A FEMALE VISITOR COMES TO ROME, GEORGIA

Matt and Steve waited on the platform for the train to come in, and as usual, it was late. Finally, with a cloud of black cinders, she was seen coming around the bend. It pulled into the depot, and with a gust of steam bellowing from her belly, she rolled to a stop. One female passenger stood out among the others that got off that day. It was Brenda Andrews, Steve's sister.

"Brenda!" Steve yelled out.

He ran to her, picked her up and twirled her around while Matt picked up her one bag.

"You've grown older, brother," she recognized as she put her feet back down on the platform. Then she turned and looked at Matt. "And you, too, Mr. Jorgensen. Oh, I see. You're a major. And Steve?"

"Still a captain, sis," he said, taking her arm and slipping it into his. "He earned his promotion. Boy did he earn it. You shoulda seen him. He captured this General and three of his officers all by hisself. I mean, he waltzed into their camp and . . ."

"I'm sure she didn't come all this way to hear about me," Matt interrupted, joining them in the walk to a carriage with two horses setting away from the platform.

"Here, you go, sis," Steve said as he helped Brenda up into the back of the carriage. He started to sit in the front seat but Matt beat him to it.

"I'll drive." Matt threw the bag in the front seat, climbed in and took the lines. He turned his head and looked back at Brenda, doffed his hat and said, "Welcome to Rome, Miss Andrews."

"Thank you, Major. And where are we going?"

Smacking the horses with the lines, he headed the team out into the road. "To a little place called Clear Creek."

"This isn't exactly the best place or time for a visit, if you ask my opinion," Matt said with his eyes on the road.

"I consented only because she kept naggin' me," Steve replied. "It might look peaceful, but we've got Yankees camped close by, sis."

"Really?" Brenda asked looking around. "If they are, I don't see any."

"We just had a skirmish the other day," Steve informed her, pointing northward. "Our scouts let us know where they are and when they're around us."

"Oh, my. You didn't get hurt or anything, now did you?"

"No, Sis."

"Well, I'm sure I'm in capable hands of two fine officers, one being a Major and all." She smiled at Matt, and flirted with her eyes.

"A minni ball doesn't know any difference in ranks, miss," Matt said as he snapped the lines to make the team go faster.

The jolt caused Brenda to fall further back into her seat.

"Really!" Brenda remarked, straightening herself to sit upright.

"Gotta get to camp," Matt remarked. "Woods aren't safe."

"It looks like we're in open country," Brenda observed, holding on to the seat rail.

"Woods up ahead."

"He's right, sis." Steve held onto her to keep her in the carriage. Matt whipped the team into a faster run, as if he were doing it out of a little anger towards her for coming there for a visit.

When Matt pulled the team to a halt at headquarters, the horse manager ran and settled them down.

Colonel Morrison came walking up to them and greeted the new visitor.

"I take it, Steve, that this is your lovely sister, Brenda Andrews," he said pleasantly, offering his hand to her as she stepped out of the carriage.

"Why, thank you, Colonel."

"Morrison, Miss," he said with a smile.

"Well. Colonel Morrison. This is your army camp?"

"Yes, it is. I trust you had an easy carriage ride."

"Easy?" She looked over at Matt standing next to the carriage with her bag in his hand. "Yes, it was."

"Fine. Then, why don't we let your brother show you around first, and then you can join me later for dinner in my tent."

"Yes. Yes, I'd like that." She let go of his hand and smiled while watching the Colonel walk to his tent.

"He's a nice gentleman," she said, looking at Matt out of the side of her eye.

"I'll take your bag to your quarters," Matt said and walked over to a tent, leaving Steve and Brenda to themselves.

"You came to see him more than me, didn't you, sis?" Steve asked, watching her stare at Matt, walking away.

"As much, Steve," she answered. "As much."

That evening in Morrison's tent was one of the finest Matt and Steve had enjoyed in a long time for the meal was of the finest beef and the wine flowed. The company was excellent for a beautiful lady graced their table.

Afterwards, Matt and Steve excused themselves and left Morrison alone while they walked Brenda outside in the evening breeze.

Feeling awkward about his presence, Matt excused himself.

"I've got some plans in my tent for tomorrow's drill," he said, walking away. "So if you two will excuse me. I think you need some time together anyway."

"Matt," Steve summoned him quickly and walked to him. "I'm the one who should be going over some plans," he whispered. "If you want to call it thet. She'd like to spend some time with you."

"Oh, hell, Steve," Matt whispered back. "I'll only be dead weight."

"Ginny?"

"I don't know. Maybe."

"Try and jest talk with her. She came all this way, and part of it was to be with you."

Matt looked back at Brenda and then asked, "You alright with this?"

"Not for me to say. It's for you."

"All right. But don't say I didn't warn you."

Steve went back to Brenda, kissed her on the cheek and said, "Matt's right. I've got some plans to look over for tomorrow."

"I thought they were his plans," she returned with a smirk on her face.

"Well, they are and I have to look at them first and then sort of pass them on to him for his approval," he replied, haltingly.

She knew that he was leaving so she could be alone with Matt.

"Okay," she said with a smile as she watched him walk away. "See you in the morning?"

"I'll call for you."

Matt stood still looking at Brenda.

Brenda waited for Matt to join her.

He turned and watched Steve as he walked away and then looked back at Brenda. "Wanna walk some?"

Sensing his awkwardness she answered and said, "Back to my tent if you don't mind. I am rather tired. And that wine didn't do me any too good."

"Me neither," he mused.

She put her arm in his and allowed him to escort her back to her tent. "Will I see you in the morning?" she asked, holding onto the flap of her tent.

"We'll be up early, putting the men through their paces. Come on down and we'll give you a show."

She smiled and said, "Steve said he'd call on me."

Matt sensed her feelings for him through her evening-colored eyes and his body trembled with delight at just wanting to grab her and kiss her. He looked around for anyone spying on them, then smiled at Brenda. "You look beautiful tonight. You know thet."

Brenda held onto the flap of the tent, turned her body into his and answered, "After traveling all day. I haven't had time to clean this dust from me."

"Maybe it's the dust thet makes me so attracted to you."

"You're being coy with me. I mean, you've never said anything like thet before when you had more of an opportunity. And if I remember correctly, you never danced with me."

"I just met you then. Besides, I had a gal."

"And now?"

"Didn't Steve tell you? She was killed. Early."

"I'm sorry, Matt." She let go of the flap and dropped her hands to her side. "He told me. How insensitive of me."

"Not really. It's been a long time."

"If you still need a warm hand, I'm here for you."

"You came all this way to see your brother. I'm impressed."

"You can't get anything straight, can you, Matt Jorgensen?" She placed her hands on her hips and looked him straight into his eyes. "Sure I came here to see Steve, but I don't think I would have made this god-awful trip for that alone. No sir. I came here, also, to see you, Matt."

He allowed silence to do the talking between them for a few seconds, and then asked, "Where's my apple pie?"

She reached out and touched his hand. "You read my note I put in your lunch, didn't you?"

He pulled it from his vest pocket. "Yep." After opening it and showing it to her, he folded it neatly in its set pattern and returned it to his vest.

"You know how to make a young lady blush."

"You're right on three counts."

"What that?" she asked. Then it dawned on her what the three points were, "Oh! Why, thank you."

Grasping her hand in his he brought her against his body. "Thet's what's been keepin' me goin' all these months. Wantin' to see you again."

"If you're gonna kiss me, we'd better go inside the tent before some soldiers come along."

The pair ducked under the flap of the tent and wrapped their arms around each other and enjoyed a passionate moment. His lips found hers in the dimness of the tent as they enjoyed each other's company.

Breaking for air but holding tight to his frame, Brenda said haltingly, "I've been waiting to be kissed like that all my life."

His arms wrapped her into his body in a moment of high ecstasy and they trembled ever so slightly, wanting to touch each other in an ethereal manner much to each other's desires. His body reached out and stroked her lightly as if to stay his distance but go further if she so desired. She felt the need to accommodate him and accepted his body with little twists. Their lips parted and the couple looked into each other's eyes.

"Don't let me go too far with you," Matt said softly.

Brenda brought his lips back down to hers and moved into his body.

His hand reached and touched the top of her dress, feeling her breasts with his fingers. She made no move to stop him but kissed him harder.

Steve's voice from a near distance called out to the couple. "Matt? Brenda?"

The couple broke for a moment and Matt whispered, "Shhh. He'll go away."

They heard the sound of his boots as he passed by the tent without stopping. "I'm gonna turn in early. If you two are anywhere around, don't wake me 'til mornin'."

The couple embraced once more and enjoyed the loving moments of each other's company as they slipped down upon the ground together.

"Do you think he knows where we are?" she asked, giggling.

"He knows."

The next morning, the bugler brought everyone up. After the horsemen chowed down, they got their horses and walked them around the field to warm them up.

From his tent, Matt saw Steve call on Brenda. He watched the couple as they came out of her tent and waited to see if she would find him.

She wore a blue cotton dress filled out with her many underskirts, and a hair bonnet to match. An escaping lock of her blond hair loosely played away from her bonnet.

With Steve's help, she found Matt and did a quick step with Steve to join him.

"Have breakfast?" he asked.

"The Colonel had it brought to my tent, thank you," she answered. "And you?"

"Long ago."

"If you two will excuse me," Steve said and walked away.

"Where's Steve gong?"

"Out there to the other end. He'll pick up his horse and they'll all be ridin' in a few moments. Wanna watch?"

One of the soldiers who noticed them standing brought a couple of chairs for them.

"Why thank you," she said as the soldier was leaving. "That's nice of that young man," Brenda said as she sat down with Matt's assistance.

"Southern boys have manners," Matt returned.

"Most do," she replied.

"How about boys from Montana?"

"I enjoyed last night. Did you?"

"Just don't get outta my sight tonight. I've got plans."

"You gonna teach me how to ride?"

Matt received the pun intended and continued to watch as Steve lined up his men.

A line of horse soldiers rode together from Steve's command to the opposite end of the field, reined up and returned.

"What are they doing?"

"Well," Matt replied, taking a cigar from his shirt pocket, "they're trotting to warm up their horses as if they had just entered a field of battle. They want their horses warmed up because Steve is going to lead them in a charge."

"Oh!"

Matt bit the end off his cigar, lit it and watched Brenda out of the side of his face while exhaling the smoke into the air. He grinned.

Steve rode his steed out to the center of the line of ten horsemen.

"What's he doing now?"

"Talking with his men."

"Well, silly. What's he saying?"

"He's telling them how to charge."

"Don't they already know how to charge?"

"Yep, but he's training them in sections. You see, these men have to learn the Terry's Texas Rangers' way."

"What's that?"

"They're the elite corps of cavalrymen who've set the standard for all other cavalrymen to follow."

"I remember Steve mentioning Colonel Terry in his letters. He got killed, didn't he?"

"Yep. He's dead, Brenda. Killed in our first battle."

"And they still call them his Rangers?"

"Always will. He was one hell of a man. The best."

"I'm sorry. You might think I'm being insensitive. I just don't know much about war."

That lightened up the air for Matt. He smiled and took a drag on his cigar.

Looking back at the riders still in a line and talking with Steve, she asked, "Where are their sabers? I understand cavalrymen carry sabers."

"Back in their tents. We don't use them."

"Why on earth not? They're to be used, aren't they? Part of the uniform?"

"In parades or on special occasions, we'll wear them," Matt answered. "In battle, our men prefer Bowie knives."

"Bowie knives?"

"Named after its maker, Jim Bowie."

"Oh. I see. The man at the Alamo."

"Thet's right."

"I know a little history. After all, I am a school teacher."

"And a pretty one, too," he answered and then pointed towards the line of horse soldiers. "They're ready to move out."

"Canter!" Steve gave the signal as he rode in front of them part way down the field..

Brenda kept her eyes on Matt, and then turned them when she heard Steve yell out.

"Charge!"

"Oh, my goodness." Watching the soldiers gallop for a few moments, she quickly stood up and pointed at them. "They're slipping off their saddles."

Once she saw the riders flip back into the saddles, she stood amazed, looked at Matt, then back at the riders and applauded. "They did that on purpose," she said with glee in her voice.

"Thet's what makes us different than the others," Matt pointed out.

"Oh, my. Why did they do that?"

"Well, you see, young lady," Matt started in, standing next to her. "It confuses the enemy."

"How?"

Matt threw his cigar down and said, "Better to show you. Excuse me. Stay here. I'll be right back."

He untied the reins of his horse from the tree beside them, mounted and rode down to Steve. After a briefing, he rode back up the hill. Dismounting, he tied the reins back to the tree.

"What did you do?"

"Watch."

In the next few moments, several soldiers ran on foot to the end of the field with their rifles. Once there, they knelt on the ground. One row of soldiers lined up behind them and stood firm. At Steve's command, the first row planted the butts of their rifles into the ground with the bayonets pointed at a fixed angle. The men in the back row stood with their bayonets pointed in between the heads of the front row soldiers.

Brenda watched and then her eyes opened up wide when she heard her brother yell at the regrouped horse soldiers again, "Trot!"

The line of soldiers trotted their horses in formation towards the soldiers at the far end.

At his command, "Canter!" the riders leaned forward, putting their horses into a canter.

Brenda put her hand to her mouth when she saw a re-enactment of a battle scene where Steve, riding in front, commanded his men. "Charge!"

The men rode fast down the field, and then slipped to the side of their saddles.

The ground soldiers in the front line stood up as if to get a better look at the charging soldiers.

"What's happening?" Brenda asked.

"The infantrymen are acting like they only see rider-less horses and they leave their rifles for the moment."

Then, just as quickly, the riders popped back up into their saddles and, to the consternation of the infantrymen, picked their shotguns up from their saddle horns, and rode hard and fast onto the ground soldiers.

"Goodness gracious!" Brenda yelled. "They're going to get killed!" She covered her eyes with her hands and leaned into Matt for safety.

The infantrymen ran behind trees as the horsemen fired their shotguns into the air.

"What happened?" Brenda questioned in excitement.

"It's all over. Your brother won again."

"Oh, golly!" Brenda exclaimed. Then she realized where her arms were and pulled herself away from Matt and straightened herself up, brushing the hair from her eyes. "Do any of them get hurt?"

"Once in a while, if they daydream or forget to duck. For the most part, it's pretty safe." He gave a look of concern, and then added, "Of course, this comes after a lot of hard and rigorous training. And thet's where . . . (ahem) . . . Steve and I come in."

She looked his way and smiled.

Later that afternoon, she met with Steve and Matt again in less strenuous conditions. What appeared to be an afternoon of pleasantries to show Brenda around turned out to be an aura of excitement again.

Before she could regain her strength from the morning's activities, she saw General John Wharton with his cavalry of some two hundred and fifty troops. Half the men were riding their steeds, while the other half were hauled in wagons.

"What in the world?" she asked.

"Hey, it's Matt and Steve, fellas!" a Ranger cried out as he saw them with Brenda.

"Thet, little lady," Matt answered, is more of Terry's Texas Rangers. Come on and I'll introduce you to them."

The whole camp got up and went out to welcome the Rangers in.

"You made it, Sir" Steve said as they watched them ride in.

"Hello, Matt. Steve," General Wharton returned the welcome. "We're here like I said we'd be. Who's the young lady?" he asked, nodding his hat to her.

"Oh, eh, this is Brenda, Sir," Steve introduced. "She's my sister."

"You look nothing like your brother, Ma'am," Wharton replied.

A one-armed officer rode up behind Wharton. It was Colonel Mitchell.

"Hello, Major," Matt yelled out to Mitchell in excitement.

"Colonel, now, Matt."

"Colonel. Damn. Well, you deserve it."

"We're here for horses, Matt," Wharton informed him.

"Colonel Morrison's the man you need to see, Sir," Matt answered.

"I know. Where is he?"

"He's around." He caught Mallory's attention. "Sergeant Mallory. Find Colonel Morrison and tell him we've got visitors."

Matt got a glimpse of O'Riley. "General. If you'll excuse me for a moment. I see an ol' buddy."

"Get reacquainted with your men, Matt."

"Yes, Sir."

Grabbing O'Riley's gloved hand, he welcomed him. "Hello, Sarge."

Steve joined in and shook hands with him as well as a few of the veteran troopers. "You here to help us?"

"Wouldn't have come otherwise," O'Riley answered.

Riding back, Matt addressed his attention back to Wharton. "How's General Bragg?"

"Since Gettysburg? Madder'n a hornet."

"I understand we lost more'n twenty-thousand men at Gettysburg," Matt continued.

"Closer to thirty. On the other hand, the Federals lost just as many."

"Never figured it'd get this bad."

"It'll get worse before it gets better, I'm afraid, gentlemen. Sherman and Grant aren't about to let up. They'll be headed this way one day."

Seeing Colonel Morrison approaching them, Matt interrupted them. "Here's Colonel James Morrison, Sir."

"It's good to see you again, John," Morrison said as he saluted the General. After Wharton returned the salute, he dismounted and reached out his hand to Morrison.

"Yes. Good to see you, too Jim. Been a while since Murfreesboro."

"A lot of water under the bridge since."

Brenda excused herself. "Gentlemen, I see you've got a lot of military things to talk about, so I'll entertain myself by walking around the camp."

"By your leave, Miss," Morrison said, taking her hand. "Sergeant Major! Escort Miss Stephens and see that she is properly treated with all courtesy."

Sergeant Major Mallory approached Morrison, saluted, and escorted Brenda away from the group of men. "No need telling me, Sir. She'll get nothin' but the best from me."

Matt noticed General Harrison coming from behind and moving his horse up towards them.

"We've been talking about Gettysburg," Wharton informed Morrison.

"Terrible," Morrison replied.. "General Rosecrans is at my back door again as we speak. We kicked the hell out of them once, with the help of these two gentlemen. How we did it is a story I've got to tell you later at suppertime."

"That, we can share. Why do you think I've got them here in Georgia? I kinda know how ya'll did it, Jim."

"Hello, Jim," Harrison greeted Morrison, moving his horse in position with Wharton's.

"You remember General Harrison, Jim?"

"I remember. How you be?" Morrison returned.

"Call me, Tom." Harrison returned.

"I remember the stories about you at Shiloh, Tom. You were the big hero of that battle."

Matt gritted his teeth as he watched Harrison receive more accolades because he remembered him taking the glory from him in that battle. He said nothing.

"I'm glad word about that got around. Made me General."

"I don't want to be so boastful as to say that we've stopped Rosecrans. No, Tom. I think he'll be coming in soon. But we'll be ready for him, again. And you?"

"That's why we're here," Wharton replied. "We need horses. Good horses."

"I've got them. I believe you said you needed three hundred and fifty."

"Thereabouts. Do you have that many good ones to spare for my Tennesseeans?" Wharton asked.

"What are you doing to the poor animals that Tennessee is scarce of them?

"Riding the hell out of them, Jim."

"I'm finding out what you mean."

Wharton eyed the camp. "I've brought down some of my best riders. These men," he referred to Matt and Steve, "trained most of them. Some are new but damn good. I won't beat around the bush, Colonel. I'm here to recruit another hundred or so men. The best we can find. Let Matt and Steve break them while we're here."

"I think that can be done. Right, gentlemen?"

"If you say so. Yes, Sir," Matt replied with Steve echoing. "We'll put the Rangers in with Morrison's Cavalry at dawn, first thing."

For the next few days, Brenda got a good look at how her brother and Matt set up a training program for the cavalry. She could not be any more proud than she was in those few days.

Matt and Steve also knew what the Rangers had in mind when a special honor was about to be bestowed upon their General. All of the Rangers, here and back in Nashville, had already informed Matt and Steve that they had taken up a collection to buy Wharton the finest Mexican saddle money could buy, and the finest charger they could find to strap it on.

The two men had searched and found a thoroughbred bay to be the perfect horse for Wharton. Matt personally trained him.

Harrison dismounted and caught up with Matt and Steve as they continued escorting Brenda around the camp.

"You got the saddle?" Harrison asked.

"Hello, Tom," Matt answered. "This is Brenda Andrews, Steve's sister. Brenda, General Tom Harrison."

"Oh, yes." Her voice was different as she had read about Harrison through Steve's letters, and they didn't flatter him any. "Nice to meet you, General," she returned. She noticed that he wasn't as tall as he appeared when she first saw him, riding in with the Rangers. She also noticed that he started to eye her a little more flirtatiously. She turned her eyes away from him.

"The saddle was shipped to my attention from San Antonio," Matt continued.

"Are we all set for tomorrow?" His eyes were staid on Brenda.

"We're ready."

"Good. I'll present it to him tomorrow during the festivities." He suddenly turned away from Brenda and asked, "Where's the horse."

Looking around to make sure Wharton wasn't within hearing distance, Matt answered, "Follow us."

In a separate area among some trees was tied a bay thoroughbred. The groomer stayed in charge of it and kept it well curried and groomed.

"The saddle is in the groomer's tent. He and the head horseman will put it on the horse just before the presentation."

Harrison looked at the animal with envy in his eye. His concentration on Brenda disappeared. He patted the horse down with both hands and examined its teeth.

"I've never seen such a beautiful horse," he remarked. "Let's look at the saddle."

The groomer led them to his tent.

"Don't bring it out," Matt said. "We'll look at it inside."

Harrison's eyes bulged when he saw the exquisitely adorned silver saddle lying in front of him. It was a Mexican saddle. He touched it and ran his hands across its cantle and fender. "It's beautiful."

"Put the blanket back on it before our General steals it," Matt humored.

Harrison took it more seriously than just a humorous remark and said, "I'll have one, some day."

Matt thought in his mind, "*Sure.*"

5 August 1863

On the next day, it appeared that the whole countryside came out and pitched tents alongside the Rangers and Morrison's Cavalry. Barbeque beef, genuine, aged in the keg whiskey and frivolity were the order of the day as the Rangers danced merrily with the ladies, and then raced against each other with their horses.

"Wouldn't have missed this for anything, Colonel," Matt replied.

Brenda had the time of her life as she kept close to Matt's side.

"Well, where's the food?" Steve asked rubbing his hands together.

"This way," Major Pat Christian said, leading the men to the tables. "Feast your eyes on all that food, gentlemen."

And that they did. The Christmas celebration at Murfreesboro was no match for this festival. The *Bloody Sixth*, Arkansas' band, played songs such as *The Girl I Left Behind Me, Dixie* and the *Rangers' Battle Song* to name a few. Morrison's Cavalry quickly learned some of the words to the Rangers' song, and how to dance to its music.

"I see at least four or five cows being barbequed," Steve said, looking over the field. "Whole cows."

"Why friends, that's Texas style!" The booming voice of General John Wharton broke through as he strutted over to the men.

"General, Sir," Matt addressed him. As he did, he noticed Brenda holding onto Wharton's arm. "Brenda," Matt said politely. "I see you two have got acquainted."

"Yes," Wharton answered, smiling down at Brenda. "A fine looking filley, if I might add, Matt. She's told me a lot about you."

"Oh?"

"Only what I know, Major," Brenda replied to Matt.

Wharton took Brenda's hand and offered it to Matt. "I'll expect a dance later." He walked off in the accompaniment of a few other ladies walking with him.

Some of the ladies, attending the cooking, shooed the men from their food as Matt cut himself off a slice of beef and offered a piece to Brenda.

"You'll not be eating a bite until we ring the bell," one of the ladies addressed him. "Now get, all of ya."

"Yes, ladies," Matt replied.

Then Matt said to Wharton. "John, if I may." He motioned with his hand for them to walk to the other part of the field where chairs were set up. As they sat, he said, "You are about to see some real excitement, now."

And excitement it was. Colonel Morrison brought out his cavalry as they paraded in front for all to see. Matt and Steve joined him in their ranks as they rode to the sidelines. Then the horse soldiers put on a show that brought back memories of the Fair at Nashville.

"I see they've been taught well, Jim," Wharton said, applauding the riders.

"Yes," Morrison answered. "Matt and Steve did a fine job. But look at the horses. These are Georgia animals, General. You'll be riding the same."

Afterwards, Matt and Steve stole some time and, with Brenda tagging along, reacquainted themselves with the visiting Rangers.

"Why don't you fellas eat?" Matt asked, chawing down on a piece of beef.

"Nothin's gonna stop us," Troy said, carving into the beef.

"You've broken Harrison, Matt," Christian said. "He's no longer scared of his shadow."

"Yeah," Troy came in. "But we hate him more than ever. He thinks he's the two of you in one. Keeps tellin' us how we should fight."

"Best part though," Christian continued, "he's got some of his confidence back. He drives right in there with us."

"Iron Pants?" Steve asked.

"Nope. No more," Troy replied. "He's a regular, but he still wears his red bandana on top his head like a banny rooster."

"Iron pants?" Brenda asked.

"Don't ask," Steve replied. "You don't want to know."

That afternoon, the Rangers and Morrison's cavalry, with ladies on their arms, took seats on the lawn and watched as

Harrison praised Wharton as the Commander of Terry's Texas Rangers.

"I've ridden with General Wharton longer than most here," Harrison bragged with his thumbs inside his gallowses. "We rode together at Manassas with Colonels Terry and Lubbock. I was there when they, and General Wharton, returned to Texas from Montgomery after they had just formed Terry's Rangers."

Wharton cleared his throat and interrupted. "The day after, Tom. We had formalized our plans in a stagecoach on the trip back to Texas when President Davis refused our support." He looked over at Doc, who was an early recruit with the Rangers, and asked, "Doc. When did you come along? "

"Colonel Harrison, at thet time, brought me in, Sir," Doc answered. "He brought a couple hundred of us in. I think only a few of us are left. Troy and Christian I reckon, a few others, maybe."

"Yes, John," Harrison corrected himself. "I remember it like it was yesterday. You said we were going to ride the best horses to glory. Only thing wrong with that was, we didn't know where we were going to get them from."

A roar of laughter filled the lawn and when it quieted down, Harrison continued. "Anyway, if you gentlemen will bring him forward."

The head horseman and his chief groomer led a magnificent bay thoroughbred gelding attired with the finest saddle and tack any horse soldier could hope for.

"General Wharton," Harrison continued, "the Rangers bought you this horse with their saved up Confederate paper."

Together, Terry's Rangers sounded out, "The finest horse Confederate money could buy."

Matt leaned over to Brenda and said, " . . . you'd have to have been there to understand."

Wharton's watery eyes focused the best they could on the mount and the saddle, which complemented the horse to the hilt.

"A Mexican saddle!" He stared in total surprise. "Where in the hell did you men find a Mexican saddle out here in Georgia?"

The saddle jingled with silver and was decorated with fine embroidery.

Harrison took the reins from the head horseman and held them as he addressed Wharton. "In honor of your services, and on behalf of Terry's Texas Rangers, it gives me great pleasure to present this horse and saddle to you.

"This was planned well ahead of time, John, your being an expert in horseflesh, and saddles. You were an inspiration for all of us not to ride McClellans."

"Thank you, General Harrison," Wharton said as he walked over to Harrison and received the reins.

"John," Harrison cleared his throat and rubbed his hands around the muscles of the fine animal, "I'm proud that the Rangers chose me to present this fine animal and saddle to you."

Wharton took the reins, put his foot into the stirrup and swung up into the saddle. He adjusted himself a bit and became accustomed to its fit. Looking at the men, he wiped his nose with his gauntlet and nudged his prize forward to the center of the field away from the barbeques and the tables. Once clear, he nudged him into an easy gait. After a few moments, he moved his horse into a faster gait and finally into a gallop.

"He rides like the wind," Harrison remarked.

"Rangers!" Matt yelled out. "What the hell are you waiting for? Mount up!"

As fast as lightning, every man who had a horse that day mounted up and galloped out into the field where they followed Wharton, Matt, Steve, and Harrison joined them. On the last lap, the men watched as Wharton prepared to ride towards the tables.

Seeing the peril that Brenda was in, Matt rode to her side, picked her up and carried her to safety. "Let's get you out of the way." He dropped her off away from Harm's Way and rode back into position and waited for Wharton's memorable ride.

Once Wharton saw the danger was over, he rode fast and cleared one of the tables for a final assault on the festivities. He reined up, dismounted and gave his horse back to the head horseman and waited for the rest of the Rangers to come in.

The Rangers without horses lined the tables up in a separate row and quickly moved out of the way for the riders to come in. Given the nod by Matt, the Rangers rode in formation of threes and hurdled the tables with their horses.

Matt and Steve entered as a finale, riding across the field like thunder and cleared the tables to the roar of the crowd. They reined up, dismounted and stood beside their horses.

"Gentlemen," Wharton began his speech. "I am proud of Terry's Texas Rangers. I've had three horses killed under me. I do not intend to have this one killed. But, like Matt said time and time again, I will not spare it to kill the enemy, nor will I spare it when my life is in imminent danger. But, devil be damned, I'm gonna have the greatest time keeping it alive, leading us into more victories."

"I remember what your mother said," Harrison added, "when you were made the Regimental Commander. She said that her son's place was at the front as long as there was need for a man there. And I agree, John. Your place is at the front. Always will be."

"You remember that, do you, Tom? And all this time I thought you weren't paying attention."

One of the ladies yelled out from the sidelines. "Now, if you'll excuse us, gentlemen. We ladies have one more thing to say."

"By all means, ladies," Wharton answered with a smile big as all out doors.

And the lady shouted, "Terry's Texas Rangers. Morrison's Cavalry. Ya'll come on and eat."

The rattle of pots and pans filled the air with excitement as the men gathered around the barbeques and filled their plates with the over abundance of food. While they filled their bellies, Wharton stepped back up to the center with pride.

"You know how proud of you men I am. There's no need telling you that. And you know how proud I am of this fine animal and saddle you've presented to me. I can't express my appreciation enough.

"And I'm proud of all these Tennesseans who came out to share with us. Watching you people do what you did, your support and all, I can only tell you how grateful I am.

"What you've done is Texas style. I mean, you've outdone yourselves. This barbeque. Some Texians must have showed you how we do it in Texas. Of that there's no doubt. But to do all of this, I'll go on record to say I would hate like hell to have to fight you. I said that about Texians and now, by gawd, I'll say it about you Tennesseans."

"What about the Georgians?" one of Morrison's riders asked almost indignantly.

"Hell, you know how I feel about Georgians," Wharton quipped right back, realizing he might be stepping on toes. "When in Rome . . . Well, hell, I was born in Tennessee, same as Davy Crockett. And for my mother to give me birth as a Tennessean, she had to be tough. But I'm a Texian, now, through and through. But you know, having met and got to know you Georgians better, I'd hate to have to fight either of you." He lit a cigar and threw the match to the wind. "But, I'd do it just to show you that I'd win."

He lightened the air as only Wharton could do in that hour, for the moment of elocution was his, and he handled it admirably, occasionally flirting with Brenda with his eyes.

The day wore into evening and the men found themselves with ladies at the dance. Steve stole out into the evening with a fine looking lass and disappeared into the night air.

Matt enjoyed Brenda's company as they danced the last dance together.

"I'm leaving in the morning," Brenda informed Matt, resting her eyes on his. "It'll probably be a long while before we'll see each other again."

Nothing was said for the rest of the dance, but Brenda thought more about the possibility that they may never see each other again. Not if a minnie ball had Matt's name on it. A tear came to her eye.

"You're crying," Matt observed in the sound of her sobs.

"Just sad that this has to be our last dance together."

Matt kept dancing and said nothing. He was at a loss for words.

150

The walk back to her tent was slow, but to them it seemed far too fast. Their hands held together tightly as neither one wanted to let go.

When they reached the tent, their bodies locked together with their arms around each other. He gently bent over and kissed her.

"You said you had plans for us tonight?" she asked looking into his eyes. "Did you mean dancing?"

"That, and other things." He kissed her again gently.

"Mmmm," she murmured through her kissed lips.

"Mmmm," he replied. He pulled open the tent and led her inside, letting the flap close behind them.

The evening air was warm as the couple began to find themselves with each other.

"It's a warm night," Brenda said as she unbuttoned his blouse, pushing her fingers inside to feel his bare skin.

"You smell just like an apple pie," he said softly.

"It'll be in the window with your initials on it."

Matt peeled her dress from her body and let it fall to the ground. His eyes could barely see her in the tent's darkness so he let his hands become his eyes as he planted a kiss on her opened mouth. He played kittenish with her long strands of hair.

The fireflies lit up against the tent and the brushing of the limbs of a nearby tree danced on its canvas while the rhythmic cadence of the pair of lovers quietly played through the night. The hooting of a close-by owl and the scurrying of a jackrabbit across the trail just outside kept the heated sounds of their romantic interlude to themselves alone. And then sleep enraptured their bodies and all thoughts of war were swept away from their minds.

Steve drove them back to the station the next morning where the train was letting out the last of its steam, as it got ready to move out. The great puff of black smoke had not belched from the smoke stack yet.

"I suppose they're waiting for me to get on board," Brenda said sheepishly as she held onto Matt's hand.

He took the bag on board with her and helped her find her seat. Once he made sure that she was comfortable, he leaned down and kissed her again.

"Yep."

"What?" she asked.

"Cinnamon. Gotta be cinnamon on it."

She looked up into his eyes and brought him back for another kiss.

Steve and Matt stood on the platform and waved Brenda off as the train passed them by. It took several minutes for the train to disappear around the bend and into the woods, but the two men stayed and watched it as it did.

"Got a great sister, huh, Matt?"

"Yep."

"Got Ginny out of your system?"

Matt looked at Steve, swallowed hard and said nothing. He climbed into the driver's seat and snapped the lines to take the team home.

For the next several weeks, Matt and Steve worked with Wharton and his men.

Then one day it happened. Matt mapped out a strategy to catch Harrison alone and he took it. Harrison had just left an outhouse and was pulling up his gallowses when Matt yelled out to him from out of range of any other soldier. "Hey, Napoleon!"

"I will be addressed as General Harrison, Major," Harrison returned. "What d'ya want?"

Matt rushed him and dragged him down the hillside. "There's no one around, Tom, just you and me. Steve and I saved your ass on many occasions and you've never once apologized for making us mark time in the freezin' rain."

"You're going to hold a grudge against me for that?" He picked himself up and brushed the dirt from his uniform. He straightened himself up and started to walk away. "I thought we were through with that at Shiloh."

152

"Shiloh! You really made off to be the hero then. Thet was when I was on your turf. You've ventured off your turf, General. You're on mine, now. Here, I'm the General. And, you're about to do mark time."

"What? You're crazy. I'll have you shot."

"Steve," Matt called out. "You ready?"

"Yep."

Steve and Matt grabbed Harrison and pushed him through the bushes to a small clearing on the other side where two other Rangers in hoods were waiting, each with a tub full of warm cow paddies in front of them and a barrel partially filled with dung.

"Take off your boots, General," Matt ordered, pushing Harrison to the ground.

Two other hooded Rangers came around the side of them and assisted Harrison with taking off his boots, and then they acted as lookouts.

"All clear, Captain," one of them said after having run up to the top of the hill to observe.

"All clear around here," the other hooded Ranger said as he looked around the lower grounds in all directions.

The other hooded Rangers stood Harrison up and held him. They then took a hold of his legs and placed him into the barrel.

Matt and Steve emptied the other tubs into the barrel spilling some on his head and clothes.

"Now, General," Matt ordered, "mark time!"

Harrison sputtered and fumed, but the harder he tried to get out of the barrel, the worse it became for him with the cow dung sticking to his legs and crawling up the back side of his pants. He fought to get loose from the iron grip of both men only to slip and slosh the dung into a gooey mess. When he attempted to wipe his face, the dung clung to his lips and nose.

"I trust you brought some clean clothes with you, General," Matt said as he motioned for his compadres to let Harrison alone and leave.

"You sons-of-bitches!" Harrison yelled and toppled over with the barrel, freeing himself. By the time he picked himself up from the ground, the men had disappeared. Soaked and stinking with cow dung, he trooped down to a stream and washed and cleaned himself off the best he could, dumping his uniform down a hole in the outhouse. Still, no matter how hard he tried to get rid of the smell, the stench lasted the whole night. He made it a point to stay hidden inside his tent the entire next day, eating alone.

Harrison never did report the incident to Wharton for fear of how he would have pictured him in his eyes as a man covered with cow manure from his head to his toes. Instead, he accepted the event as a baptism into Matt and Steve's elite circle of Texas Rangers. He put on a clean set of clothes and went about the following day as if nothing happened.

The day finally came for Wharton and Harrison to return to Bragg's Brigade. Sitting in his Mexican silver saddle, Wharton reached down and shook Morrison's hand.

"Thank you, Jim, for your hospitality. Our prayers are with you."

"And ours with you, John. Tom."

"Good-bye, General," Matt addressed Wharton. Steve gave a nod and waved to the other horse soldiers.

Wharton looked at the two, rubbed his nose and winked at the two men, because somehow he had found out what had happened. He then looked over at Harrison. He spurred his new bay and rode off. Harrison followed him without looking back

As the rest of the Rangers followed, a few of them, including O'Riley and Christian, waved a fond farewell to their beloved friends, Major Matt Jorgensen and Captain Steve Andrews. Four hundred and twelve Rangers rode away on Georgian horses that morning back to Tennessee.

One man stayed behind, Chaplain Robert Franklin Bunting. Matt saw him walking away, and ran to catch up with him "Chaplain," Matt whispered as he sided him.

Bunting stopped and faced Matt. "Oh, hello, Matt. I saw you, but you were too busy, so I didn't bother to let you know I was here."

"Why aren't you leaving with them?" Matt asked, starting his walk with the chaplain.

"It seems my need is more important here. So, I chose to stay." He looked at Matt and kept walking. "I've been keeping up with your battles. You're still with us."

"Yep. Sometimes, I still wonder why."

"Do you want to talk some, Matt?"

Matt nodded and the two men paused under a magnolia tree and sat on the grass. "Best place I know of.," Bunting said, laying the Bible beside him. "I usually find a tree to park under when I'm meditating with God."

He watched Matt picking at the grass. "Still wondering why you're alive when other great men are dying?"

"Just thet, I suppose," Matt answered. "Ginny, too."

"Ginny?" Bunting asked, quizzically, realizing that Matt had not mentioned her before.

"My girl, Chaplain. I lost her, too."

"I'm sorry."

"My fault. You see, when I mustered into this War, I wrote her, telling her I would be parading in Richmond with Terry's Texas Rangers."

"And, you didn't."

"No, Sir. We changed courses because of our need for horses. Wound up in Kentucky."

"And Ginny?"

"She rode out from her home in Tennesse to meet me in Richmond." He paused, looked up at the sky and said nothing.

"Where is she now, Matt?"

"Dead, I suppose."

"How?"

Matt groped for words. "A young Blue-belly shot her, thinking she was a Johnny."

"That must have been two years ago."

"About." Matt stood up and grabbed the overlying branch to lean on. "Why her, Chaplain? Why her?"

"You never discussed her. Just Terry, Lubbock and Johnston. I'd like to learn more about her."

Bunting continued to counsel with Matt for the next few hours, as Matt slowly brought Bunting up to date with his hopes that Ginny was still alive.

"I have thet strong feeling, a strange feeling, if you know what I mean, Chaplain," Matt continued, now sitting on the grass, looking down the long road the Rangers rode a few hours before. "She's out there somewhere. I can feel it all the time. It's not just a fantasy with me. It's real. More real, it seems, when I'm in Tennessee." He stopped, realizing then that most of his battles were fought in Tennessee.

"What, Matt? You were saying?" Bunting realized that a moment of truth was about to be revealed.

Matt looked down at the ground, picked around more at the grass, then looked up and out into the sky as if searching for something, or someone.

"She haunts my dreams, Chaplain. She stays with me as if she's a living part of me. I can't explain it any better."

"And she's dead?"

Matt said nothing for a long while. And then, with tight lips, he answered, "Every chance I get, I ride into Tennessee to find her. To find anything I can about her. I – I've not even found a trace. Not a trace."

"I'll ask again, Matt. Is she dead?"

"No!" Matt rose and walked away. Then he stopped and stared out into the distance without saying a word. Finally, he quietly answered, "I suppose."

"Then, we have to settle for that, Matt. She's gone, and you're left with the memories. Those memories are what haunt you."

Matt turned his face and looked into Bunting's eyes. After another brief moment, he said, "Then why? If there's a God, why did He take her from me?"

"The Lord giveth, and the Lord taketh away. Blessed is the name of the Lord."

"The Good Book?" Matt surmised.

"Job had the same question, Matt. He's one of the men in the Bible. In fact, a whole book is written about him and his problems. Makes ours seem insignificant. It seems that God took everything he had away from him, even his ten children and all in a day. Yet, he never complained. Not once. Oh, he could have, I suppose, but he kept God first in his mind. He was faithful, and more than that, he was a patient man."

"He had something to say to God? What would it be?" Matt asked, clinching his fist.

"Well, Matt," Bunting answered, opening the Good Book, "let's find out." After flipping a few pages, he read, *I cry to you, O God, but you do not answer.* "That's where I think you are, Matt."

"Right on the nose."

"There's more." *The churning inside me never stops, days of suffering comfort me.* "You see, Matt. You're punishing yourself for what you think you did to Ginny. Else, you're going to continue living in guilt, and that's what I think is happening with you, right now. Let go, Matt. Let her go."

Matt stood up, looked around and then sternly looked back at Bunting standing next to him.

"I hoped I've helped you, Matt. Have I?"

"Some. But I can tell you the answer is not in thet Book."

Bunting watched Matt walk away. He closed the Bible , turned and walked towards the chapel.

10 September 1863

Steve returned, attempting to keep up with Matt's long stride.

Morrison was standing outside his headquarters, watching the Rangers as they rode away.. "Fine group of men you trained, gentlemen. I'm proud to have you serve under me."

"Well, Sir," Matt interrupted, "we've got a request."

"You'd like to ride with General Wharton and the Rangers again," Morrison surmised.

"What?" Steve shouted with angry eyes focused on Matt.

"Yes, Sir," Matt answered. "We've no more horse soldiers showing up right now, so we could take this lull and fight the Yankees with General Wharton."

"Don't I get to say nothin'?" Steve asked, crushing his hat in his hands.

"Go ahead, friend," Matt told Steve.

Steve looked at Morrison, then back at Matt. He punched his hat back into a blocked position. Then he looked around the camp. "It is kinda deserted around here now without the Rangers."

Morrison smiled and turned his look towards the two men. "In a few days, I'll be moving out with a regiment, too. You've trained them well, and now I'm waiting for some more men to regroup with me. I'd like to send them to you so you can shape them up before we go."

"Where're you headed for, Colonel?" Matt inquired.

"Not too far away. The other side of the Hiawassee. A place called Chickamaugua. We'll be in good hands. Forrest will be there. And Bragg." He turned and walked away.

Steve removed his hat, scratched his head and asked, "Chickamaugua?"

Matt turned towards Steve, smiled and repeated, "Chicamaugua?"

"What's in Chickamaugua?"

"Some place to be, I recken," Matt answered as he untied Skeeter and rode away. Steve mounted his stallion and followed.

Eight days later, Chaplain Bunting met with Matt and Steve as they were preparing for an afternoon ride.

"Wonder what's up," Steve asked as he threw a blanket over his mount. He watched Bunting approach him.

"Got bad news, Matt," Bunting said, haltingly, holding up a wire.

Matt looked at the wire Bunting handed him.

"What's it say?" Steve asked, looking at the saddened Bunting. "Somebody killed?"

"Almost," Matt answered. "First of all, *to let you know, the battle at Chickamaugua. General Wharton . . . . we won.*" Matt flipped the wire with his hand. "How about that! Our John Wharton." He opened the wire again and continued, ". . . *Bragg and . . . Forrest.*" Matt skip-read the wire. Steve interrupted, saying, "Hell, they should 'av won with that team."

"Not necessarily," Matt commented. Forrest was not Bragg's fair-haired boy, and let me tell ya somethin', friend. You remember thet Bragg was not too well liked by Forrest either. Forrest lost a lot of respect for thet general."

"Read on, Matt," Bunting said solemnly with his hands clasped together as if in prayer.

"But I'll say this. Thet's what makes heroes. They might have hated one another, but they fought bravely together."

"Something like Harrison with us?" Steve asked.

"Yeah. Guess so." Matt continued reading. "And *Colonel George G. Dibrell, 8th Tennessee Cavalry.*" Matt paused and looked up. "If my memory serves me right, Dibrell's cavalry unit was not all thet well-trained. Coulda helped him, had he asked." He went back to reading. "Still . . . *Colonel Morrison with Georgia, Tennessee and North Carolina Battalions, and. . . some eighteen-hundred men savagely beaten at Chickamauga.*"

"Colonel Morrison is headed back," Bunting added. "He'll be with his torn and battered."

"What about Forrest?"

"Don't know. Suppose he made it. We'll know more when Morrison returns. Guess I best get ready."

Matt reined up, took in a breath of fresh air deep into his lungs and smiled. "So much for volunteering," Matt said, taking his makings out of his shirt pocket.

"Whatcha doin', friend?" Steve asked, turning his steed around to face Matt. "You're looking like an angry man who witnessed a major defeat."

"Chickamaugua? You're right, ol' buddy," Matt answered, looking westward.

"Had we been there, would it have made a difference?" Steve asked.

"Yep. Probably should have"

December, 1863

As clockwork, Christmas came again to Rome, Georgia that year. Soldiers licked their wounds. Some went back into battle. Some died. Others healed up. Forrest had made it out with a slight scratch when he lost another good horse.

2 May 1864

The leaves of Spring fell upon the Southern soil. The Union Armies were pressing in on Georgia. A tired and wearisome rider came into camp and warned Morrison that Union horse soldiers were heading their way.

Morrison met with his officers and commanded them to meet the enemy.

"Matt," he addressed him from his headquarters, "I don't know how many, or who at this time, but take as many men as you need and stop them. I'll follow behind."

"Alright, men," Matt yelled out at a cavalry company readied to move out, "let's ride!"

Steve immediately followed with his company.

Some hours into their ride, one of the men cried out in a low voice, "Matt! Across the ravine. Wagon tracks."

"I see them." Matt scoured the path further towards a ridge. "Smoke! I'll bet the Blue Bellies burned the bridge. Their loss. They can't run away."

Within minutes, a regiment of Confederate soldiers headed their way from Matt's left flank. A young lady sat the rump of a horse ridden by none other than, General Nathan Bedford Forrest. He reined up and sided Matt.

"Well, hello, son," Forrest addressed a bewildered Matt. "Nice meeting you in the thickets. Ain't seen ya in a coon's age."

"Nathan," Matt returned. "What's happening?" Looking at the young lady, Matt then asked, "And who's the young lady?"

"Oh, Matt, allow me to interduce you to her. Emma, this is Major Matt Jorgensen, a Texas Ranger. Matt, this is Emma." He looked back at Emma. "I forgot your last name."

"Sansom," Emma replied, holding tight to Nathan's belt.

"She sorta came along for the ride. You see, since the bridge was burned, we couldn't cross the river. She found us a cattle ford. Had it not been for her, we'd not be here."

"Those Yankees don't know how to shoot," Emma remarked with a grin. "They filled the air with a lot of noise and didn't hit any of us'n."

The men around them smiled and kept their laughter light.

"Colonel Streight, Matt," Forrest informed him. "Abel D. He's headed towards Rome.

"I count four regiments of infantry, two companies of cavalry, and two mountain howitzers."

A crackle of gunshots opened the air behind them as Steve and his company rode in.

"Now you've done it," Matt exclaimed, smacking his gauntlet against his leg.

"General Forrest, Sir," Steve yelled out.

"Steve. Good to see you, fella," Forrest returned.

"We've lost any element of surprise," Matt said with grit teeth.

"Oh, they knew we were here," Forrest enlightened him. "Even with the noise of all their equipment, they knew we were here."

"Smells around here," Steve added, lifting his hat off his head. "Do my eyes deceive me?"

"Yep," Forrest answered, giving Emma a hand to slide off his mount. "Noisy, too. Aren't they?"

"What are they?" Matt asked.

"Looks like mules," Steve answered. "About a thousand, I recken."

Matt watched Emma walk back into the woods away from the units.

"Close to, I figure," Forrest agreed. "You two, take your companies to the right and left. I'll attack head on."

"Kinda risky, Sir," Matt returned. "Seems to me you'll ride into a hail of bullets."

"Hell, Matt, they'll die of fright. Take another good look. Have you ever seen a more worn-out cavalry unit in your life? They're barely hanging in their saddles. Hell, I've been chasing them around in circles for the past few days 'til they don't know which end is up."

And they didn't. Forrest charged head on with Matt's unit, and Steve's company following, the Federals surrendered quite easily.

"How the hell did you do it?" Streight asked Forrest as he handed over his saber.

"Strategy, Colonel Streight. Pure strategy. I figured you wore yourselves out with all the weight of your heavy equipment, mules and all. Then I figured, all I had to do was to keep you moving, depriving you of sleep and starve you into surrendering. Not much to it."

Colonel Morrison met General Forrest and rode ahead and waited at camp while the *Lightning Mule Brigade* was offered an escort into Rome. When provisions were made for the prisoners, mules and all, the parties began, which lasted for several days and nights.

Morrison proposed a toast as he stood at the end of the table and offered up his best sherry. "To General Nathan Bedford Forrest. The best cavalryman in the Confederate army."

Forrest stood up with his drink held by his belt. "Some would challenge that, seeing how I fight my way, and not by the book. But," raising his glass, he continued, "thank you." Then, looking over at Matt, he added, "And to two fine officers whom I am very proud of. Major Matt Jorgensen and Captain Steve Andrews. Two of the finest cavalry officers in this man's army."

The officers around the table and standing in Morrison's headquarters saluted with the toast and then, as they walked around the table, they threw the glasses into the fireplace.

"And now," Morrison announced, "knowing how you have lost another good horse under you. How many does that make, Nathan?"

"Oh, twenty or so, but who's counting," Forrest returned with laughter.

"Well, regardless of how many, the Romans would like to present you with one of their best steeds in stock."

A horse wrangler walked into the room with a beautiful thoroughbred bay quarter horse with three white socks and a flash across its nose. It was adorned with Forrest's saddle all polished.

"Now, that, gentlemen," Forrest addressed the men, "is what I call a fine animal."

The horse lifted its tail, and all Forrest could add was, "Now get him the hell out of here before he spoils my dinner."

Laughter filled the air while the men spilled their drinks and continued the party that night. Matt and Steve waddled around camp and settled next to an old oak. Their flag rested against its bark where Steve sat. He looked at it and cleared his eyes.

"Do I count right?" Steve asked, counting the stars on the flag with his fingers. "You count them."

"What, friend?"

"There are eleven stars," Steve remarked, looking pie-eyed at Matt.

"Nah. Twelve," Matt returned, tipping up a bottle to finish its contents.

"Eleven," Steve returned.

"Eleven?" Matt echoed.

"We started with twelve.

"Somebody added another star?" Matt surmised.

The two officers quibbled about the flag's missing star until they fell asleep.

Actually, there was no missing star. The confederacy had added Georgia as the thirteenth state earlier and eliminated Kentucky and Missouri as Union States. These made up the eleven stars on the flag that the two officers counted, remembering their twelve original stars. And, the motto on the flag no longer read *We Conquer or Die*, but was changed that year to read *God Defend the Faith.* The flag only saw battle for that one month with the Rangers. She was ripped off its pole by some branches in a later skirmish and fell into the hands of a Yankee soldier. She appeared later with the words in Latin, *Ducit Amor Patria,* meaning the same. But for Matt and Steve, their favorite would always be *We Conquer or Die.*

Early the next morning, Forrest and his regiment left Rome before they could accept the grand barbeque that was to be set up in their honor.

Peace came to Rome once again, and Matt and Steve continued training new recruits and working with veterans who were either recuperated from being wounded and or simply transferred to Rome for *R & R* and more training. Once in a while they would engage in a few skirmishes with Federals closing in on Rome. But for the most part, they spent the remainder of the war with " . . . tighten your girths. Trot! Canter! Charge!"

A wire came to Rome from Major General Wharton. He had one last field battle, that in Louisiana at the Red River campaign. Chaplain Bunting received the wire at headquarters from Colonel Morrison and carried it personally to Matt and Steve.

The two young officers were at the stables readying their mounts for a ride.

"You're headed out for some more training, Matt?" Bunting inquired.

"Nope," Matt answered as he swung himself into the saddle. "Over to see the old man. Got word he received a wire for us."

"I know. He gave this to me to give to you." He handed the wire to Matt.

"What's it about?" Steve asked, watching Matt read it.

"Looks like our services here are just about over, big buddy."

"How's that?"

"Seems that Wharton needs us in Texas. He's been transferred to General John Bankhead Magruder's command in Texas. And we're to go along with him."

"Texas?" Steve yelled out. "Yahoo! We're going to Texas."

"Yep. He's got a celebration for us when we arrive at his home."

"He's expecting us post haste, boys," Bunting added.

"Us?" Matt asked.

"You saw who the wire was addressed to? Major Matt Jorgensen, Captains Robert Bunting and Steve Andrews."

"You, too? I'll be a . . . ."

"Don't say it, Steve," Bunting chided. "I'll have to ask you to help in the chapel."

On the train ride to Texas, Bunting filled in the blanks to Matt and Steve. "Wharton actually wrote President Davis for a transfer to General Magruder's command. He's John Bankhead Magruder, a man with high ambitions. His objective, I may add, includes Wharton. From what I understand, Magruder pulled some strings to get him there.

"And of course, Wharton's counting on us to be with him. Where we're headed is just two days from the wealthiest region of all Texas, somewhere on the Matagorda Peninsula. It appears that some Federal forces are threatening their position, and we're needed. Magruder's biggest argument is that Wharton's expertise is in his own back yard more than on the eastern arena."

"Sounds to me like we've got a job to do." Matt looked at Bunting and smiled. "And Jeff Davis thought Texas wouldn't get into the war."

Bunting continued. "I've heard through the grapevine that Wharton's seriously thinking about running for governor of Texas. I want to be there when that happens. Besides, he has a wife and daughter, boys," Bunting added.

"Well," Matt joined in, "he's got us. Right, friend?" he asked Steve with a smile.

The trio rode on and caught the train to Houston. Unbeknown to the men as they rode through the northern part of

Alabama, Forrest was defeated in Selma by Major General James H. Wilson. He survived and finished out the War.

September - November 1864

When General Ulysses S. Grant became General of all the Union armies, he appointed General Tecumseh Sherman supreme commander of the armies in the West. The red-haired Ohioan, Sherman began his march towards Atlanta. On 1 September 1864, Grant captured Atlanta and marched on Rome. In November, he ordered all the buildings on Broad Street burned except a few along with some churches that were turned into hospitals. The Railroad Depots, Foundry and every thing of value to the enemy in Rome were destroyed. All the way from Rome to Kingston the road was lined with *contrabands* of all ages sizes and sexes

Sherman plunged towards Savannah and sent a wire to President Abraham Lincoln, saying that he was presenting him the city of Savannah as a Christmas gift.

CHAPTER 12

THE FOURTH FALLEN
BRAZORIAN SABER

The ride was over when the three men stepped from the Texas and New Orleans Railroad and were met by General Wharton himself.

"Gentlemen," Wharton addressed them as he stood tall on the platform beside his carriage, "it's been a long time."

Matt looked at the handsome general and without taking his eyes off of him, answered, "Too long, General."

Mrs. Eliza Wharton and her daughter Penelope sat in the carriage. Mrs. Eliza Wharton was an attractive woman, roughly the same age as the General, and was the daughter of David Johnson, the one-time governor of South Carolina. She wore her hair elegantly in a bun with her curls pushed back under her finely laced bonnet. Her dress adorned the front seat of the two-horse carriage, leaving little room for the General as the driver.

"Welcome to Houston, Matt . . . Steve . . . Chaplain Bunting." Wharton said warmly. "This is my wife, Eliza, and our daughter, Penelope. She prefers to be called *Penny*."

Matt doffed his hat, took Eliza's hand and kissed it. "Mrs. Wharton. It is indeed my pleasure."

Steve followed suit but clumsily took Eliza's hand, and without kissing it, said, "Mine, too, Mrs. Wharton."

Penny giggled a little, looked at her daddy and settled down.

Bunting removed his hat in like manner and bowed to the family. "My blessings upon you and your family, General."

"I'll drive, if you show me the way," Matt suggested in a smiling gesture.

"No need, Matt. It's right down the road. You just enjoy Penny's company and I'll be grateful. We've got you rooms at my headquarters at Hempstead," the General informed them as he snapped the lines to the team of horses.

The road led to the estate a short distant from the depot.

"This is called the Liendo Plantation, gentlemen. It's one of Texas' earliest cotton plantations, built by Leonard Waller Groce. He just happened to be one of the largest and most respected landowners in Texas.

When the General and his party arrived in site of the house, Wharton announced, "Not much, but it's my headquarters, and it's attractive. I haven't been home for almost three years, and any house with my family is worth it." He smiled at Eliza and Penny.

Over his shoulder, he noticed the men staring at the slaves who were working the land. "I see you're impressed, gentlemen," he gleamed. "There are over three hundred slaves you're seeing all around you. It's a completely self-contained community with no needs from the outside world whatsoever. And, I may add, this is just typical of what we are fighting for in Texas. The North shall never take this away from us."

"It's a beautiful way of living," Matt sized up as he watched the slaves move as if orchestrated in some fashion with little supervision that he could see. A picture of the McBride Plantation flashed through his mind with him being the foreman over slaves. "I can readily see our importance of being here."

When the carriage came to a halt, some male slaves met the entourage and carried their things into the house. The two-story house had a porch on the main floor and a balcony above it.

It was set back off the main road to a little girl like Penny, every bit of a hundred miles.

"You'll be made comfortable," Wharton assured them as he led them into the main house. Once settled in, the Wharton's met with the three men in the front room. A warm fire in the fireplace took the chill from the early April air.

"I trust your quarters are satisfactory," Eliza queried, watching her House Negro pass by towards her private quarters.

"Yes, Ma'm," Matt returned, as he stood by the fireplace. "Sure nice fire."

And that's the way the evening went right on through supper served by the Negro couple. Of course, Penny had to flirt with Steve as the two toyed with each other to the delight of her parents.

"In the morning, we'll be going into Houston where you'll be introduced to General Magruder."

5 April 1865

On the morrow, Wharton drove the two gentlemen to the Fannin House in Houston. It was evening time when they arrived. General John Bankhead Magruder was having dinner, awaiting their arrival.

After the introductions and at the request of Magruder, the General and his staff sat down and joined in dinner.

"Matt, Steve, and Chaplain Bunting," Magruder began, "The reason why John brought you to Houston is simply this. My force needed a proven officer with the confidence of Texians, and I chose General Wharton. Not by chance, let me tell you. He asked for this transfer, stating that east of the Mississippi had enough well-qualified leaders. And Texas needed a Texian."

"Well, Texas has the best," Matt responded. "Not undermining you in any way. I've heard of your great exploits. But, Steve and I've fought many battles under General Wharton."

"Picked him up when he got injured, and nursed him when he needed us," Steve added.

"And that's another thing I had to contend with. My constituents felt that John was not in the best of health back east and needed to come to Texas to dry out."

"Smart men," Matt acknowledged.

"Did they mention about his being wounded so many times?" Steve asked, forking a potato.

"They know," Wharton answered, looking around the room. "But that was just an excuse to get me here. General Magruder needed that excuse. As you can see, I'm as healthy as an ox."

"Not true." Magruder chimed in, biting the end of a cigar while watching the men finish their meals. "He has a ruptured vessel in his leg, but he tells us, riding is good exercise for it. But, we are not going to coddle him any." Lighting the cigar, he continued. "Our contention is that the Trans-Mississippi Department needed a capable officer. One who could deal with cattle, Texas style. Particularly, red Brahmans. John's expertise and experience is just what we need."

Matt looked at Steve for the longest time, without really seeing him. His mind wandered back to Montana on his father's Double O Ranch, and then he returned. "Smells more like something political, I'm a thinkin', brother Steve."

"How's thet, brother Matt?" Steve came back, not realizing what Matt had in mind.

Magruder looked at Wharton and the two men smiled. "You might have something there, Matt," Magruder suggested, watching the cigar smoke waft to the ceiling. He stared at the men as they pushed back their plates and wiped their mouths as if in unison with Wharton. He took out four cigars and offered them to the men. "Want a cigar, gentlemen?"

Magruder smiled and suggested, "Someone's been talking?"

"Not me, Mac," Wharton answered, lighting the cigar. "Oh, hell. What harm can it do?" He leaned forward and paused for a moment to collect his thoughts. "Harrison kinda planted a thought in my head a few years back."

"Our *Harrison?*" Steve asked with eyes wide open.

"Tom. Yes," Wharton answered.

"What'd he say?" Matt wondered.

"When he talked about all he wanted out of this god-awful war was to become governor of Texas like Lubbock's brother."

"Whoa!" Matt replied with hands out in the open. "What a neat thing."

"Doesn't mean a thing, yet, boys," Magruder stepped in. "By some suggestions, the Tri-Weekly Telegraph ran an article about the three possible contenders for the office, and John's name was among them. Can't say how it got there, but, well, let's just say, it got there. In big print, too."

6 April 1865

The night went on, and the men drank and smoked well into it, as the lanterns dimmed and eyelids fell heavy. But came dawn, each of the men were up and hard at work about their business. Magruder was already headed for breakfast when Matt walked by his table.

"Mornin', General," Matt said, saluting him politely.

"Good morning, Matt," Magruder returned. "Got some time? I'm just having breakfast."

"Well, thank you, Sir," Matt said, sliding his legs over the back of a chair and landing, taking a seat. "Real hungry this mornin' after some good heavy talkin' like last night." He gestered with his hands around a tilted glass.

Steve walked up and joined them, taking another empty chair at the table.

Before Steve got his coffee poured, two officers stopped at their table and acknowledged the General.

"Colonel Baylor, Major Sorell," Magruder addressed them. "I'd like you to meet Major Jorgensen and Captain Andrews."

Baylor was thirty-three years old, six feet two inches tall, sporting a neatly-trimmed moustache and long beard. He seemed to be a fine type of frontier gentleman, coming from a long line of Indian fighters..

Baylor looked sternly at Matt and then held out his hand, blatantly. "Terry's Texas Rangers. Under General Wharton. We fought some battles together."

Matt nodded. "I remember you. George, isn't it? In fact Colonel, I do remember you. Seems to me I heard something about your brother creating a university here in Texas, wasn't it?"

"My name is George Wythe Baylor," Major," he clarified it for him. "My brother, Robert, helped organize an educational society for the Texas Union Baptists out Waco way. We Baylors are proud people." He threw out his chest and stood up straight. "And I recognize you, too as the big man who showed some of the Rangers how to fight."

"Most. We tried. Some stayed alive. "

"You're here because . . .?" Baylor asked, his eyes waiting for a negative answer.

"General Wharton," Matt returned.

"You're his friend?"

"Aren't we all?" Matt asked, taking out a cigar from his shirt pocket.

Baylor nodded to Magruder, and then with his partner, walked away.

"Bad blood, that one," Magruder said, starting in on his newly arrived breakfast as the waiter poured him some coffee. "Nothing like his brother, I don't suppose. His brother also beat out Harrison some years before the War for district judge. Like he hinted, his family is full of fighters."

"Our Harrison. Terry's Rangers?" Matt asked, with a surprised look on his face.

"What's he got agin Wharton?" Matt asked, striking his match on his belt buckle and lighting his cigar.

"There had long been bad blood between the two officers, going back I suppose to even when you two joined the Rangers. Don't think he ever liked Wharton for his fast promotions and such. But John earned them, as you men well know."

"Hell, I know that General. We were there, every step of the way."

Steve sided next to Matt. "Wharton was promoted over everyone else. Including ol' Iron Sides."

Magruder laughed. "I heard about what happened in Georgia."

Matt and Steve looked surprised and then joined in with laughter. "I thought it was a well-kept secret," Matt said, throwing his cigar down and crushing it with his foot.

"Oh, hell, Matt. You know there's no *well-kept secret* in this man's army." He took a swig of his coffee. About Baylor, John and he came to blows at the Red River Campaign where Wharton lost a big battle. Hell, it was.even before the Red River Campaign. But it was because of the Red River Campaign that Baylor became belligerent and accused Wharton of misconduct in leading his men into battle. That was the straw that set them dangerously apart."

"Wharton couldn't do that," Steve piped in. "We know him. He's too good an officer. We've seen him lead in too many battles. He's good."

"I don't think there's any truth in it. But Baylor voiced his resentment of Wharton loud and clear in front of other officers. He said, *Your charge, Mister Wharton, was malice and without thorough planning. You cost me my men.*

"So, why's he still on a rampage?" Matt asked, looking back at Baylor and Sorell walking by the window.

"He's like that," Magruder came back, mopping up his plate with a biscuit. "Had it not been for his family's background, I don't think I'd even like him under my command. But, he came with Wharton's request, like it or not."

"Where's General Wharton, now, Sir?" Matt asked, taking a plate of eggs from Steve as Steve had already put half of them on his plate.

"He's getting ready to go back to Hemstead. Early riser. General Harrison, James Harrison, not Tom. He's with him." He took the pot of coffee and offered some to Matt, who declined. "You two take a leave for the day. When Wharton returns, we'll have some work for you to do."

Matt continued to watch out the window as Baylor and Sorell mounted their horses and rode out towards the railroad depot.

"You say Wharton's going back to Hempstead?" Matt asked Magruder, keeping his eyes affixed on Baylor's unit.

"Should be at the depot right about now, Matt. Why?"

Matt took another swig of coffee, grabbed Steve by the arm and left the table. "Think we need to be riding, Steve. Sorry, General. Thanks for the breakfast."

Steve almost fell over his chair as Matt pulled him. "But, I ain't through."

"Thanks again, General." Matt saluted as he and Steve ran out the door.

They quickly ran across the campus to the livery stable, saddled their horses, and tore out after Baylor and Sorell.

"What's the matter?" Steve asked, holding on to his hat.

"You know how I can instinctively smell trouble? Well, I smell it now, friend. Let's ride."

Colonel Baylor with Major Sorell by his side stopped at the edge of the depot. They walked in to where a carriage was standing. Wharton sat in the back seat of the carriage while Brigadier General James E. Harrison sat in front bringing the team of horses to a halt at the railroad cars.

"Baylor's arrived," Harrison advised Wharton as the two men watched Baylor and Sorell approach them.

"General Wharton!" Baylor called out.

Wharton stood up and acknowledged Baylor. "Colonel Baylor. I thought you were in Hempstead with your command." He removed his gloves and asked, "Why aren't you?"

"Well, you can never have a kind word to say to me, now can you, Wharton."

"General Wharton, Mister. And I'll ask you only once more, why aren't you with your command?"

"My command? You put my junior in charge of them. Made a fool of me right in front of them. Was I to stay under those conditions."

Harrison tied the reins to the carriage and smarted back at Baylor. "You, Mister, will not talk in that manner to your superior. Do you hear me?"

"I hear you, Sir," Baylor returned.

"Then why aren't you in Hempstead?"

"Because, Sir," Baylor continued, "I must discuss the situation with General Wharton about my men deserting."

"Your men deserting?" Wharton asked, laughingly, almost sarcastically. "Why in heaven's name would your men desert?"

"Because of you, dammit!" Baylor snapped back. "You got a lot of my men killed by your stupid order at Red River, and don't think they'll forget it. Or me."

"You're a damn liar!" Wharton charged him. Then he looked at Baylor with a look of remembrance. "You, Mister, retreated. You were ordered to hold on. Banks was losing it." He referred to Union officer, Major General Nathaniel P. Banks in a series of battles fought along the Red River in Louisiana. "If any of your men deserted, it was because of your running away, not my commands."

Baylor stepped up into the carriage with a clinched fist. "No, Sir. You're the damn liar and a demagogue. I want the whole damned army to know of your incompetence as a leader."

The jolting of the carriage as he entered caused the team of horses to move a little further as Baylor swung hard at Wharton. The movement caused his fist to miss its mark.

Matt and Steve reined up at Sorell's position and Steve quickly stayed Sorell's hand as it appeared he was going for his Colt. Matt dismounted and cocked his pistol at Baylor's head.

"Climb back down nice and easy, Mister," Matt commanded.

Wharton composed himself as he watched Matt and Steve take control. "You're under arrest, Colonel Baylor, for insubordination and an assault against your superior officer. Matt, take him to Hempstead."

"You heard him," Matt echoed. He turned into him and pulled him up by his coat collar. "Get on your horse." Matt's mistake was not taking his pistol away from him, for Baylor was one of he best shots in the cavalry. Matt had thought about it, but he felt that the officer would act as a gentleman and that it was not necessary to remove him of his pistol.

Complying with Matt's command, Baylor climbed back into his saddle. "I apologize, General Wharton, for my actions. I realize what I have done and I ask that I place myself under arrest with General Magruder instead, Sir."

"Why?" Wharton asked, putting his gloves back on and stepping outside the carriage.

"Because, I can't face my command in Hempstead if I'm under arrest. I just can't face them."

Wharton looked at tears streaming down Baylor's cheeks and felt that Baylor was feeling remorse for his actions. "Stop your damn crying. You will immediately report to Hempstead and place your self under arrest there." He looked at Sorell and added, "But you, you sorrowful thing of an officer, will report to Hempstead under arrest right now. And you will tell Baylor's command all that went on here." He watched Sorell as he sat his horse, watching Baylor cry. "Understand me?"

"Yes, Sir," Sorell answered. He saluted the superior officers. "By your leave, Sir." After receiving Wharton's salute, he turned his horse and rode towards Hempstead.

"I'll see you there, Major," Wharton promised him.

Matt remounted, saluted Wharton, and with Steve, followed Baylor for a short distance and then rode ahead of him to the Hening House. They rejoined Magruder at the Hening House and explained to him about Baylor.

Baylor showed up afterwards and placed himself under arrest.

"Needless to say, George," Magruder started in without rising from his table. "You have been a disappointment to me for quite awhile, although I overlooked it. But now. Now, George, I'm simply ashamed of you."

Baylor's face was reddened from crying so hard. His chest muscles ached from his panted breaths. "I'm – I'm sorry, Sir."

"Sorry won't cut it with me. You know that." He looked at the sulking officer standing before him, poured his cup of coffee on the floor in disgust and said, "Get upstairs. My room is at the top. Use it and clean yourself up. I'll deal with you later."

He watched the pitiful man walk away, unescorted, and then said, "Sit down, gentlemen. Pour me another cup of coffee, Matt, and tell me all about it."

"Don't we get anything but coffee?" Steve asked, eyeing the empty plates left on the table.

"The cook in the back room will fix you up something," Magruder informed Steve. "Tell him I told you."

Matt sat and enjoyed his coffee. But before his second cup, Magruder excused himself and went out back. While he was gone, Matt saw Wharton and Harrison drive up in a carriage. "Excuse me, Steve, but I think we're going to be needed."

Matt greeted the two officers at the front door away from the dining room.

"If you're looking for Baylor, he's upstairs in Magruder's room," Matt informed Wharton. "Mac told him to compose himself. He wants to talk with him afterwards."

"I want to talk with Magruder. Go with me, Matt," Wharton requested, pushing Matt in front of him for him to follow. "I don't want this to get out of hand. I need to talk with Magruder."

"I understand, Sir," Matt replied. "I suppose an incident like this could do a lot of harm to your political career."

If anyone could straighten it out, Matt knew it would be General Magruder. He clumsily climbed the stairs with the two Generals.

From behind the closed door, the three officers could hear the sobs of a beaten man. Matt knocked on the door, and Wharton opened it, hoping to find Magruder. Instead, he saw Baylor sitting on his bed with his head in his hands.

"Where's Magruder?" Wharton asked.

"Probably relieving himself," Matt answered. "I'll go get him."

Wharton looked at Baylor and said sarcastically, "You are the sorriest looking thing I've ever seen. You're not fit to be called an officer. You couldn't have made a call for your men to charge because you never had the guts to watch them get slaughtered."

Matt stopped by the door and watched Wharton, hoping he would restrain himself.

Harrison took a hold of Wharton's arm and pulled him gently to a side. "Calm down, Wharton. He's not worth your words. Matt, go find Magruder."

Baylor looked up into Wharton's angry eyes and cried the louder.

Wharton stared sternly into his face. "Do you hear me, Baylor. You are nothing but a yellow-livered coward who doesn't deserve to be an officer."

He turned and walked away. Matt sensed that the fight had ended and went to open the door for Wharton. Instead, Wharton turned, and with clinched fists, went back and confronted Baylor.

Feeling that Wharton was going to do something that he would regret, Harrison stepped between the two men. "Wharton, he's not worth it. Leave a dead horse lie, dammit."

Baylor pulled his Colt and cocked it, but Harrison grabbed his hand and stopped him from pulling the trigger.

Matt, hearing from down the hall what was happening, quickly returned and went to Wharton's side. Before he could reach him, Baylor had pulled his hand loose from Harrison's grip, pulled the Colt up and into Wharton's left side. Without any hesitation, he discharged his revolver.

The bullet penetrated his heart. Wharton died instantly. Harrison cradled his lifeless body in his arms as the blood seeped from his side.

Matt's rugged left fist found its target in Baylor's face, sending him wheeling across the room and smashing into the wood beams supporting the ceiling. Before Baylor could fall, Matt's right fist sent him over his bed, causing him to hit the floor hard with his face.

Steve ran through the door and stopped Matt from going any further. "No need, Matt. He's out cold."

Matt gasped, bit hard on his lip, causing it to bleed. He broke Steve's grip, picked Baylor up and slammed his body into the bulkhead, bringing his backhand across his bloody face, and then again and again until Steve stopped him. Matt finally let go of Baylor, letting him slink to the floor.

General Magruder had followed Steve into the room, and seeing Wharton on the floor, knelt at his side. Holding onto his hand, he placed the other on Harrison's shoulder. "How the hell did this happen, Jim?"

"God only knows, Mac. God only knows."

Matt walked over to Magruder, knelt down and bowed his head. "The greatest of all leaders. Gone to his Maker."

At Magruder's insistence, Matt commanded three soldiers who had been at the scene to arrest Baylor.

"He's to be charged him with murder," General Harrison added and then, joining Magruder and Matt, knelt down at Wharton's side. "Get that murderer out of my sight before I kill him."

CHAPTER 13

A MONUMENT ERECTED FOR
THE FOUR BRAZORIAN SABERS

9 April 1865

The sun hid behind the clouds that morning and waited for the coffin to be lowered into the ground before the clouds let their tears fall upon the funeral. General John Wharton was buried with full military honors in Hempstead. As before, Captain Bunting gave the eulogy for the General, the fourth Southern Civil War leader from Brazoria County, Texas to meet his Maker. And as before, Bunting removed the Confederate flag, folded it, and along with Wharton's saber, placed them among his personal belongings in his room in Houston.

A few days later, General Magruder summoned Chaplain Bunting to his office.

"Yes, Sir?" Bunting greeted the General as he came to attention at Magruder's desk.

Magruder stood up and returned Bunting's salute. Walking around the desk, he sat on its edge and looked somberly into Bunting's eyes. "We've got to make a visit. Sit down."

"Yes, sir?" Bunting answered and took a chair in front of Magruder.

Magruder took a file from his desk and opened it. "Colonel George Wythe Baylor. Good record. Not a trouble maker. No where in here does it spell out anything like that."

"Where are we going, General?" Bunting interrupted.

"To welcome his uncle, Robert. I understand he's arriving to attend his nephew's trial. He's a district judge and we need to talk with him."

"I think that would be proper, Sir. Got anything else in his file that would help me in talking with him?"

Magruder handed the file to Bunting and returned to his seat behind his desk. "Take it with you. Read it. And then get back to me within the hour."

"Yes, Sir," Bunting said, rising and saluting the General.

Running down the steps outside the building, he ran into Matt and Steve. "Hold up, guys!"

"We were jest sauntering over for some chow," Matt informed him. "Watcha got?"

"File on Baylor."

"Don't wanna see it,"Matt returned.

"I think you'll need to, Matt. His uncle, Robert, should be here sometime today. The General wants to make him feel comfortable while on the post."

"Whew!" Steve came back. "I thought for a moment you wanted us to go with you."

"Exactly."

"He said *you*, Chaplain," Matt reminded him. He would always call him *Chaplain* when he wanted to get his goat.

"And since you two are close to this situation, I figure you'd want to side with us." He looked into their eyes as they tried to turn away from him. "Right?"

"Oh, awright," Matt replied and stepped in pace with Bunting as they headed for his office.

"We have ta?" Steve asked, siding the two men. "Huh?"

"Yep," Matt returned.

With a tin cup of coffee in his hand, Matt made himself comfortable in Bunting's office.

Matt looked back at Bunting. "Baylor's going to be tried for murder. Sad thet it happened. Real sad."

"That's why we've got to talk with his uncle," Bunting responded.

"You're suggesting that Baylor was a pretty good soldier?" He wrestled with a match in his mouth, sliding it to the side in his mouth when he took a sip of coffee. "Well, to tell you the truth, I can't say I remember seein' him mixed up in anythin'. You, Steve?"

"He commanded a regiment of cavalry during the Red River campaign.

"Well," Matt continued, "it seemed to me thet he was one thet never wanted to follow Wharton's tactics much."

"Matt," Bunting addressed him softly, "he broke. I've seen it happen to too many good men. Cried a lot. Crying is a relief of months and months of constant battles, and some times, like in Baylor's case, years of intense stress brought on by being a leader."

"I can relate to that," Matt answered. A lull fell over their conversation for a moment while they continued to walk. Then Matt asked, "What do you think will happen to him?"

"Depends."

"On what?" Steve interrupted. "He killed a man. General Wharton."

"Oh, no doubt about his being guilty as sin on that account, Steve. But, he had a good war record. The circumstances, his mental and physical health all play an important part in the court deciding whether or not he should be tried as a killer. And then . . ." He paused for a moment, laid his luggage down and looked out onto the campus at Hempstead, and then over to where Wharton was laid to rest. A light drizzle still fell upon the green that day.

"What?" Matt asked.

"This War, Matt. It's over. We saw it coming. That's why Wharton called us here. He knew it was just a matter of a time. He had ridden out the war, become a hero, and was now being considered for a political position."

"And the last bullet killed a great man," Matt interjected. "Hell, he was destined to be great. Just think, had General Wharton kept on going to Hempstead, and not bothered going back to take the matter of Baylor up with Magruder, that last bullet never would have been directed at him."

Bunting watched Matt's eyes light up. "I think you're beginning to see that every man has a mission in life, Matt. Mine, I believe, is to keep these moments in history alive. You, on the other hand, Matt, have a deep mission to make history."

Matt looked around and then back at Bunting. "Me? Nah, Chaplain. You've got it wrong there. Yeah! You're here to keep the history alive for generations to come. No doubt about that with all them notes you keep taking. But, me. I don't make history. Those who died made history. I just pick up the pieces and keep on going."

Bunting mused in his mind what Matt had said, and smiled. "You taught Terry's Rangers well. Terry would have been proud of you, as he foresaw your potential from the beginning, as I see it. You trained the men to meet their highest potential as horse soldiers. They became the *fierce devils* Someone had to do."

Matt saw the pride in Bunting's eyes, turned and walked away; a little taller.

Matt and Steve waited for Judge Robert Baylor to step down from the train. When the steam from the locomotive cleared, they saw a well-dressed man step off.

"Judge Baylor?" Matt asked, walking up to the man in his seventies, tall in stature and relatively good looking, sporting a full-length beard.

The meeting with Magruder and Bunting proved to be beneficial for the judge, for the outcome was, George Baylor was released in his custody. The two men took the next train to Waco.

Matt and Steve stopped by the Chaplain's office where Bunting was packed and waiting for them.

"Gentlemen," Bunting addressed them, clasping his arms behind him, "we have come a long way to be going back so soon. Are you ready?"

"Ready, Chaplain," Matt answered, lifting his luggage as a sign of readiness.

Bunting showed Steve his baggage containing the four sabers of the fallen heroes and the flags that had draped their coffins.

Steve pointed to Bunting's luggage and said, "You,ve got four sabers in your bag there. What cha aimin' to do with 'em?"

"The sabers?" Bunting repeated. "Like I said, I want to make a tribute of some kind for our leaders."

"A memorial, right?" Matt asked.

"That's my intention."

"Well, I want to see it happen," Matt replied and walked out the door and down the walk of the campus.

"Yes, Sir," Steve replied, and picked up his luggage, and with Bunting, followed Matt.

.

Matt looked over at Chaplain Bunting and asked, "President Davis?"

"We don't know anything, Matt."

Matt stopped on the green, turned to his two companions and said, "Terry promised something to President Davis."

"What's thet?" Steve asked, again putting the luggage down. He removed his hat and looked out across the campus into the sun, showing his yellowed teeth as if to smile at Mother Nature.

"To march in front of President Davis with his Rangers."

"He did say thet, alright," Steve agreed.

"Well. We're goin' to do somethin' like thet, gentlemen. You with us, Chaplain?"

"I hear you loud and clear, Matt, and I'm all for it. Wouldn't miss it for the world." Bunting did not exactly know what Matt had up his sleeve, but he knew it would add to his vast pile of notes he kept of the war.

Matt rubbed his chin and said, "It's a cinch we can't parade in front of Jeff Davis like Terry wanted us to." Matt kept the pace going. "But we can parade in front of Magruder."

Bunting pondered on what Matt had said, and then spoke. "I like the idea. He smiled, watched Steve grin and then said, "And I want to erect a memorial for our four fallen Brazorian Sabers."

He sat his bag down and pointing to it, said, "I have four sabers in this bag. I'm going to request that a monument with these sabers be erected here in Houston as a memorial for our four heroes. I'm headed for Magruder's headquarters now. Want to join me?"

"Well," Matt came back excitedly, "Why can't we do both?"

"It's worth a try," Bunting agreed. "But let's do one thing first. That's the military way. Then, we'll have Magruder agree on having Terry's Rangers ride in front of him. I don't think he'd mind."

"I know he'd go for it. And if we get the General's approval," Matt continued, "I'll have Terry's Texas Rangers readied for the event in no time." Matt stood tall, grinned and nodded his head.

The three men turned and continued their walk across the campus towards General Magruder's headquarters. The General was standing outside when he saw them approach him. He lit his cigar, and waited for the men to near him.

When he heard of the plan to erect the memorial, and saw the sabers, he was speechless for a moment. Then he said, "Damnation! It's a good idea. Sorry for the language, Chaplain. But . . . you have my permission. Now that Governor Murrah is out of my hair, we might get it pushed through immediately. Pendleton and I never saw things eye to eye, so to speak. He was always quarreling with us over the conscription of troops. God knows we needed them. Finally, once he heard that the Union

Army was about to move into Texas, he vacated the seat and turned it over to Lieutenant Fletcher Stockdale." He looked at Matt, and then at Steve and finally at Bunting. He humphed and said, "I think we might have a chance. Where do you suggest we erect it?"

Without any hesitation, Chaplain Bunting answered with a smile, "Houston. That's where Colonels Terry and Lubbock are buried. Think of it, Matt," Bunting went on, using four fingers to make his point, "Each man is from Brazoria County. The cemetery in Houston holds great memories for our Texians who fought in this War. Let's lift up our leaders here where their spirits will always remain free."

"But what about Wharton?" Matt asked, pointing towards his burial site there in Hempstead. "He's here."

"And General Johnston is laid to rest in New Orleans," Bunting reminded him. "I highly suggest Houston because that's where the first Rangers are buried. And, after all, it's where Texas started."

Magruder agreed. "I can go along with that."

Matt looked at Magruder, turned and smiled at Bunting. "Houston sounds like a good resting place." He turned to Steve and added, "Don't plan on me being here, though."

"Get the masons on it right away. I'll issue you an order. Got any ideas of how it should look, Chaplain?"

"Some," he said out of the side of his mouth, for he had laid out drawings for the three sabers before Wharton's, and now all he had to do was add his. "Kind of like this," and he took a piece of paper from his jacket pocket and made a drawing for Magruder..

The masons had the stone memorial made in quick order and loaded onto a buggy ready to take to the main cemetery in Houston. Constant drizzle only marred the trip as Terry's Texas Rangers rode behind the wagon. Lieutenant Governor Fletcher Stockdale joined General Magruder and his adjutant as they led the procession. Matt, Steve and Chaplain Bunting rode in the second carriage.

By the time they reached the place for erecting the monument, the sun cleared the clouds and sent the drizzle on its way as if to say *God is in His Heaven and all was at peace with the world.*

The monument was covered with a purple cloth, but the four Confederate flags were raised and flew beside it. Two cavalrymen from Terry's Texas Rangers sat their steeds at the ends of the monument, facing the podium.

Lieutenant Governor Stockdale was the first to speak. He spoke eloquently, slowly reading from his notes. He afterwards introduced General Magruder and then sat down.

Magruder took his turn at the podium, thanked Lieutenant Governor Stockdale and then addressed the crowd of soldiers and civilians alike.

He began. "General John Austin Wharton was my friend. He was your friend. But more than that, he was our savior. Well, one of them, for today we are honoring four saviors.

"For the past four years, General Wharton showed constant valor and courage in his duty, ranking him one of the greatest heroes of this blood-awful War. We laid him at rest in Hempstead. Colonels Benjamin Franklin Terry and Tom Saltus Lubbock are laid in their resting places here.

"I did not know Colonel Terry, or Colonel Lubbock. I knew of them and of their vigor in wanting to protect the South and her heritage. I can only bestow praise for their splendid valor, courage and honor to this cause.

About General Albert Sidney Johnston. He was a friend. More than that, he was one of the bravest soldiers who ever fought in any war. For my money, he could have been our next president."

The audience was silent up until that moment when a slight clap of a few hands grew into a thunderous applause. They had heard many times about Johnston's leadership at Shiloh and other places.

Magruder kept talking above the applause. "No words can fully describe the love, honor and respect we want to show these four great heroes today. Each one of them accomplished the goal they had set out to achieve. Of this, I am certain."

He waited for the applause to settle down and for the people to sit back down before he continued.

"I'd like to turn the rest of this service over to the man who has made this moment of grandeur possible, Regimental Chaplain Robert Franklin Bunting, and our de facto war correspondent, if I may add. He has kept a log of what has been happening in this God-awful War, that if you read any of it, you'd understand more clearly why we are erecting this monument to these four men today. Ladies and gentlemen, Chaplain Bunting."

Bunting, who had been sitting on the side with Matt and Steve, rose and walked stiffly to the podium, shook Stockdale's hand, then Magruder's and waited for the two men to be seated along with Magruder's adjutant. Matt and Steve watched from behind the podium but at the opposite end of the platform than that of the three men of distinction.

"Thank you, General Magruder."

Bunting began with the usual remarks and thanks and then looked over the audience as if waiting for an inspiration as to what words to say.

"It is true that I have kept volumes of records about this War. General Magruder called it what it is . . . *God-awful*. But except for these four men, it could have been worse. And it probably would have been. I knew each of them, as did Major Matthew Jorgensen and Captain Steve Andrews, sitting here with me on the platform.

"Colonels Benjamin Franklin Terry and Thomas Saltus Lubbock formed what became the famous, or infamous by some, Terry's Texas Rangers. Both men died in the first engagement.

"General Albert Sidney Johnston refused to die. It wasn't in his nature to die. But, die he did at Shiloh. I could describe in detail how each of these men died, but rest assured, it would not be necessary to give you this pain.

"General John Austin Wharton. Like General Magruder said about General Johnston, the same could be said about General Wharton on a local scale. If he were standing next to me right now, you would be looking at your next governor." He turned and smiled at Stockdale, winning his approval. "I assure you. He was that good of a man. The sad thing was, we buried him just a few days ago in another cemetery. In Hempstead."

He continued his speech for the next thirty minutes, taking time only to swallow sips of water and to occasionally wipe a tear from his eye, which he tried to hide.

Then he concluded, saying, "I removed each man's saber, along with the flag that draped his coffin, in order that I may present it as a memorial to that person. I did not know that it would be for four men. Only God knew that.

"I am honored to have done so, because had I not had the brass with which to do so . . . "He allowed the audience to join in laughter. And then he continued. "Had I not taken the sabers, they would have been lost forever. I saw much more in this gain. I saw Colonel Terry's saber as a symbol of freedom for the State of Texas. I next saw Colonel Lubbock's saber as the courage of the State of Texas."

The audience responded loudly with clapping and a few *amens*.

"With General Johnston's saber, it goes further than that. I see the unification of this great land of ours. And by General Wharton's saber, I see the growth and strength of our great state.

"I stand in front of you, ladies and gentlemen, not as an eloquent spokesman, but as a proud man, and yet as a humble man, who has had the opportunity to have witnessed the works and deaths of all of these great men. I ask not that you accept this monument as a stone to remember these men by, but that you accept their sabers inside this stone as the means by which our freedom has been accomplished.

"We know not what the future holds for Texas or for the South. We know not what side will eventually win, although the wind seems to be blowing from the North." With that, he received some laughter, and some snickers, and some boos. "God holds these certainties in His almighty hand.

"I ask only that you remember Texas and the South through the lives, the victories and the deaths of our leaders.

"People of Texas – Texians – together with people of our Confederacy, I give you the Sabers of Colonel Benjamin Franklin

190

Terry, Colonel Thomas Saltus Lubbock, General Albert Sidney Johnston, and General John Austin Wharton."

He next asked the audience to stand, and they proudly obeyed. The officers and soldiers gave their salute. The two cavalrymen, still sitting in their saddles, removed the purple cloth and revealed the monument. There was a breathless moment throughout the audience.

"Man, that is what I call a monument," Steve whispered over to Matt.

It had Terry's saber fully encased at a slant with the other three sabers plunged downward in a parallel fashion with each other. The handles were exposed just above the point in the saber that was left unsharpened. Each sported a gold-plated steel braid. The plaque read:

The Brazorian Sabers

Colonel Benjamin Franklin Terry
Colonel Thomas Saltus Lubbock
General Albert Sidney Johnston
General John Austin Wharton

May the South forever stand because of these heroes

Remember the Alamo
Also Remember the Brazorian Sabers

14 April 1885

Chaplain Bunting, having had the foresight to make certain that the widows of the fallen heroes would be there, presented the flag that had lain with the sabers to each of them.

The sun slid behind her clouds and the rains put a benediction to a perfect memorial service as the horses and carriages carried the people homeward. A streak of sunlight broke through the clouds for a moment and glistened across the handles on the sabers to shine brighter than ever, and then it disappeared.

The covered carriage that carried the four officers from the ceremony became lost among the others as they disappeared on the road that was decorated with crosses and stone heads. The rain continued.

Word by wire reached Hempstead that the War was over.

Seeing General Magruder heading for the Hening House for his breakfast, Matt walked over to him.

"Hell," Matt said, "we knew thet after we laid General Wharton to rest, Sir."

"Yes, Matt. But President Davis is still nowhere to be found. He was last heard leaving Danville, Virginia's capital.

"Sir," Matt said, turning swiftly in to Magruder's path as the two walked together. "I have a request."

"Another one? Make it, son."

"Terry's hope was to some day have his cavalry unit parade in front of President Davis."

"And . . .?"

"I know it's too far away, but the War is over. Well . . ."

"You and Bunting are two of a kind. You want another ceremony?"

"Right here at Hempstead. We've a hundred or so Rangers with us. And you." He rubbed his chin as if to look for words. "Let's dress up, and ride in front of you and the rest of the officers as a tribute to President Davis, Sir."

"Do it in honor of our President? What am I, Matt, a soft touch?"

Steve caught up with the two officers as he munched on a biscuit. "What's up?"

"Sir, it sounds ridiculous, but let me tell you something," Matt continued as he kept pace with Magruder's fast steps. "Our men have put on celebrations across the South. Let them put on a final demonstration in front of you and your company."

"You're really into this, aren't you, Matt?"

"The War's over, Sir. One last hurrah!"

"I'm for thet," Steve added.

The three men stopped and looked out onto the campus, the buildings, and out into the fields where the slaves were standing about.

A long moment of silence almost gave Matt a feeling of defeat. Then, he saw a big smile come across Magruder's face.

Hitting his leg with his glove, Magruder commanded with most enthusiasm. "Do it!"

Matt knew it might have been with a little egotism and pride that this parade was directed at Magruder, but regardless, he accepted his command, and in his heart said, *Thank you, God.*

The three men smiled, and Magruder asked, "Now, may I go to breakfast?"

The time came three days later when over one hundred of Terry's Texas Rangers, adorned with polished boots, and clean clothes, rode in groups of ten men with a non-com riding at their side.

Matt rode point while Steve rode behind as second. Four horse soldiers on foot each led a rider-less horse with boots in the stirrups pointed backwards, representing the officers who died.

The ladies came out to watch them. The men saluted with drinks in their hands. General Magruder and his command sat in the shade and watched the splendor.

When the parade was over, the men formed two sides to prepare for a re-enactment of a battle like they performed as the first Wild West Show east of the Mississippi. The show began with loud blasts from the canons behind them, and shots ringing in the air. They charged each other with a rebel yell.

Afterwards, to the thrill of the audience, and specially to the ladies, special picked horse soldiers rode out into the arena and picked up coins tossed by the ladies. And, again, McTavish, Troy, Doc and a few well-trained horse soldiers rode out and plucked the coins from the bosoms of some of the ladies lying in the middle of the campus. To the astonishment of other ladies, and some men, no one was hurt, and all took it in with laughter and applause.

The finale came when the cavalrymen joined up and rode in splendor and style in front of General Magruder and his officers.

Matt and Steve rode up to Magruder. Doffiing his hat at Mrs. Magruder, Matt said politely, "Ma'am. We certainly hope that you and your husband enjoyed our little demonstration." The two officers saluted Magruder, and Matt said, "Sir, we salute you. We salute the Confederacy. And, we salute President Jefferson Davis."

After Magruder's returned salute, they turned their steeds and rode back to join the rest, giving their rebel yell. They dismissed the horse soldiers, and all rode off to join their ladies and drink the rest of the day away.

EPILOGUE

Easter week, 1865

Matt found a rock under a tree, sat down, tipped his hat back, took a pencil from his shirt pocket and a piece of scorched scratch paper he had found and looked out into the distance as if to find words good enough to write Ginny another letter. His style of writing was without punctuation marks because he wrote randomly as he would talk to her had she been there.

Dear Ginny.

My guts tell me you're out there, Honey. I feel your free spirit with me every time a breeze blows . . . or a tree whistles . . . or a brook sings her melodic song as she rushes over a bed of large boulders.

Well, it's over, Gin. It's over. Been one hell of a war. I'm glad it's all over. I owe my life to my Creator for keeping me safe. So many times I saw a saber lunge towards me and miss. At times I felt a musket ball whisk by me. Oh, I've some scars, not many, just enough to show my red badge of courage.

195

*Some others weren't so lucky.   From Brazoria County,
Texas.   You probably don't know where that's at . . . South of
here, Honey.   Colonels Benjamin Franklin Terry and John
Lubbock had a dream.   It's hard to believe they're gone . . . way
before the War had fatally plunged its fangs into the nation.   And
they carved their victories with their sabers.   The Brazorian sabers
– Terry's Texas Rangers.   And . . . so many . . . so many perished
by the sword with them.*

*My friend, Steve . . . Andrews . . . and Bob Bunting, our
chaplain. Both played a big part in it, too.   We're proud . . . loyal
to our commanders, and to the South.   Bob got a call to the First
Presbyterian Church in Nashville.   Left this morning.   It's funny.
He never mentioned being Presbyterian.   I guess I kinda thought
all chaplains were Baptists.*

*Now you know I'm not the religious type.   I live and let live.
Thet's my motto.   But Chaplain Bob never once preached to me.
Oh, he talked to me a lot, but thet's because we're friends.   Gonna
miss him.*

*You know, someone told me that we had lost more than a
half million men, women and boys in this damn war.   And you
know the worst part . . . I'm thinking that most of them died from
diseases.   I saw them, Gin.   And them I didn't see who went to
prison, I heard lots of them died there . . . both sides.*

*Can you imagine?   The North had twice as many men as us
Rebs, so stands to reason, I recken, they must have had twice as
many killed.   It's hard to realize that more than a whole state went
to meet Jesus.   Hard to believe.   God help us all if our nation, or
any nation, rises up against itself again.   And for what?*

*Honey, you and Jim and I talked for many hours about the
grandeur of this country of ours . . . its resources, its wealth, its
people . . . so much God offers us . . . gives us . . . and I suppose we
destroyed most of it.   For what?   So that there would be no more
slaves?   I hardly think so, for I can imagine negroes still working
on plantations.   I recken they'd be fools to leave a good home,
work, and food and clothes for their families.   Yet, as I write this
letter, I see miles of slaves moving North to work in factories.*

A rider-less horse rode by Matt at break-neck speed,

breaking his train of thought. The sound echoed through Matt's mind as he watched the sight of the horse grow smaller as it ran across a meadow.

Freedom! Freedom, dear Ginny. As free as that Appy that ran past me just now. She doesn't know where she's going, only that she's free. Free, dear Ginny. Free. She musta had a master who cared for her, fed her barley and oats, brushed her down, combed her mane and dressed up her tail. She had no cares in the world, 'cept for her master's weight and a bit in her mouth when he wanted to go for a ride.

She's free from being ridden . . . and I suppose I'd break and run across the meadow to be free like her. But where the hell would I go? Where would she wind up? Just as soon as someone sees her, she'll be captured and ridden again. But, she'll be fed and cared for once more . . . by another master. Would a foreman in a plant become the slave's new master and work him to death for crumbs?

Finishing up on a piece of burnt chicken, Steve walked up behind Matt and broke the silence of the moment. "Thinking, Pal?" He looked at Matt as he intensively surveyed the trail of the rider-less horse. "Writing Ginny another love letter?"

Matt turned towards Steve and answered softly, "Yep. Like I said, she's with me wherever I go. I can feel her spirit as sure as you're standing here with me, now. I know she's alive . . . somewhere. And one day, I'm gonna find her."

"We'll find her, Friend. Together, we'll find her."

Gulping down his last bite, Steve threw the chicken bones in the dying embers of the campfire. "Where to, Pal?"

Matt broke, stood up, took his letter in hand and threw it to the wind. He walked over to Skeeter who was saddled and ready to ride. "Back to the McBride Plantation."

"Again? You've scoured the place already. What do ya expect to find?" He swung his body onto his horse, watched the letter sail on the wind, and sidled Matt.

"Something, Steve," Matt nodded. "I feel Ginny's leading me there."

"Wull, Friend," Steve gestured, pulling the brim of his hat down, "it's on to McBride's." Then he smiled at Matt and added, "Don't mind if we stop off at Brenda's on the way, do ya?"

Matt returned the smile and nodded. "I look forward to a hot apple pie any day, friend."

The two men rode together as one, their youth hard-beaten by the Civil War that had lasted over a hundred years, but neither man was bitter; just glad that it was over and that they were on their way home. Home, an ethereal place far back in the recesses of their minds where a female friend and sister watched anxiously on the porch of a small farm while the wind danced fancifully around her, kicking up dust along the dry road that stretched for miles into the horizon.

The easy gait through part of Texas was peaceful and uneventful, and both men enjoyed it after the many battles they had fought together.

The aroma of an apple pie sweetened the crisp morning air as it wafted gently in the breeze. A letter dangled from her hands, as she held tight to her calico apron. In the note, the words simply read, "I'm bringing him home, sis. The war's over." When Brenda Andrews read the letter from her brother, Steve, her heart raced for time, for she took it to mean that Matt Jorgensen could be coming with him.

Matt and Brenda's brother stopped off in Nacogdoches to unwind from the war, then onward to Brenda. It was Easter week, 1865. The dew was lifting off the leaf-trodden road that morning that led up to Brenda's house. The sun split her rays between the cottonwoods and streaked across the rolling hillside, cutting through the curtains hanging in the kitchen window. Brenda watched through the kitchen window as the riders got closer.

When they reached the ridge of Steve's farm, a small unpretentious piece of land, Steve pointed excitedly towards the house centered on it.

As the riders' shadows appeared through the dawning light, Brenda recognized the shadowy features and she knew right away that the two men in her life were finally home. The men rode wearily with their heads down as if the ride had been long and tedious. One raised his head and smiled. It was Steve, Brenda's brother.

Quickly, she ran back to her house, whisked through the door and into her bedroom where she dressed and primped herself up to meet her guests.

Steve rode on to the house and called out, "Brenda!"

Matt sauntered his horse up to the house and dismounted.

Bucky went into a fast spin and began barking and yelping, and ran towards a familiar voice.

"Brenda!" Steve called out again.

Brenda walked slowly to the front room and waited breathlessly in the middle of the room as she saw the front door open and Steve bounce in.

She ran to his arms, hugged him and looked into his smiling face. "Oh, Steve!" she exclaimed, repeatedly with tears in her eyes. Then she broke from his grip and looked behind him to see if Matt was there.

"He's outside? She asked as she pushed past Steve and rushed out the door to the porch.

Sitting on the swing, digging into the apple pie with his fingers was Matt. He looked up at her and smiled with applesauce all over his lips.

"I see you made two."

He stood up and received a warm hug of appreciation, not like that of a sweetheart. He looked into her puzzling eyes, smiled and kissed her cheek. "Got a fork?" he asked with a smile.

In the meantime, Steve's eyes had caught the site of a baby crib in the front room. His eyes widened for he had not heard about Brenda having a baby. He took his hat and threw it in the corner and then walked over to the crib and touched it.

Matt and Brenda entered the room with their arms around each other, but stopped short at the site of the crib. Matt's arm dropped from around Brenda.

"A crib?" was all Matt could ask as he stood stunned. "Whose?" He thought for the moment about when Brenda had visited him in Rome, Georgia.

Brenda stood at the door and then slowly walked over to the crib where she picked up a small blanket and held it to her bosom. She turned and looked into Matt's eyes for what seemed an eternity, hoping to choose the right words.

Then she lightly spoke. "I'm married, Matt." She watched Matt's face turn ashen. "I have a son."

She sat in a chair, caressed the blanket tenderly, and told the story to the two men. Matt stood while Steve sat in the door way. "I know it sounds crude, but you never answered any of my letters. Oh, Steve did, but he never said anything that you might have said about me. So I began giving up on you." She looked intently into Matt's eyes, while Steve just sat on the stoop and stared at the crib. "Ooh! Matt Jorgensen. You can bring out the devil in me."

"What? What did I do?" Matt replied, looking around for a fork.

"Well, I didn't want to become a spinster. And who knows, you might have gone off and got yourself killed, and me alone here on this farm with no one."

Brenda found a fork and gave it to Matt.

"Thanks," Matt responded. "You were starting to tell us."

Brenda turned and wiped a tear from her eye. Then she turned back to Matt and explained how the event happened a few months after she had returned from Rome.

It was on a like morning when the dew was lifting from the leaf-trodden road leading up to Brenda's house. The sound of slow-moving hoof beats broke the silence of the air and echoed against the door of the lonely home, awakening her owner.

Brenda threw on a light robe, grabbed her rifle from its hook above the doorway, opened the front door and looked out into the woods as her pointed-ear, yelping mongrel sided her. The sounds kept coming closer and she knew them too well for they were those of horses moving towards her. She had heard them fearfully enough through the war, waiting to see whether the riders wore gray or blue; she was particular to the color of gray. She walked down the wagon-wheel gutted road as the rooster met the dawn and the chickens flapped their feathers. Her cow sauntered towards the railed fence and followed Brenda with her eyes while chewing on a wet cud.

"Keep quiet, Bucky," Brenda said softly as she bent lowly to shush her mongrel pal. "I suspect they might be friendly."

When the riders' shadows appeared through the dawning light, Brenda's countenance fell as she discovered the men were not who she had expected. Both men wore the rebel uniform, had scraggy beards and were very unkempt, saddle-tired, hungry and bone dry. They smelled as if they had been in their saddles for the entire war. Brenda covered her mouth and nose and turned her head.

One of the men looked at Brenda and asked, "Got food?" His body was limp in the saddle as if he were glued to it. The other man eked out a small grin, exposing his yellowed teeth, those that had remained

Brenda turned back to the men and took her hand away from her mouth, realizing the need at hand for two suffering soldiers. She grabbed hold of the reins and led the one to her house while the other followed. Bucky yelped and bit at the hooves of the horses as if in total dislike for the muddied critters.

The two soldiers eyed one another and looked over the farm and landscape around them. As Brenda stopped the horse at the trough, she suggested to its rider, "Slide off and you can clean up here. I've got biscuits on the stove. I'll run in and make some eggs."

The rider reached down and grabbed Brenda's shoulder as he fell from his saddle.

She winced from his grip and ran to the house as the other rider tumbled out of his saddle.

Neither man was well enough to chase her so they laid for the moment on the ground near the trough. One looked up into the sky and watched the clouds form together. "Damn. Gonna storm, Skinny."

Skinny laid face down in the dirt around the trough. He raised himself up, threw an arm into the trough and pulled himself up to its edge where he doused his face and watched the filth muddy up the water. "Wash up, Clem. We gonna eat."

Clem, the shortest of the pair, raised himself up and

crawled over to the trough where he threw himself in, clothes and all. Skinny grabbed hold of Clem's dirty yellow hair and pushed him down into the water, which was getting murkier by the minute. Clem reached up and pulled Skinny into the trough with him and the two wrestled until they were both spit tired and fell out of the trough. The water did little good for cleaning them, but it did get rid of some of their filth. The clothes only seemed to get tougher as it soaked into the dirt. The men seemed to know every cuss word in the book as they rolled around the dirt together, pulling at each other's torn and tattered uniform until they finally fell apart from each other's hold and passed out.

Brenda watched the pair for several minutes and finally saw her chance to walk back outside. She grabbed her rifle and walked cautiously while Bucky slowly sneaked up on the pair. Realizing that they were of no present danger to her, Brenda took a bar of soap and a scrub brush from the nearby barn and tossed it at them. Neither man budged. She dipped a bucket of water from the trough and threw it on the two men who only sniffed and snorted. She sat down on a tree stump, placed the rifle across her lap and watched the pair sleep.

"You know something, Bucky. These men are deserters. They're not real soldiers. I can tell. Real soldiers keep clean. Why their pistols are filthy and rusty even. But, they're human beings just the same and we've got to treat them as such. Just we better be watching our backs, if you get my drift."

She rose up and walked back to the house. Leaving the rifle in the house, she came back with a pan of eggs, biscuits and gravy and laid them on the stump beside the men. She returned to the house and came back out with two cups of coffee. She watched the men lay there, neither of them moving. She took her time walking back to the house where she picked up her rifle. She slowly walked back outside and poked its barrel into the sky, and let the burst of two bullets echo off the barn and dissipate across the farmland.

The sounds stirred the men as they jumped into each other's arms where they realized their situation and backed away from each other rather sheepishly. They looked around and saw

202

Brenda holding a smoking rifle.

"Your food is on the stump," she said, aiming the rifle in their direction. "Eat up and then get!"

When Brenda paused in her story, she rose, placed the blanket back inside the crib, turned and looked into the two men's faces as they sat, seemingly in a trance at what they had just heard.

Matt set his pie down, turned and buried his fist into a nearby post, causing skin to peel back and bleed. "Damn!" He took his neckerchief, rubbed the blood from his hand and turned back to Brenda. "Go on. Finish it."

Brenda looked deeply into Matt's eyes and continued. "They didn't leave right away. They stayed a few days, got up on their feet and had an argument."

"Over you, I bet!" Matt said in disgust as he leaned against the wall..

"Yes," Brenda answered. "One wanted to have his way with me. The younger one, Clem, argued with him and stopped him. Then both men rode away."

"But one of them . . . ?" Matt asked, haltingly.

"Clem came back a few months later. I didn't recognize him. He had returned to his unit."

"And the baby?"

Steve rose and walked back towards Brenda. "If he's about two years old with blonde hair, he's sitting on a horse out here."

Brenda ran to the door and Matt slowly followed, moving past Steve. There sat Clem with a small child sitting in front of him.

"Matt," Brenda said as she removed the baby from the arms of the rider, "this is Junior." Brenda looked at Steve and smiled. "My son."

Steve walked over to Brenda and reached out for the boy. He tenderly held the boy at arms length, as if to examine him and allow his mind to grasp what he was hearing. "Oh my god," was all Steve could say. "Hmph. I'm an uncle!"

"And this is my husband," Brenda continued, "Clem Conley."

Matt looked up at a clean cut gentleman with a neatly

trimmed beard, nothing like the description Brenda had earlier described. He was impressed but still dismayed with the sudden news that he had been jilted; not that he had any intentions of marrying Brenda, but the fact that she was married and already a mother. "Hello. I'm Matt Jorgensen." Then he noticed the stripe on Bob's trousers. "A Yankee!"

"7th Cavalry, Tennessee," Conley answered. M'name's Clement Jonathon Conley."

Matt looked at Clem and after a few silent moments, he broke and said, "Clem," and, picking up his pie, he walked over and handed Clem the remains of it with the looks that he'd been dipping into earlier and said, "Here, I guess this is yours."

"Thanks, but she made two," Clem returned. "We can eat 'em after supper . . . thet is, if'n you're stayin'."

Matt kept his pie, and smiled at Clem as if showing his pleasure of knowing the man. Then he turned and went back into the house.

He felt no animosity towards Clem, but was a little hurt about Brenda, only that he hadn't heard of the marriage. Thinking to himself, he smiled and said, *God, I'm glad she found a half-way decent man. Loved her, thet I did, but not with the love I have for Ginny. No, Sir. Thank you, Lord.*

On the next day, Brenda walked out to greet the postman at the edge of the road and Matt carried Junior. They had talked all morning since breakfast and made amends. She yelled back at Steve, "A letter for you, brother. You got some mail."

"Nothing for me," Matt jestered with a pout, looking at Junior. "Matt never gets nothin'."

"Nothin', Uncle Matt," Junior said with a grin.

Brenda heard Matt, looked his way and smiled an assuring smile that could only be measured by two in the same heartbeat.

Steve ran down to the couple and retrieved the mail from Brenda. "Hello, Junior," he addressed the baby, taking a hold of its hand. "It's to both of us," Steve answered, pulling his finger away from Junior.

"Both of us?"

"Yep. It's from Chaplain Bunting."

It still took Matt and Steve time to realize that the War was really over. Sharing this moment together was like mail call with them.

Brenda took Junior off Matt's hands and walked back to the house.

"Good news about Johnston and Wharton," Steve said as he read the letter. He says that both Generals Albert Sidney Johnston and John Austin Wharton were reentered in the Texas State Cemetery, Houston, Texas. Now ain't thet something. I'd say the monument was adequately placed."

"Oh? What else he got to say?" Matt asked, clipping off a chaw of tobacco.

"Wull. Listen to this. *I received word from Jeff Davis. He was pleased about our parade. He told me to tell you that you're a man of your word.*

Boys, I don't know how it will turn out, but our Jeff Davis was indicted for treason against the United States government. Word has it that he entered Fort Monroe, Virginia just this week for his sentence.

He continued reading. *On the lighter side, men, I found out that, our General Tom Harrison did get his red badge of courage at Johnsonville, North Carolina. He gave up aspiring for the Governor's seat. But I hear he's running for the district judge position in Waco.*

Matt let out a laugh that startled the horses, and Steve joined in. "That's it," Steve concluded, folding the letter and putting it back in his shirt pocket. He took out his tobacco and joined Matt in a chewing break.

Steve continued to read. *Well, that's it from me for now. Write when you can or drop by when you're in the neighborhood.*
Bob

Matt stayed with Steve and Brenda for a few more days and got acquainted with his new friend, Clem Conley and a baby named, Junior. After learning about Conley's courtship with Brenda once he returned as a soldier, he showed his appreciation for the couple's marriage. Although he was curious about the

205

timing of Junior's birth, he said nothing so as not to upset the state of their marriage.

Steve showed Matt some of the work Conley did to the farm from last time they saw it. They liked Conley's handy work and determination as he welcomed the role of husband and father, settling down in Texas amid men who fought his kind a few months prior.

On Easter Sunday, Matt and Steve stood on the porch and waved to the young family as they left for church just over the hill. "Wull," Matt started in as he mounted Skeeter, "you comin' with me, friend?"

"Where you headed, pal?" Steve asked, as he hurdled the porch rail and untied his horse.

"Nacadoches, for starters. Get drunk. Reckon I deserve it. Then off to find Ginny."

"Not gonna tell Brenda?"

"Done told her." Matt pulled the brim of his hat down and rode off.

"Whoa up a bit." Steve took a gulp as he watched Matt spur his horse back down the hillside. "I have ta tell Brenda, too, ya know."

"Done told her thet, too. She fixed your blanket roll, pal."

Steve mounted his steed and loped behind Matt. He yelled, "What about Ginny? We still gonna look for her?"

The wind carried his voice across the plains and dissipated into thin air without Matt ever looking back. But he got the gist of it when he heard Ginny's name.

Matt reined up, looked behind and answered him. "She's a ghost right now, Steve. Jest a ghost. But I'm gonna find her. You comin' or not?"

Steve joined up with Matt and they rode off that Easter morning. The funny thing was that Steve had bottled up a secret that he hid deep inside himself. Brenda had told him the first night back that Junior was Matt's son, and not Conley's. Conley knew, but it made no difference to him. He had fallen in love with her and she with him, and he accepted the hand that was dealt him. And now, Steve had a secret that was burning inside him and he wanted to tell someone, but had no one to tell, for he had made a promise to Brenda.

Matt looked towards Nacadoches and smiled. "Junior. She jest had to name him *Junior*.

The Ghost of Ginny McBride

PREFACE

1865 April 2

The bursts from a battery of canons shook the early morning air in Virginia, but nothing was going to disturb the leaves or the squirrels in Richmond, for they had grown accustomed to the noise.

But this day was different from all the rest. The War was over and Richmond had fallen into the hands of the Federals. As Petersburg fell, Richmond was evacuated, and so leaves fell and squirrels ran for cover.

Fate is a word which, seemingly no one can describe, yet it is one of the most powerful nouns in the English language. One may call it *predestination* or *foreordainment* or simply *plain old luck..* However one calls it, the fact remains that it is real for any one believing in and accepting it.

Beth Paterson, a young lady in her early twenties from a plantation in Tennessee, believed that fate put her and her sweetheart, a cowboy on the run from Montana, together. Following this belief so strongly, she rode to meet him as he was to ride from Texas with Terry's Texas Rangers and be in a parade in Richmond, Virginia. But as fate would have it, she was felled by a young Federal's musketball on her ride, and lost the trail of her lover.

Today, she stood in her bedroom tall and straight wearing the clothes she wore when she was shot; black pants, blouse and hat with a whip and a .38 strapped to her side. She pulled back the drape that covered her window and looked out over Richmond, watching the many colors of orange fire envelope her buildings with plumes of smoke climbing up to the night sky.

Why, she asked herself, *am I here? And why now? Who am I? Why can't I remember? Why? Why can't I remember even my own name?*

A rap on the door interrupted her thoughts and she closed the drape.

"Yes?"

"It's been a while since supper, Beth," Emma answered in a soft voice.

"Come on in, Emma."

Emma was the wife of a physician in the Federal Army, Captain Henry Paterson. He found Beth and had nursed her back to health on a battlefield somewhere in Tennessee. After having saved her from her a wound and a bout with pneumonia, he discovered that she also suffered from a sense of deep, dark amnesia. Because of the unique nature of her illness, which he seemed all but given up on healing her, he charged that she be transported to his home in Virginia so that he could personally tend to her illness once he returned from the War; figuring he would be home soon. However, as the War progressed, he stayed on the battlefield by choice and the War lasted longer than he expected.

The task of tending to Beth was turned over to Emma who fought at first the duty laid upon her, but soon became attached to Beth in a mother-daughter relationship.

"Our Union Soldiers are taking Richmond. The fires were set by the Rebs turning tail and running."

For some strange reason, Beth felt a cringe inside her soul at what Emma had just said.

Seeing Beth for the first time in this outfit, Emma was taken aback at the sight. For the past four years, Emma had put her through finishing school and then watched her graduate from William and Mary as a lawyer. Emma was proud of her adopted daughter, a lady of refinement and intelligence, now looking like a hard-hitting fighter with vengeance in her heart.

Beth looked at the startled look in Emma's eyes and attempted to explain.

"This get up? I found it in my old duffle bag under my bed. I thought if I put it on, somehow it might spark something to bring back my memory as to who I really am."

"Anything?"

"Not a thing, Emma," Beth responded. "Not a blasted thing. Excuse me. But somehow, it does make me think that I must have been some sort of rebel or something. Where would I be, using a whip and a gun?"

Emma watched as Beth began to undress. "You and I have asked the same question many times. I swear I don't know."

Emma's house nigger walked up and stood outside Beth's bedroom and overheard the conversation.

"Excuse me, Missy Paterson."

"Yes, Penny. What is it?" Emma asked, relieving Beth of her weapons.

"I think I might know who she be, Mum."

"You what?" Emma asked, turning quickly around with the whip and gun in her hands.

"You know who I am?" Beth asked. "Who?"

"Wull, not who, but I know them things you have in your hands."

"These?" Emma asked. "A whip and a pistol?" She turned to Beth, and handing the gun back to Beth, said, "Oh my goodness. Is that thing loaded?"

Beth took it, opened the cylinder and examined it. "Nope. It's clean. Suspect they unloaded it when they found me."

Beth looked at Penny while Emma began unbuttoning her bodice. "Go on, Penny. What need would I have had with them."

"Wull," Penny began, pulling her blouse away from her shoulder to show scars.

"The whip?" Emma gasped. "How come I never saw them?"

"Cause you neber had no cause to see dem. You neber used the whip."

"You mean to tell me that somebody whipped you?" Beth asked, climbing out of her pants.

"Why, child, you can see she was," Emma addressed Beth. She touched the scars with her finger tips. "They are whelps, Beth."

"Yes, Mum," Penny replied. "Bigger ones on my back, too."

"Your master?" Emma surmised. "The man who sold you to us."

"Yes, Mum."

"Your master?" Beth asked. "Your master did this to you?"

"Yes, Child," Emma said, still looking at Penny's scars. "Some masters will use a whip on their slaves." Then she turned to Beth, and with wide-opened eyes exclaimed, "Oh, my lord, could you have been a maser?"

"Me?" Beth asked, slipping her arms into her blouse. "Me?" She laughed and then stopped abruptly. "Could I have been? Nah! Not me."

"You don't know that for sure," Emma returned. "It's something to go on. I'll write Henry and inform him about this possibility."

That night, Beth slept very little as she let the thought of the possibility of her being a master kept her up most of the night. Her thoughts carried her back to when she first came to the Paterson Estate four year prior.

15 December 1861

A young soldier boy drove the one-horse military wagon through a pair of iron gates and brought it to a halt in front of the steps of the Paterson Manor on a slight incline overlooking Richmond.

"We're here," he addressed Ginny as he went around the wagon to help her from the wagon. He watched her as she eyed the manor. "Yep. She's a biggun. Real big, you ask me."

"You sure we got the right place?" Ginny asked, picking up her duffle bag.

"Here, let me get thet for ya." The boy quickly took the bag from her grip and escorted her up the stairs

At the door, he pulled the chain which summoned a black male servant to their assistance. Beth looked startled at first at the

212

sight of a black man opening the door and bowing to her, and then gained her composure.

A lady in her forties appeared at the door behind him. It was Mrs. Emma Paterson, the wife of Captain Henry Paterson who had been attending to Ginny. It had only been a few months since Emma Paterson took her in as her husband's patient.

At first Emma was reticent about having a strange, yet beautiful young lady as a border in her house, knowing her husband to be a man of vanity. Yet, to follow her husband's demands as a professional man, she bowed to his wishes and looked towards taking her in.

"Well, dear," she addressed Ginny, seeing her for the first time dressed in a horse soldier's outfit and pinned for size, "you have to be Beth."

Beth nodded and smiled. "Yes, Ma'am."

"Well, let's get you inside and changed from those awful looking clothes. You must be tired from you journey. I can tell from the looks of you that you must be starved."

She looked at the soldier boy who escorted her from the one-horse military wagon to the door of the stately Paterson manor. "Thank you, son. You can quit goggling over her, and get back to wherever you're heading." She shooed him easy back down the steps in a kind movement.

The lad gulped, and apologized, "Yes, Ma'am. Sorry, Ma'am." He nearly fell down the steps as he turned and ran back to the wagon.

The house Negro escorted Ginny inside the house as a Negro man servant took Ginny's duffle bag filled with her belongings. The act of the two servants appeared odd to her at first, then she reeled back into her consciousness and realized they were black people being subservient to their masters; something she felt connected with in her past.

"What is it, Child?" Emma asked, watching Ginny changed expressions on her face at the sight of the servants.

"I . . . I don't know. I've seen Negroes along the way here. That's what you call them, isn't it?"

Emma nodded and took Ginny's hand from the house Negro and brought Ginny into the foyer which led to a spiral staircase in the middle. She led Ginny to the right of the staircase into a large living room filled with two large divans and four overstuffed chairs. Off to the side of the living room was an expansive dining area with a large table set for eight.

"We call them that. What would you call them?"

Ginny thought a while and watched the two servants as they scurried off attending to their duties. "I . . . I don't know. I have no idea. Just seems an odd name for me to remember."

"Well, no matter," Emma continued, "we've more important things to attend to at the moment. Your room is at the top of the stairs. Would you like to sit and talk a while, or lie down. I suspect you might be tired."

"Oh, yes, I am, "Ginny agreed, "but I want to know more about this house." Her eyes grew large as she eyed her surroundings. "This is a house."

"Oh, my, yes, dear," Emma agreed politely. "It's called a manor. It was built by Doctor Paterson's father and his father before him." She stopped and rested her hand on Ginny's shoulder. "What kind of house did you come from?"

Ginny looked around the house as if Emma was not present. Emma followed her from room to room. When Ginny stopped to look into the dining room, she turned and met Emma. "It's large."

"Yes, it is," Emma returned. "As I asked before, what kind of house did you live in? Can you remember?"

Ginny looked at Emma for a moment as in a glaze, trying to recollect her earlier surroundings.

"I remember a living room this big," she started recollecting. "No. It was bigger."

"Bigger?" Emma returned with a surprise look. She thought to herself, *Nah. She can't have come from a rich family. Not the way Henry described her.*

"Yes. At least twice as big." She gazed at Emma as if she looked right through her. "Why did I say that? I don't know any such thing." She wrapped her arms around Emma and cried. "Oh, Mrs. Paterson."

For the first time in a long time, Emma felt a sense of being needed by another human being, having no children of her own. And, even though Ginny was in her early twenties, she knew Ginny needed her, and as an added feeling, she felt the need of a *daughter.* Doctor Paterson seemed to have made a wise choice in sending Ginny to her. Even though, she could not get the thought out of her mind that this amnesia might be faked.

Emma took a handkerchief from her sleeve and wiped Ginny's eyes. "Do we have a name?" she asked, hoping she would not cause a disruption in Ginny's psyche.

Ginny returned the handkerchief, looked at Emma and walked away. She turned and smiled and said, "Nope!"

"My house Negro has served up her special, smoked ham." She referred to her house Negro who had the appearance of not only being a good cook, serving up a good supper but showing it on herself as well. "

While they shared the supper moment together, Emma opened the Doctor's last letter, which inquired about Ginny's condition upon her arrival at the manor.

"This will be somewhat of a revelation to tell him," she conversed with Ginny. "A small one, yes, but a revelation, to say the least."

Penny refilled Emma's cup of tea and did likewise with Ginny's cup as Emma continued talking with excitement. She waited for what seemed like forever before Ginny would start talking.

"Mrs. Paterson, I'm just not sure what I saw."

"Tell me, Child. Anything that comes to your mind. Anything will help the Doctor in speeding up your recovery." She continued to wait for Ginny to talk about her vision in the dining room. "Anything."

Ginny shrugged her shoulders, smiled, shoved a biscuit in her lovely mouth and kept eating. She appeared to Emma to be nonchalant about her self, but the truth of the matter was, she simply could not recall anything that would be of help. So, she figured that the best thing for the moment was to get on with her breakfast.

Christmas came and Ginny was made sure she was a part of the family. She awoke that morning and walked softly through the hall and down the staircase to the living room. There she saw the tree she, Emma, Penny and her husband, Jeremiah brought in and decorated. Under the branches of the evergreen were presents. Upon examining them, she found one with her name on it.

Emma had followed Beth down the staircase without her knowing it as Jeremiah and Penny watched stealthily through the opened kitchen door.

Beth sat cross-legged in front of the tree and stared at her present, wondering what was inside. She heard a giggle come from the kitchen, looked up and saw Emma walking into the room.

"Merry Christmas, Child," Emma said with a smile only a mother could share with her offspring.

Penny led Jeremiah by the hand and they moved in behind Emma.

"Child," Jeremiah said with glee, "you done made this heah family proud."

"Open it," Emma said as she stood clothed in her bathrobe next to Jeremiah and Penny.

Fumbling through the paper wrapping, she uncovered a dark blue dress and bonnet to match. "Oh, my!" was all she could exclaim as she held the dress up to her bosom.

"You start finishing school the first week n January, Beth. You'll be needing these. Keep going. We have another present for you."

She followed Emma's advice and opened another smaller present. It was a pair of high-laced shoes. And then Emma pointed to a bonnet lying on the divan.

Beth remembered those presents as so important to her more than anything she could imagine. She so looked forward to finishing school, although she felt she was slightly a little older than she should have been for that. But then, she did not even know how old she really was, so she accepted the opportunity to become a lady; a task she thought was next to being impossible. After all, she had taken on all the appearances of being a man; even to the extent of being mistaken for one and shot as one. Those were the facts pointed out to her by Doctor Paterson.

It was a moderately cool February evening in 1862 when Ginny succumbed to heavy sleep from a tiresome day at finishing school and being tutored in the evening.

As she lay on her back, the appearance of a battlefield appeared to Ginny in a dream. She could see the canons exploding in the near distance and men dressed in a an array of different clothing manning them. She saw the battery of explosions set off in cadence and heard the echo vibrate throughout the woods. And then all was quiet for a long while. She followed one horseman as he rode towards her and dismounted. As quickly as the scene of fire and smoke appeared, it disappeared as fast, leaving only the man in her vision as he tied his steed to a tree branch and sat on a log.

He looked towards her and took a pencil and paper in hand. And then only his face appeared shrouded by a mist which enveloped his appearance to where she could not clearly see his face.

The face seemed to stand in mid air in the far off corner of her bedroom. As he began to write, he talked, and occasionally he would stare towards Ginny.

She twitched and turned in her bed as she fought the fear of her nightmare. But, to her, it was no nightmare, as the face seemed to pay attention to her, as if it knew her. And, somehow, she sensed an awareness as to who the man was, but could not see him or hear him clear enough to ascertain his identity. He spoke in an even, pleasant tone as one addressing his lover, softly, almost to a whisper as he wrote.

Dear Ginny.

I'm still in Tennessee. The winter is cold. Bitterly cold. Eighty-four Rangers died before January ended. Only five from battle. Seems we're plagued with a really bad winter. We have less than half the men prepared for duty.

Colonel Terry's gone. So is Colonel Lubbock. Brave men, both. The Brazorian Sabers. We're still calling ourselves, Terry's Texas Rangers. God I admired Colonel Terry! Did you know he was a rich man? He was wealthy. But none of it went with him. Only his fame and his glory. Colonel Wharton is now in command. I suppose he'll prove to be a good leader. He was in command of Company B.

Whatever happens, I suppose now I have to sorta live up to Terry's legend. Don't you worry, darling, Steve and I will keep his name alive as long as this War lasts.

They tell me a young girl was shot by a blue boy who had no sense. Somewhere close by. I suppose that's why I keep coming back here, fighting and trying to figure all this out. I can't believe it was you who he could have shot. But if it was, I know you're still alive, darling. I feel it. I feel it as if you were sitting here on this stupid log with me right now.

Maybe you are.

I love you so, darling. And I miss you so very much.

Your Matt

As Ginny slept, her closed eyes moved as if intently listening to each word carefully. She wanted to rise out of bed and touch the words with her long fingers. For fear of the face disappearing, she remained in bed and kept her eyes shut tight, and held onto each syllable.

Her lips pursed up into a smile and her fingers reached out and grabbed a tight hold of the sheet that covered her, pulling it to her body. For what seemed like hours, she continued reading the words over and over.

Then a sense of ecstasy moved across the room towards her bed. She let go of her hold on the sheet and let it slide off her onto the floor, exposing her alabaster body clad in a thin night gown. She felt the wisp of cool air seemingly caress her and tenderly kiss her moist lips.

Then the apparition left as quickly as it had appeared, leaving no trace of its having been there. Ginny slept on, hoping he would come back and tell her who he was, and possibly reveal who she is.

When she awoke the next morning, she walked over to the wall where the ghostly figure had appeared. There was no sign of anything out of the ordinary having been there; nothing was disturbed. She turned and looked at her bed, messed up from her restless sleep, and then spun around in the room with her arms outstretched and a broad smile of contentment on her face.

Whoever you are, mister, she said to herself, *I'm going to see you again.*

She was quick to dress and run down the stairs where she was met by Emma.

"Good morning, Child," Emma greeted her. "Have a good night sleep, I take it?"

Ginny stopped, looked at Emma for a moment, looked around the room and outside in the garden, and answered her. "Yes, Ma'am. A very good sleep." Then she smiled and sheepishly said, "I've got something to tell you."

"Breakfast is on the veranda, Child. Let's talk about it over some scrambled eggs and biscuits. Penny made them the way you like."

The two ladies sat at the table, and Penny had already started serving them breakfast. During the course, Beth told Emma about her dream.

"It was real! I could almost reach out and touch his face, that's how real it was. And . . . "

Emma waited for Beth to continue. When she kept looking as if in the distance, she asked, "And, what, Child?"

"That face. It looked so familiar. So, so familiar. Like someone I know . . . or should know."

"Oh. Can you describe it in any detail that could help us?

Beth put her chin in her hands and placed her elbows on the table. "Handsome. Beyond words. He knew me, Emma. He addressed his letter to me. I forget what he said in it. But it was addressed to me. He . . . had blue eyes. Sparkling blue eyes. I think."

"You think?"

"Yes. Because, we don't dream in color, do we?"

"But you saw them as blue."

"Maybe. Maybe they were blue because they looked blue . . . to me. Oh, he is handsome. If I don't know him, I should. I want to know him, Emma."

Emma buttered her biscuit in a hurried fashion, and took a sip of her orange juice. Then she said, "And I've got news for you. We've been making preparations for you to enter William and Mary. Henry and I. You've said you wanted to become a lawyer. Well, here's your chance."

Beth sat up straight, removed her elbows from the table and looked at Emma straight forward. "William and Mary? Oh, Emma."

Beth began to find herself again that Indian Summer, but she still resigned herself that she was no longer in any hurry to really learn who she was. The world was a happy place for her and she was content in keeping it that way.

On the other side of the world, though, Matt Jorgensen was still intent on finding her at whatever the cost.

1865 April 2

There was no moon the night Confederate President Jefferson Davis and his cabinet escaped Richmond by taking the Richmond and Danville Railroad to Danville.

Retreating, the Confederate soldiers set fire to the military establishments and arsenals throughout town, but the wind knew no boundaries. The fire consumed Richmond.

ARTICLES, BOOKS and WEB SITES

Years of research and study goes into the making of a novel, keeping with historical accuracies, even of the minute kind. I want to acknowledge the following authors and internet sites, which have helped me in this endeavor.

Civil War Historian, Los Angeles, CA

Years of research and study goes into the making of a novel keeping with historical accuracies, even of the minute kind. I want to acknowledge the following internet sites which have helped me in this endeavor:

"Causes of the Civil War"
http://members.aol.com/jfepperson/causes.html

"Americas Civil War"
http://www.thehistorynet.com/AmericasCivilWar/articles/1997/0997_text.htm

http://www.crt.state.la.us/crt/tourism/civilwar/generals.htm

"Ad for Runaway Slaves, Feb. 10, 1864"
http://jefferson.village.virginia.edu/vcdh/fellows/runaway.html

"Letter from Juliana Dorsey to General Cocke"

"Letter from Nelia W. of Edge Hill plantation"
http://jefferson.village.virginia.edu/vcdh/fellows/women1.html

http://www.ninetyone.canby.k12.or.us/Classrooms/wigow
sky/civilwar/civilwar.htm

http://www.civilwarhome.com/ftsumter.htm

"Document of slave life"
http://www.campus.ccsd.k12.co.us/ss/SONY/psbeta2/slavpho2.ht
m

"A poster asking for the return of a runaway slave"
http://www.campus.ccsd.k12.co.us/ss/SONY/psbeta2/shriver.htm

"Cotton Gin" by a student in Mr. Munzel's 8th grade
Social Studies class of 99
http://www.pausd.paloalto.ca.us/jls/virtualmuseum/ushistory/cott
on/

"Gin Helped Expand Cotton Industry",
http://www.concentric.net/~Pgarber/gin.html

"The Online Archive of Terry's Texas Rangers

Sharing & preserving the history of the 8th Texas Cavalry
Regiment, 1861-1865 http://www.terrystexasrangers.org/

"Notable Notes about the Terry's Texas Rangers"
http://www.tyler.net/stark/notable.htm

"Eighth Texas Cavalry"
http://www.tsha.utexas.edu/handbook/online/articles/view/EE/qk
e2.html

"Horse Artillery of Terry's Texas Rangers 8th Texas
Cavalry" http://home.flash.net/~porterjh/whitesbattery/

"AEC Cemetery #2 – Slave Cemetery"
http://www.roanetn.com/slave/part6.htm

"East Tennessee's Mountain War"
http://www.state.tn.s/environment/hist/PathDivided/east_tn.htm

http://www.hrticket.com/top/1,1419,N-HRTicket-History-X!ArticleDetail-6598,00.html

Steven A. Bridges huskyfan@ix.netcom.com

Terry's Texas Rangers
http://www.terrystexasrangers.org/library/bibliography.html

Chronological Order of Events Leading
to the Battle of Corinth
October 3rd and 4th, 1862 , By Hugh Horton

Corinth 1861-1865 By Margaret Greene Rogers

http://www.terrystexasrangers.org/library/southern_bivou
ac/v1n3.html Annette Wetzel

Ranger Chaplain Robert F. Bunting 8th Cavalry

http://www.interment.net/data/us/tx/brazoria/sandypoint/s
andypoint.htm

"History of the Tenth New York Cavalry" Captain
Vanderbilt

http://www2.cr.nps.gov/abpp/battles/ky004.htm

http://www.bufordsboys.com/McClellanSaddle.htm

http://www.nonebuttexians.com/Texians.pdf

http://www.civilwarhome.com/shilohdescription.htm

http://www.civilwarhome.com/civilwarcavalry.htm

http://www.nytimes.com/learning/general/onthisday/bday/0427.html

http://library.thinkquest.org/3055/graphics/people/beauregard.html

http://americancivilwar.com/campaigns/Stones_River_Campaign_Map.html

"The Atlas of the Civil War" by James M. McPherson

"Green   Ones   and   Black   Ones"
The   Most   Common   Field   Pieces   of   the   Civil   War
By James Morgan

The Civil War Society's "Encyclopedia of the Civil War and Mark M. Boatner's "Civil War Dictionary."

http://www.civilwarhome.com/potpourr.htm

"None But Texians", A History of Terry's Texas Rangers, Jeffrey D. Murrah http://www.nonebuttexians.com/Texians.pdf

http://www.civilwar.org/historyclassroom/hc_stonesriverhist.htm

Ranger Chaplain Robert F. Burning's account in a contemporary newspaper, 1861

http://home.neo.rr.com/ohiocav/rangers.htm

"The Handbook of Texas Online", Thomas W. Cutrer http://www.tsha.utexas.edu/handbook/online/articles/view/EE/qke2.html

Texas Rangers

Libraryhttp://www.terrystexasrangers.org/library/official_reports/1862_04_12.html

http://www.keathleywebs.com/terrysrangers/terry1.htm

http://www.civilwarhome.com/hillatchickamauga.htm

http://www.nostalgiaville.com/travel/Tennessee/Warren/warren.htm

http://blueandgraytrail.com/date/August_21

http://en.wikipedia.org/wiki/History_of_African_Americans_in_the_Civil_War

The Army Of The Cumberland" (Chapter VII) By Henry M. Cist, Brevet Brigadier-General U. S. V.; A. A. G. On The Staff of Major General Rosecrans, And The Staff Of Major-General Thomas; Secretary Of The Society Of The, Army Of The Cumberland
http://www.civilwarhome.com/advancetomurfreesboro.htm

http://members.tripod.com/~douglk/nathan_bedford_forrest/Nathan_Bedford_Forrest.htm

http://www.civilwarhome.com/stones.htm

http://www.civilwarhome.come/stones.htm

http://www.civilwarhome.com/CMHmurfreesboro.htm

http://www.cr.nps.gov/hps/abpp/battles/tn006.htm

http://www.cr.nps.gov/hps/abpp/battles/tn006.htm

http://www.ngeorgia.com/people/forrest.html

http://education.yahoo.com/reference/encyclopedia/entry/

ForrestN

http://www.ngeorgia.com/people/forrest.html

http://www.tsha.utexas.edu/handbook/online/articles/WW/fwh4.html

http://www.gthcenter.org/collections/mscrpt/W-Z/wharton.htm

http://www.answers.com/topic/john-a-wharton

http://www.terrystexasrangers.org/biographical_notes/h/harrison_t.html

http://faculty.washington.edu/kendo/terrys.html

http://www.b17.com/mosb/generals/harrisont.htm

http://www.keathleywebs.com/terrysrangers/terry3.htm

http://www.terrystexasrangers.org/histories/fitzhugh/terrys_texas_rangers.html#1

http://www.tsha.utexas.edu/publications/journals/shq/online/v019/n3/article_5.html

http://www.tsha.utexas.edu/handbook/online/articles/LL/flu2.html

http://www.texasranger.org/dispatch/19/BR-%20Albert_Sidney_Johnston/Johnston.htm

http://en.wikipedia.org/wiki/Nathan_Bedford_Forrest

http://www.indianainthecivilwar.com/hoosier/crittend.htm

Kate Scurry Terrell, "Terry's Texas Rangers," in *A Comprehensive History of Texas, 1685 to 1897*, ed. by Dudley G. Wooten (2 vols.; Dallas: William G. Scarff, 1898), Vol. II, p. 682;

Clarence R. Wharton, *History of Fort Bend County* (San Antonio: The Naylor Company, 1939), p. 169.

http://www.city-data.com/picfilesc/picc13414.php

http://www.thc.state.tx.us/publications/brochures/CivilWar.pdf

http://www.thc.state.tx.us/heritagetourism/htcivilwar.html

http://www.liendo.org/

http://www.thc.state.tx.us/publications/brochures/CivilWar.pdf

"John A. Wharton: The Forgotten General", Paul R.Scott, http://www.terrystexasrangers.org/biographies/submitted/wharton.html

http://www.tsha.utexas.edu/handbook/online/articles/BB/kbb5.html

http://www.tsha.utexas.edu/handbook/online/articles/HH/fhaaf.html

http://www.rosecity.net/genealogy/bledsoe/fam/fam00060.html.

http://www.cemetery.state.tx.us/pub/user_form.asp?step=1&pers_id=69

http://www.tsha.utexas.edu/handbook/online/articles/WW/fwh4.html

http://www.tsha.utexas.edu/handbook/online/articles/MM/fmu15.html

http://www.terrystexasrangers.org/histories/scott_thesis.html

Eighth Texas Cavalry Regiment, CSA
By Paul Robert Scott

The University of Texas at Arlington July 1977

Our Trust Is in the God of Battles: The Civil War Letters of Robert Franklin Bunting, Chaplain, Terry's Texas Rangers: R. F. Bunting, Thomas W. Cutrer Hardcover, 2006 University of Tennessee Press http://en.wikipedia.org/wiki/Albert_Sidney_Johnston http://www.terrystexasrangers.org/biographies/submitted/wharton.html

http://en.wikipedia.org/wiki/Fort_Monroe%2C_Virginia

http://www.edinburgh-tattoo.co.uk/tattoo-experience/fact.html

http://en.wikipedia.org/wiki/Battle_of_Murfreesboro

http://www.historynet.com/magazines/american_civil_war/3032626.html

An article on Murfreesboro written by Michael Haskew and originally appeared in the January 1997 issue of *America's Civil War* magazine.

http://www.civilwarhome.com/kniffinstonesriver.htm

http://www.answers.com/topic/battle-of-stones-river

http://www.civilwarhome.com/CMHmurfreesboro.htm

http://www.southerntradewind.net/1stgacavalry.html

http://www.georgiaencyclopedia.org/nge/Article.jsp?id=h-2211

http://home.earthlink.net/~larsrbl/CW/Romepage.htm

From the journal of Kate Cumming, Confederate nurse, July 30, 1863: http://romegeorgia.com/history.html

http://en.wikipedia.org/wiki/Rome,_GA

Cornelius C. Platter Civil War Diary, 1864 - 1865 Pages 1 – 6 Author: Platter, Cornelius C.

http://dlg.galileo.usg.edu/hargrett/platter/001.php

hhttp://www.cgsc.army.mil/carl/resources/csi/Robertson3/robertson3.asp

And last, but certainly not the least, I want to thank the many Civil War re-enactors I have met and talked with at many events, and especially to those from Terry's Rangers.